LARA CROFT
TOMB
RAIDER

LARA CROFT
TOMB
RAIDER

Novelization by Dave Stern

Based on the Screenplay Written by
Patrick Massett & John Zinman and Simon West

POCKET BOOKS

NEW YORK   LONDON   TORONTO   SYDNEY   SINGAPORE

This book is a work of fiction. Names, characters, places and incidents are products of the author's imagination or are used fictitiously. Any resemblance to actual events or locales or persons living or dead is entirely coincidental.

An *Original* Publication of POCKET BOOKS

 POCKET BOOKS, a division of Simon & Schuster, Inc.
1230 Avenue of the Americas, New York, NY 10020

ISBN: 0-7434-2429-8

First Pocketbooks printing June 2001

10 9 8 7 6 5 4 3 2 1

POCKET and colophon are registered
trademarks of Simon & Schuster, Inc.

Photography by David La Chapelle and Alex Bailey

Interior design by Jaime Putorti

Printed in the U.S.A.

Prelude

ħ
Ᵽ
⚵
⊕
♈
☊
⚇
⚸

Time was fast running out, Croft knew that, and yet he still could not decide what to do. In just a few short days, he'd be on a plane bound for Novaya Zemlya. There were a million details remaining to be sorted out regarding the expedition: he should be on the phone, talking with Lobdynin, lining up the workers, paying court to the government functionaries and museum officials whose support was essential to the expedition's success. He should be arranging the supplies, making sure the food was edible this time out, that no matter what the weather, they would have adequate shelter.

But he couldn't think about the expedition right now.

All he could think about were the pages of Manethon's *Aegyptica*, put back on his desk in the wrong order.

Two nights ago, he had been out, at the Royal

Ballet's holiday performance of the *Nutcracker*. When he returned home, it was still early; he decided to continue working on his translation. He'd gone to the study, where he found his dictionaries and reference books arranged neatly on his desk, as he'd left them. The reproduced pages of the papyrus were there too, except . . .

They had been rearranged.

Someone had been in his study while he was gone.

Croft knew instantly who that someone had to be. And Croft—Lord Henshingly Croft, of Croft Manor, scion and heir to one of the realm's most revered and influential families—knew one other thing as well. At that instant, despite all his wealth, and standing, and supposed power, he was utterly and totally alone in the world. Those he had counted his friends were to be trusted no more— were indeed, to be regarded as his mortal enemies.

So now Croft sat at his desk, wondering who he could count on, who would share the burden of his knowledge, and act on it, should the need arise.

At his right hand was a stack of stationery; half a dozen sheets lay in the wastebasket already, the scribbling of letters he'd started, reconsidered, and ultimately decided to throw away.

At his left was a half-filled cup of Earl Grey and a half-eaten croissant: he didn't remember having had the other half of either. Were they from this morning, last night . . . ? He couldn't recall. As a matter of fact, he couldn't recall dinner last night, either.

Croft stood, and walked to the Library window.

The house grounds were already carpeted in white,

and more snow was predicted before nightfall. Not enough to delay his going, he'd been assured. But nothing could have stopped Croft at this point, not even a blizzard equal to the one that had prevented him from reaching the Tunguska crater last February. The stakes were too great.

Croft turned away from the window and faced the fireplace. Above the mantel, set directly into the chimneypiece, was a tiled mosaic of his ancestor Robert Croft, a portrait done in ten thousand colored stones. The earl (the first of the Crofts to bear that title) posed in his councilor's robes, an enigmatic smile on his sharp-featured face, his beard neatly trimmed, his eyes twinkling with the confidence of a man, who knows something you don't.

The mosaic (which Croft had recently learned had been made in Venice and shipped to the Manor as a gift—irony of ironies) depicted the earl at the height of his power and influence, that moment in time when Robert, as his father William had been before him, was Queen Elizabeth I's most trusted adviser. Croft had tried, in his own way, to continue in the family tradition, to give the benefit of his wisdom to those in power.

Now, though . . .

Those in power no longer trusted him, it was clear. And so Croft returned to his desk, and his dilemma: Who could he trust?

There was Edward, his cousin, a banker in London—as righteous a soul as ever lived, as scrupulous and tight-lipped as a banker could be. The most recent letter Croft had started had been to him, but even before he finished the first few paragraphs, he realized Edward was a bad choice. Edward believed the world was as it appeared, that the powers that be were in fact, the powers that be. God, Queen, and Country.

Edward would have a hard time swallowing the truth.

So Edward would not do.

Then there was Franklin. Franklin Clive, his oldest friend, now his lawyer. With Franklin, there would be no need to explain. With Franklin, he could simply instruct, and those instructions would be followed to the letter. Except . . .

Franklin was a man of the law, bound by its strictures and precedents. If the law confronted Franklin, he would obey it. Not just obey it: Franklin would trust in the law to do what was right.

So Franklin would not do.

But then, who?

There was a knock on the door.

"Come."

The door pushed open, and right about at the level of the doorknob, a little face appeared. Lara.

Croft smiled.

At the *Nutcracker*, he'd finally noticed what his friends had been telling him for the past year. His daughter was the spitting image of her mother. She had gone to the ballet in a green velvet dress, pinning her dark hair up in a French twist that made her look dignified beyond her years, all seven of them. Watching Lara at the ballet, as she sat down and smoothed her dress, as she clapped her hands together in delight and smiled at every new character that took the stage, was like watching his wife come alive again before him. Even looking at her today, dressed in slacks and a jumper, the resemblance was striking. The feeling Croft had when he looked at Lara now . . . was the very definition of bittersweet.

"I brought you some lunch, Daddy."

"That is the best news I've had all day."

Wilson appeared around the end of the door carrying a tray. "We brought you some lunch."

"Well, I made it," Lara said.

"That you did, my girl. That you did. Sliced the apples herself, sir." Wilson crossed the room and set the tray down on the console at Croft's left hand. "Wields the knife like a little Gypsy woman, if you ask me."

Lara came and stood next to the serving platter. "It's apples and brie, Daddy." She pointed with one little finger. "And potato crisps, and hummus and tahini."

Lara had picked up a taste for Middle Eastern food on the expedition last summer: While Croft had been preoccupied with the dig, Lara and Olivia, who'd come along as her companion, had wandered the alleys of Al Iskandariya for provisions, bringing back delicacy after delicacy.

"It looks wonderful. Thank you, angel." He held out his arms, and Lara came into them.

"You're welcome, Daddy."

Croft tousled her hair.

"Would you care to join me, mademoiselle?"

Lara grinned.

Croft stood, pulled over another chair to the desk, and held it out for his daughter.

Wilson remained standing. "Have you heard from Lobdynin?"

Croft shook his head, picked up a slice of apple, and spread some of the brie on it. Wilson and he had been friends for over twenty years: Up until two days ago, Croft would have trusted him with his life. Now he could barely bring himself to look at the man.

Wilson must have sensed something was the matter. When Lara excused herself to go to the bathroom, he set down his tea and spoke.

"You seem troubled, Croft."

"Well," Croft said, and now he forced himself to look up and give Wilson a halfhearted smile. "It's the usual: too much to do, too little time to do it in."

Wilson nodded. "If you like, I could handle some of the arrangements."

"Thank you, Paul." Croft wondered if perhaps he was wrong, at least about Wilson's involvement. The two of them had been close for so long, and the man was like a godfather to Lara. Was Wilson capable of such a betrayal?

Perhaps not, but . . . the problem wasn't just Wilson. It was those who, for all intents and purposes, ran things. Gareth, Mrs. King, and Ravenna, and their distinguished leader, they were the ones Croft couldn't trust.

None of which impacted on the expedition, so after lunch, he gave in and asked Wilson if he wouldn't mind making a call to Lobdynin, and gave himself a break in the form of a game of chess with Lara. But halfway through he lost his concentration, and Lara came very close to beating him, which she had never done. She accused him of not trying to do his best, and refused to believe his denials, so he had to take her into the kitchen and give her some ice cream as a distraction.

They returned to the study together, and sat in front of the fire. He read her a little from Haliburton, and then left her to browse through the rest of the volume, while he returned to his desk and the never-ending question: Whom could he trust?

"Daddy?"

"Yes, Lara?"

"Why can't I come with you this time?" She had put the Haliburton down, and was across the room, spinning the big globe.

"In case you've forgotten, you have school."

"School is silly. It's all baby stuff."

Croft hid his smile, as Lara's complaint was one he himself had echoed to her teachers. She was well ahead of the rest of her class. "You need to go to school, Lara."

"Daddy, I have an idea. I could get a tutor. Bobby Cecil has a tutor."

"Yes, well, that's Bobby Cecil. I think it's important for you to learn amongst your peers."

"But I want to stay with you, Daddy. And you know everything they're going to teach me in school. Maybe you could be my tutor."

"I'm sorry, angel."

Lara stuck out her lower lip.

"But next year, I can come with you, can't I, Daddy?"

"We'll see. It depends on where we go."

"You said Cambodia, before. I want to go to Cambodia."

"Lara, Cambodia is no place for a little girl."

"I'm not that little. You said so yourself."

"True enough."

"And besides, I can help."

"Really?" Croft smiled then, at the image of Lara, carrying a backpack full of equipment down the Khmer Trail.

"Don't laugh. I really can help, you'll see," Lara said, suddenly sounding twenty years older, her voice and expression so earnest and grown-up that Croft, looking into the future, pitied anyone who crossed paths with his daughter.

Looking into the future.

Croft stared at Lara.

"What?" she asked.

Whom to trust, he had wondered, and the answer had been staring him in the face all along.

"Lara," he said slowly, "can you find Cambodia on the globe for me?"

She frowned. "I think so."

"Go on, then." Croft reached into the top drawer of his desk and pulled out a sheet of onionskin and picked up his pen.

Across the room, Lara was hunched over the globe, her eyes and fingers searching for the target Croft had given her.

Above the fireplace, Robert Croft looked down from his mosaic on his descendants, and the current Lord Croft remembered how William, his father, had trained his son to take up his duties, his service, where he had left off.

For God, Queen, and Country.

Well, then, now it was time for the latest generation of Crofts to be of service.

Croft began writing.

My darling daughter.

His pen wavered for a moment. His eyes sought out Lara's, and they shared a smile.

If you are reading this letter, then I am no longer with you. And I miss you, and I love you always, and forever.

Croft bent over his paper again.

Outside, snow began to fall.

I. Manfred Powell rode into Venice like a king.

The procession felt natural to him, like putting on a favorite old suit he'd forgotten in the corner of his closet. Comfortable.

Pimms, on the other hand, looked anything but. He kept shivering, and trying to hide it, kept trying to zip up the front of his orange windbreaker higher, to insulate himself from the sea spray and the gusting wind.

Powell leaned into his ear and whispered, "I'm getting angry with you, Pimms."

The man went pale.

"Sir?"

"I said, I'm getting angry." At that moment, the *commandante*, who was steering the motorboat, turned around and smiled at Powell. Powell smiled back, and surreptitiously nudged Pimms, who smiled as well. "This is a great honor we have been given, to ride with these gentlemen, and you look like you'd rather be anyplace else."

There were five of them in the boat: Powell, Pimms, and three members of the *Venezia Brigati*, Venice's canal-based firefighters. All were dressed identically, in orange foul-weather gear and black firefighters' helmets with wide yellow stripes around them.

"Sorry, sir." Pimms's longish sandy-brown hair peeked out from underneath his helmet. "It's just that I hadn't expected it to be this cold."

Powell drew in a breath. "Pimms."

"Yes, sir?"

"You're whining. You know how I detest whining."

"Sorry, sir."

"So look like you're enjoying yourself—please."

"Yes, sir." Pimms clasped his hands behind his back and made his mouth into a grimacing sort of shape that—Powell supposed—was intended as a smile. Then Pimms cleared his throat.

"What a privilege to be here, and now, with you gentlemen, and in this boat," Pimms declared, much too loudly.

The three men, who had been talking amongst themselves, suddenly stopped. The *commandante* turned left, and then right, and then back toward Pimms.

"*Grazi, signore,*" he said. The other two nodded. Pimms, in turn, nodded at Powell, and gave him the thumbs-up.

Powell sighed. *Good help was so hard to find these days.*

It had been overcast this morning, and chilly, but now, as they came up the Grand Canal, past San Marco on their right, and then on under the Ponte de-

Accademicia, the sun broke through the clouds, light struck the water, and the great parade of marble buildings on either side of the canal shone spectacularly. This was the Venice he had fallen in love with on his first trip to the city thirty years ago, when he was just a young, impressionable lawyer. Now Powell had become, in fact, by virtue of his legitimate business interests, a very important man in the city of Venice. Hence the invitation on the fireboat's inaugural ride.

The *commandante* docked the boat, as Powell had instructed, at a small quay in the shadow of the Palazzo Grassi. Powell climbed off, shaking hands and smiling with the men, Pimms a step behind.

The two of them walked at a brisk pace, squeezing their way among tourists and tourist trappers, hurrying down the Calle di Mandela, and turned into an alleyway that was so small people often passed by it unknowingly. They emerged into a surprisingly large courtyard.

Before them stood a massive stone building that during the late sixteenth century had served as headquarters for the Council of Three, the secret society that had then ruled the republic. For the last few hundred years, it had served a similar purpose, for a similar organization.

The building's exterior gave no clue to what lay within, though, save for a single stone gargoyle perched high above its entrance. A sharp-eyed observer might note that this gargoyle differed from the usual Renaissance statuary found throughout Venice. It seemed out of place somehow: Venice presented a face of wealth and opulence to the world, a face that asked observers to enjoy its beauty.

This gargoyle presented a face that said, simply, "Go away."

That same sharp-eyed observer might also note that the stone gargoyle held something in its hands: a triangle, with an eye in the middle of it. The eye in the pyramid.

The symbol of the Illuminati.

Powell, Pimms walking a step behind him, passed underneath the gargoyle, into the building, and out of sight.

If the exterior of the building did little to call attention to itself, the Grand Hall was just the opposite.

It was the size of a football field, with vaulted ceilings five stories high, immaculate ivory columns spaced the length of the room, elaborate, gilt-edged scrollwork, a huge, floor-to-ceiling mural on one end, and two massive iron doors at the other.

Along the length of the room, long oak conference tables provided enough seating for the Order's ninety-nine voting members. Underneath the huge mural, seven chairs sat on a raised dais. Seven chairs, for the seven members of the High Council. Six of the chairs were occupied, only the center chair, directly to Powell's left, was empty.

Across the empty center chair, Powell saw Gareth fidgeting, and looking at his watch. Mrs. King crossed her legs. Ravenna folded his arms and sighed.

Powell allowed himself a small smile. Gathered in this room were some of the most powerful men and women in the world, business and political leaders, people used to giving commands, being waited on hand and foot at all hours of the day. Now they were the ones doing the waiting.

A chime sounded, and a door at the back of the room opened.

A tall, distinguished-looking gentleman walked through.

He appeared to be in his early sixties—but no one knew exactly how old he was. He spoke eight languages (that Powell knew of) without the trace of an accent. No one knew where he'd been born. No one could recall a time when he had not sat on the Order's High Council. Twenty-seven years ago, on the death of Madame Simon, he had been named their leader by universal acclamation. No balloting was necessary.

A good thing, because the man had no name.

Within the Order, he was known simply as the distinguished gentleman.

He sat down, between Powell and Gareth, and cleared his throat.

"Brothers and Sisters, it seems we are running out of time. This is not acceptable."

He stressed the last two words, and then allowed the room to be silent a moment.

At the floor tables, Powell sensed as much as saw the younger members shifting, growing nervous. The distinguished-looking gentleman often absented himself from the Order's monthly meetings, allowing Gareth to run those proceedings. Gareth, who had all the presence of a mole rat, and hemmed and hawed, rarely speaking in absolutes. The presence of their leader, here and now, brought home the importance of this meeting to the Order.

"Mr. Powell." The distinguished-looking gentleman turned to him. "The explanation for this, please?"

Powell held the older man's gaze a moment, without flinching. He was no neophyte, no toady. He was his own man. Their leader had recognized that by putting him in charge of the most important project in the Order's history.

A folder appeared before Powell, a folder held by Pimms, who was bending over, offering, he saw, the latest results from Miss Holcomb's team. Powell waved him off.

"I have no 'explanation,' and certainly no excuses, except to once again—respectfully—" his eyes caught Gareth's on that last word, "remind the Council that our calculations involve an almost inconceivable number of iterative operations. We are working from clues based on ancient cosmological models, older than Ptolemy, pre-dating Aristotle, before Plato, models of the universe derived from hypotheses never recorded in the pages of history. Correlation between these models and the actual universe as we know it has proved somewhat of a code-breaking challenge. But I am happy to announce that we are almost ready. And I am supremely confident that we will have our answer in time for the relevant planetary alignment."

"In one week," the man said.

"Yes. In one week."

"That's good news then, Mr. Powell. Because remember, we have only one opportunity to find what we are looking for. And if we fail, we must wait another five thousand years."

Powell smiled. "Well, I don't know about you but

that's more time than I am prepared to commit to this enterprise."

The room fell silent.

Behind the distinguished-looking gentleman, Powell saw Gareth, looking shocked, and Mrs. King, looking worried. Of course, Powell remembered a previous incident involving the distinguished-looking gentleman and another member of the Order who attempted a joke. A protégé of Mrs. King's, who ended up with a dagger in the throat for her efforts.

The Illuminati in general, and their leader in particular, frowned on humor.

Powell tended to be the exception. Generally.

Now he and the distinguished-looking gentleman locked eyes. Finally the older man smiled.

"So we will be ready."

Powell nodded. "Trust me."

The meeting continued. Powell summarized the results of their research in English, and then he had Miss Holcomb stand and go over the methodology used to achieve those results in greater detail. Powell was intimately familiar with the work—he'd supervised virtually all of it—so as she spoke, he allowed his mind to wander.

He had, in fact, lied to the leader of the Order.

They were no closer to finding the object of their search today than they had been six months, or six years, ago. The clues they were working from, the pages from the traitor's diary, the sketches the man had made, were hopelessly fragmented, and often contradictory. This morning, he'd awoken with the nagging sensation that they were running down blind alley after blind alley in their work, that something—to quote the bard—was rotten in Denmark.

Perhaps it would be worth another search through the Order's own records. Or maybe another expedition to Al Iskandariya, in search of the Tenth Diary, the one that recorded the High Priest's own words. Legend said it recorded not just the location of the piece they sought but documented the building of the device that was to be used to find the object.

Perhaps. He did want to continue his rise through the Illuminati organization, and certainly the successful completion of this task would let him take that next step closer to the top. At the same time . . .

Powell crossed his legs, and felt the dagger blade pressing against his ankle, where he'd hidden it—there were other ways to ascend to a position of leadership.

When the meeting ended, he rose and exited the Hall as quickly as possible, not wanting to be bogged down with questions from the other members of the Council. He took the staircase up, and out onto the colonnade overlooking the Great Hall. Pimms trotted along, a step behind him.

Powell pulled out his dagger and played with it idly.

"We're not ready now, are we?" Pimms asked.

Powell turned and gave him an icy glare. "No."

"Oh my God. My God. We need a miracle."

"Pimms."

"Yes, sir?"

"If you're so convinced it's a miracle we need, you need to stop whining, and start praying."

"Yes, sir."

"And in the meantime . . ." Powell shook his head in disgust, studying the man a moment. He looked utterly, totally defeated.

What he needed was a dash of cold water in the face. Failing that . . .

Powell threw his knife into the wall, and smiled at Pimms.

"Fetch," he said.

"Miss Holcomb." Powell made his voice sharper than it had been. "We have one week."

"Yes, sir."

"And now you are suggesting we abandon this—"

"Not abandon. Refocus."

"Do you have a specific new approach in mind?"

"There are references to a device that was intended to be used as a guide to finding the Triangle. That particular search may be more productive—"

Powell put up a hand. "I am as familiar with those references as anyone, Miss Holcomb. But tell me, where would you suggest beginning such a search?"

She was silent for a moment. "That is not my field of expertise," she said finally.

He nodded. "The device is a fairy tale, Miss Holcomb. Continue with your work, please."

She nodded and left the room.

Powell stood and walked to the window, which overlooked one of the lesser canals. The setting sun reflected off the water, a thousand different shades of orange and yellow and red, casting a fiery light on the marbled exteriors of the buildings that lined the canal.

A device. Ridiculous. Impossible.

He heard the doors swing open again, and turned to see Pimms reenter the Hall.

"They were impressed?"

"Yes. Yes, they were, I believe. Of course, once they started asking questions, how we were able to secure so many valuable pieces, it was difficult to get them to stop, and I knew you needed me back at work right away, so—"

"Pimms."

"Yes, sir."

"A simple 'yes' will do."

"Yes. Of course." Pimms nodded. "Yes, sir. Then, yes."

"Excellent."

"Sir?"

"Yes, Pimms?"

"They asked again, would we be ready? And I repeated just what you said—that we would be ready next week."

"We will be."

"But we're not ready now, are we?"

Powell sighed. "No."

"And in the meantime . . ." Powell returned to the table, and closed up his laptop, ". . . see if you can book a table for three this evening at eight at La Caravella." The restaurant was Danielle's favorite; he felt she deserved a little something special for having the Beluga flown in for him.

Pimms looked surprised. "Dinner, sir? Tonight? With a week left?"

"Dinner, Pimms. Eight o'clock sharp. La Caravella. A private booth, if possible."

Powell picked up his laptop and left the room.

2.

It was the fifteenth of May.

And Lara Croft was not a happy camper.

She'd stubbed her toe getting out of bed, then she'd gotten dressed, only to find a rip in her favorite shorts.

She'd gone downstairs for breakfast, and found a card from Alex West propped up against the vase in the center of the table.

"Thinking of you in your time of difficulty," it said.

Lara crumpled it up and threw it into the trash.

"I need to hit something," she announced.

"Well, don't look at me." Hillary, at the stove, kept stirring the oatmeal.

Bryce, sitting at one end of the breakfast table wearing sunglasses, failed to move.

Lara picked up her coffee, took a sip, and scalded her tongue.

"Bloody hell." She put an ice cube on her tongue. "I'm going back to bed until tomorrow."

"Wait." Bryce lowered his sunglasses. "I've got an idea."

Sweat beaded on her forehead. Lara felt the drop gather, and then roll, not down into her eyes, but up, into her hair, which hung down from her head in a single long braid. Suspended upside down in midair from a rope tied to one of the chamber's main support beams, Lara let the rope out, hand over hand, lowering herself toward the floor.

Two dozen feet up, she let go, spun around, and with a soft *thwack!* of her combat boots, landed.

Landed, and listened.

Something was coming.

Metal scraping on stone.

Something big. And now she did recognize the sound, and smiled to herself.

Bryce. You tried to warn me, didn't you?

The thing was moving around the outside of the chamber, hidden behind the columns and statues she had seen before, heading toward the far corner of the room. Trying to cut her off.

So, therefore, that was where the disk was. That was where she had to go.

Lara sprang to her feet and started sprinting.

The statues whose shadows she had glimpsed from above were closer than she thought: at the first one, a bastardized midget relative of the Easter Island monoliths, she dodged left. Behind it was another, and she dodged right.

Light flashed ahead of her: the disk?

Lara changed direction in mid-stride, and jumped over a stone and then she was running full-speed again toward the disk.

Only it wasn't the disk, after all.

Lara realized her mistake just in time, and dived behind a statue, just as something metal shot out of the darkness. A rod, an arm, with sharp, glistening edges. It slammed into the stone, made a loud thumping, crumbling noise, and the air was suddenly full of powder.

Lara rolled to her right, behind another statue, just as metal flashed again, smashed again, and the statue literally disintegrated. Then she was back on her feet, flipping open her holsters, grabbing her guns, and hoping that bullets would mean something to the thing that was chasing her.

She rounded a corner, and there, suspended in a shaft of light before her, was the disk.

She put on an extra burst of speed. She was twenty feet away . . . fifteen . . . ten . . . She was moving to holster one of her guns when—

—something whooshed over her head, and a monster dropped out of the sky and landed directly between her and the disk.

Lara cursed under her breath and dropped, drawing her guns as she did so, skidding on her butt, firing even as she got her first good look at the thing in front of her. It was a ten-foot-tall, six-limbed monstrosity of metal and wire and high-tech circuitry—a droid. It charged her even as the stone and sand scraped against the back of her thighs. The thing took every round she fired. Bullets dented it but did no real harm. She targeted its abdomen as she got closer, and the chamber echoed with the clang of metal on metal. She was almost out of bullets and wondering where the hell the droid's brain was when suddenly she realized she had stopped skidding on the floor and was—

Right under the droid.

Not good.

The droid pivoted on its waist and bent over her. A metal arm slammed down, straight for her face. She rolled right, and another arm slammed down. She rolled left, and then she was trapped tight between the two arms, metal digging into her shoulders. She kicked out, pushed off the floor, and started to squeeze herself through the arms, just as she became aware that somewhere nearby a chainsaw started to whir.

Lara looked up and saw another one of the droid's arms coming toward her, and on the end of that arm was a very sharp-looking blade, spinning rapidly, spinning toward her face.

This was getting serious.

"Oh no." Lara gritted her teeth. "Oh, I don't think so."

She pushed her palms against the floor, bracing herself, and then kicked up with all her strength, planting both her boots squarely in the droid's crotch. She wasn't counting on the droid having a weak spot there; it didn't—the blade continued heading straight for her. But now—

She had some leverage.

Lara arched her back, and thrust up with all her strength.

Suddenly a spinning drill was an inch away from her face.

"Unnnhhh!!!"

Lara arched higher.

The droid lifted an inch off the ground, and the drill moved with it.

The droid pivoted, mimicking confusion. It was unbalanced now; its arms flailed for a second, and then it toppled over Lara's head, and smashed to the floor, holding its arms out in front as it fell.

Lara jumped to her feet, her leg muscles quivering. That thing had to weigh several hundred pounds; a long, hot soak would be called for when this was done.

But it wasn't done yet.

The droid pulled off its ruined arms, and rose up again to face Lara. Jagged shards of metal protruded from the ends of its other set of arms, and suddenly it snapped toward her, sliding on the ground as if it were on a greased track. Lara barely had time to get her hands up before her and parry the thing's claws with her guns. Metal sparked. The claws came again, Lara thrust forward, and just barely got her right hand up in time to block the thing. She was halfway through an eagle strike, so she came all the way around, swinging her leg, kicking the thing in what would have been its butt—if it had a butt, but all it had was a thick sheath of cable. Her boot bounced, but the impact threw it off-balance again. Now Lara was on the attack, legs and arms thrusting forward, driving the droid left, right, right, and then right again. As it spun, she saw a dull black metal plate halfway down its back, and a little green light blinking there. She smiled.

Target acquired.

The droid righted itself, and charged again.

Its right arm came up, and Lara countered. She backed away, it feinted, and now they were circling the disk, the droid feinting, then Lara, then the droid again. It moved with a hitch now, probably the result of losing the two arms, and it seemed to be as concerned with keeping her away from the disk as it was with killing her.

Time to end this little dance.

Lara kicked out. The droid took a boot to the shoulder, and wobbled, raising its arm, which was a mistake. Lara had moved away, and now her foot was coming around again. It caught the droid square on the shoulder, and it spun all the way around. In that split second Lara leaped on its back and began pulling at the metal plate.

Gears and servos wailed: It was as if the droid were screaming at her to get off. It tried to reach around and pull Lara off, but the arms it had left hadn't been designed for that. They flailed away ineffectively at Lara as she flailed away ineffectively at the backplate, which seemed to be welded onto the droid's exoskeletal structure.

Lara pulled out one of her guns and started blasting away at the plate. Dangerous to do at point-blank range, she supposed, the possibility of a ricochet hitting her of course existed, but she was counting on being lucky. She was. Metal was flying off the plate she was ripping at with her hands, and the droid was twisting and bucking, trying to get her off. But now she had hold of the plate; she wrenched it off and found herself looking at thousands of wires stranded together. She reached in, grabbed hold, and yanked as hard as she could.

Her hand came away holding wires, with circuit boards and PROMS and lots of other miniaturized mechanical components she couldn't even begin to identify dangling from the broken ends. As she sat on the droid's back, staring at its mangled innards, it gave a last shudder and stopped moving.

Lara jumped off just as it collapsed and crashed to the floor.

"Next time, pick on someone your own size," she said.

Lara walked calmly over to the disk and removed it from the beam of light. There was writing on one side of it, but the writing was unimportant.

The information the disk contained was crucial. The droid had sacrificed its life to prevent Lara from obtaining it. Which only proved—

A whirring noise came from behind her.

Lara turned just in time to see one of the droid's arms reaching for her, metal pincers snapping at the end of it.

"Stop!" She put up a hand.

It stopped.

Lara walked closer, and bent over it. The droid lay on its back, oozing a thick, viscous fluid from its chest area—oil, or an internal lubricant of some kind. She reached down, wiped away the fluid, and poked around the inside of the chest panel until she found the button she was looking for.

Then she pressed it.

A small tray popped straight up in the air toward her.

It held a disk similar to the one in her hand, but the writing on it was different.

Scrawled in black Magic Marker on the droid's disk were the words: KILL LARA CROFT.

The one in Lara's hand, the one she'd taken as her prize, also had three words written on it: LARA'S PARTY MIX.

Lara switched the disks, and pushed the tray back in.

Music started playing—very loudly. L.E.D.s arranged around the droid's chest pulsed in time. Klieg lights suddenly lit up the chamber, piercing the darkness with bright columns of light.

Lara stood in the huge ballroom of Croft Manor. Three of its walls were made up to simulate the inside of an Egyptian tomb—her exercise chamber. The fourth was a series of stone archways, inset with glass walls. Behind the glass, in the Tech Room, Bryce sat at his control station, staring out at Lara.

Then he stood, tore off his headphones, and started shouting something. The exercise chamber was soundproof, and the music was loud, so Lara couldn't hear a thing, but she got the gist of it.

She didn't feel sorry for him, though. He'd been the one to suggest this little exercise for today, the fifteenth of May.

Bryce should have known: That was never a good day.

Lara grabbed the ruined droid by the head, and started dragging it over to the Tech Room.

The Tech Room—Bryce's command center, as he liked to call it—was an impressive sight on its own, made all the more striking by contrast between it and the grandeur of the past that the rest of the manor presented.

Instead of stone, wood, and fabric, the room was chrome and steel, its center occupied by a workstation of some fifteen computers—laptops, desktops, CRTs and flat-screen monitors—arrayed in a circle. Audio and video linkups from each CPU fed into a single command control center. There was a metal tech bench, with an impressive array of diagnostic equipment, several storage cabinets full of equipment whose function Lara could only guess at, and in the corner of the room, a refrigerator. Lara had instructed Hillary to clear it out at the end of each day without fail; otherwise, the meals Bryce's well-meaning Aunt Tillie brought—meals which Bryce himself never touched—would certainly fester and turn into the kind of hazardous waste that Bryce seemed inclined to live in.

As Lara walked in, trailing the droid behind her, Bryce set down his headphones and began walking toward her.

"Oh, bugger."

Lara watched Bryce frown as he ran his hands over the bullet holes in the droid's armor. He got down on his hands and knees, stared at dents, dings, and tears, frowned again, and grunted.

Lara was more intent on stretching out her sore muscles than dealing with Bryce at the moment. Her legs were still quivering slightly from the strain of lifting the droid; it felt as if she'd just come off multiple sets on the leg press, or done a few dozen too many squat thrusts. She needed that hot bath—or a shower, at the least.

Bryce got to his feet, finally.

"Jesus Christ, Lara," he said. "Live rounds? Did you have to use live rounds?"

Her shoulders, Lara noticed, were also aching, the right one in particular, so she grabbed her right wrist with her left hand and pulled, stretching out the trapezius. She did the same with the other arm, then rotated her right in a circle, expanding it until she was doing shoulder shrugs. That hurt; that damn robot had hit something there, a nerve of some kind, that sent a fresh shot of pain straight up her spine and into her head every time the arm moved in the socket a certain way. Damn.

Hot shower, and a massage.

"Hmmphh." Bryce knelt down next to the droid again, and, with a noticeable effort—noticeable at least, to Lara. She really had to do something about getting him into the gym and into some kind of shape, otherwise in another year or so she'd be carrying in the groceries for him, for God's sake—managed to turn it over.

"Oh . . . my . . . God."

He sounded upset. In between more stretches, Lara noticed that the back of the droid did look somewhat worse than the front, particularly the dozens of wires dangling out of the back of its skull, which had been split in half, she guessed, either by one of the rounds she'd fired at point-blank range or by the act of ripping off its control plate.

"Oh. Oh," Bryce said, his eyes widening. "This is . . . this is . . ." He searched for the words. "This is brutal. This is a major remodeling. A disaster. Lara. Lara. Live rounds? Give me a break."

Give him a break? Lara suddenly stopped stretching, and turned to face Bryce. Did she hear that right?

"Excuse me, but was the drill programmed to stop?"

Bryce, all of a sudden, seemed to have a hard time hearing her over the music.

"What?"

Lara took a step closer, and raised her voice. "Was the drill programmed to stop before it mashed my face?"

Bryce offered a weak smile. "Ah, that would be 'no.' "

"Well, then."

"But you said it had to be challenging."

Lara nodded. "Yes. Hence, the live fire."

At that moment the glass door on the other side of the control chamber opened, and Hillary entered, carrying a stack of white towels.

"The laundry is done, Lady Croft, and lunch will be—"

He saw the droid and his eyebrows lifted.

"Live rounds again?"

"Keeps it interesting," Lara said.

"Yes, well, if we're going to play those games"—Hillary pointed toward the cornices at the top of the room—"we'd better take the proper precautions."

Lara looked up, and saw a six-foot section of stone cornice high above, where the two rooms joined, was riddled with bullet holes.

"Bugger," Bryce said.

"Oops," Lara added.

"Three hundred-fifty years of Crofts in this house, Lara, and those are the first bullet holes to grace the

Manor. Might I suggest you take precautions in the future, to avoid a repeat of this incident?"

He addressed the last comment to Bryce, who nodded agreement, as did Lara, though she thought Hillary was, once again, enjoying his role as the elder statesman of the house just a little too much. He was entitled, she supposed, in that he was the son of her father's chief of household; he had lived here even longer than she had, knew more of the Manor's history than she did, but still . . .

Hillary, at the ripe old age of thirty-nine, seemed to enjoy acting like a man in his seventies just a little too much.

"It would be easiest if you simply agreed not to use live rounds during these exercises, of course," he offered.

"Not use live rounds?"

She and Bryce looked at each other.

"I don't know about that," Bryce said.

"I agree." Lara smiled. "Otherwise, I mean, why bother?"

Hillary rolled his eyes.

"Probably wouldn't even work up a sweat, then," she added, grabbing a towel off the stack he held.

"My clothes are upstairs?"

Hillary grunted something, which she took for a "yes."

"Thanks," she called over her shoulder as she walked away, "for the towel."

Lara slid open the control chamber door and stepped out into the Marble Hall.

"Is there a way to turn off this music?" she heard Hillary ask.

"What do you think I'm trying to do?" Bryce responded.

A shower, she decided, and headed for the stairway and her bedroom upstairs.

People who came to stay at Croft Manor—Lara, like her father before her, enjoyed having guests in the house, at least up until the last few years, when she seemed to spend far more time away from the Manor than in it—often had a hard time getting comfortable. Lara used to think it was due to the sheer scale of the place, but now she felt it had more to do with history, the associations that so many of the rooms had, down to the fact that so many of them had names, rather than simply functional designations. You didn't stay in a guest room, you were in the King James Bedroom, or the Queen's Room, the Van Dyke Room, or the Playwright's Room. You didn't take tea in the kitchen, you had it in the Summer Drawing Room, under the watchful eye of Queen Elizabeth, or the King James Drawing Room, the neutral ground where—legend had it—Churchill and Chamberlain, at her grandfather's urging, had met to try to smooth over their differences.

Lara understood, intellectually, how so much history could be overwhelming, intimidating even, but it never had seemed that way to her. For Lara, history was something to be examined, probed, prodded, its innermost secrets uncovered and brought to light. That was why being an archaeologist—a "Tomb Raider," as the press had taken to calling her, thank you very much, Alex— came so naturally to her. Possibly, she reflected, that was why becoming a photographer had appealed to her as well.

At any rate, she'd grown up treating Croft Manor like somewhat of an archaeological site. Much more of the house was open then, and she spent hours going from wing to wing, room to room, looking at the paintings, the statues, the furniture, and then returning to her father with a hundred questions: Whose picture is that? Who lived in this room? Why is this there, that here?— and on and on ad infinitum. Most of the time, her father had the answers, and if he didn't, he'd search the Library for a book that did. And even that time when she'd accidentally broken a vase in the Yew Room, he'd never stopped her from exploring, just asked that she continue to be careful.

Her father had also hinted at the possibility of secret passageways, hidden rooms, and trapdoors running through the house. When she was younger, she used to go down to the basement, or into the sealed-off floors below the Clock Tower, and rap on panels along the walls, listening for echoes. Now, of course, she knew he'd been having her on the whole time in that regard, but part of her still looked at Croft Manor as something to be explored, a place that just might hold a few surprises for her.

Lara shut off the shower, and pulled a towel into the stall. She put her hair up in a bun, then wrapped the towel around her and walked into the adjoining bedroom.

Hillary was arranging a bouquet of irises in a vase on her dresser.

"I need to get dressed," Lara said. She let the towel drop.

Hillary gasped and covered his eyes.

"Please," she said. "Don't even pretend you care."

He peered out from behind his hand, then lowered it entirely. "Beauty is truth."

"Oh really." Lara walked to the closet and opened it. Her clothes were all missing: inside, instead, was a single, white dress.

She turned to Hillary.

"Very funny."

"I haven't finished putting the laundry away," he said.

"Where did this come from?" she asked, holding up the dress.

"Harrod's. Last Christmas. Perhaps you remember?"

Lara thought for a moment, and then she did. "Why, Hillary. This was your Christmas present to me. Before Crete."

"That's right."

"And you were hoping I would put it on."

"Well . . ." He shrugged.

She frowned, remembering something else. "Wasn't there a bet between you and Bryce, about when—or if—I would actually wear this?"

"Er." He looked down at the floor.

"Hillary." She looked up at the clock. It was ten minutes to one—ten minutes till lunch. "I shall come down to the table naked, if the rest of my clothes are not—"

"I'm going, I'm going," he said, hurrying off. Lara hung the dress back up in the closet, thinking it was sweet of Hillary to try to distract her this way, but it wasn't going to be quite that easy.

On the night table next to her bed was a black-and-white picture in a silver frame: a little girl in a green velvet dress, a man in a tuxedo, smiling at the camera from a private box at Covent Garden. Lara and her father, just prior to a performance of the *Nutcracker*.

Six months later, he was gone.

Hillary brought her clothes and left. Lara dressed and made her way downstairs, thinking about the *Nutcracker*, and the months that had followed her father's departure.

It was a horrible school year for her, every other child in the village (with the exception of Bobby Cecil) having somehow developed the idea that she was a stuck-up prig, and determined to rub her face in the dirt—figuratively and literally.

In retrospect, maybe she had been a bit of a bitch that year, or at least the last few months of it, since her father had left—bossy, selfish, and nasty, telling everyone what they should be doing for her. The Clark girl hadn't listened too well, which was why the two of them were rolling around on the football field, slapping at each other.

During a lull, Lara looked up and saw her teacher, Mrs. Welsh and Mr. Shannon, the gardener at Croft Manor, walking across the fields toward her. That struck her as strange, and so she stopped fighting.

As Mr. Shannon got closer, she saw a big white kerchief sticking out of his pocket, and his eyes were all red. He'd been crying.

She remembered thinking right then and there: *Someone's dead, but why is Mr. Shannon here to fetch me, and not Mr. Hillary?* Then she realized it was probably old Mr. Hillary who'd passed; he'd been sick a long while. Or maybe it was another one of the staff—Mrs. Bigsbee or Miss Tompkins—but there was no chance Mr. Shannon's being here had anything to do with her father. He was a thousand miles away, and besides, if it was her father, it would be old Mr. Hillary coming for her, so it wasn't her father. Not her father.

And then Mr. Shannon, whom she'd barely said a dozen words to in her life, put his hand on her shoulder and said, "Lara, y'need to come home now," and she knew then. It was her worst nightmare come true, and she burst into tears.

Her eyes were full now, as well.

"Lara?"

She'd made her way, unconsciously, into her father's study. She looked up, and saw Hillary standing in the doorway, carrying an armful of manila folders.

"What are you doing in here?"

Hillary walked past slip-covered furniture and stood before the desk. He picked a file from the stack in his arm and tossed it in front of her.

"A few potential jobs. Thought you might like a look."

She frowned. Hillary was trying—as she supposed Bryce had been—to help her forget. Sweet, but . . .

Hillary cleared his throat, waiting.

Oh, what the hell, Lara decided, and flipped open the folder.

There was a photo of Zoser's Pyramid on top.

For God's sake, she thought, *Zoser's Pyramid?* Ridiculous that anyone believed there could still be anything of historical significance or economic value within a hundred miles of that place. She glanced through the abstract. It was ridiculous as well—an argument for beginning a new dig based on a mathematical extrapolation of locations from historical sources. Ridiculous. Stupid, even. And besides . . .

"I don't want to go to Egypt again. Pyramids. Sand." She tossed the folder aside.

Hillary nodded. "I know. Gets everywhere. In the cracks. How about a Spanish galleon?" He handed her another folder.

"To photograph, or plunder?"

"Either. Perhaps both."

Lara shrugged; the idea didn't thrill her. A few old doubloons? Trunks of rotting silks on the ocean floor? She opened the folder and leafed through it. The pictures didn't do much for her, either. A ship's mast, a mound of sand that might or might not be an under-hull. . . . More shoddy archaelogical work, if you asked her. Not worth the time or the effort.

She appreciated Hillary's efforts, but it was silly for her to even try to think of working right now, and that needed to get said.

"Do you know what day it is today, Hillary?"

"Yes," he said quietly. "Of course. The fifteenth."

Lara nodded, and tossed the folder she held in her hand on top of the first one.

"That's right. And that's never a good day."

She looked up at Hillary, and then beyond him, past

the mosaic of Robert Croft in the chimneypiece, the Steinway beyond that, and to the huge oil painting that hung on the far wall of the Study.

She had had it commissioned a few years ago, based on photos Sullah had sent from the last expedition, as well as a sketch she'd done from memory of the expedition the year before. So it was larger-than-life and perfectly detailed at the same time. Just as her father had been.

Lara stood, and approached the painting.

Lord Henshingly Croft was posed in the classic tradition of the great explorers, of Sir Richard Burton, Ernest Shackleton, and Arne Sacknussem, standing proudly in front of a field tent, dressed in full explorer's gear. Behind him the desert sand swirled, and the Union Jack waved from a pole. It was her father against the elements, standing tall, flashing his devil-may-care smile, an expression that Lara had rarely seen him wear, she suddenly realized, the last few days they were together.

Hmmm.

Underneath the painting was a plaque that said: LORD CROFT 1917–1981.

It was hard to believe he'd been gone for twenty years—twenty years ago today that Mr. Shannon had led her into the chapel at Croft Manor, and her Aunt Liate had swallowed her up in her arms, sobbing hysterically. Lara had just shut herself down; she didn't need these strangers intruding on her world and asking her over and over again if she was all right, how awful this all was, putting out clothes for her to wear, telling her what to feel, watching her every second.

Her feelings, then, as now, were her own. Her father would have understood—respected—that.

She locked eyes with his portrait for a moment, and returned her father's smile.

"Never a good day," Hillary said.

"No," Lara agreed. "Never a good day. But an important one."

Without another word, she turned her back on Hillary and the Study, and walked out into the Long Gallery. She went past the Library, then the Chapel, and then out the West Entrance to the manor. A balustraded terrace there overlooked formal gardens below: an outer ring of lime trees surrounding a meticulously arranged planting of flowers, the flowers in turn surrounding a pool of water lilies, the water lilies encircling a sculptured fountain.

Directly before her though, the garden's symmetry had been broken. A short flight of steps led down to a break in the row of trees, and a more simple planting of jasmine, Poet's jasmine.

Next to the bushes stood a stone replica of the field tent in the painting of her father. Strangely, it was even more evocative of his presence than the portrait, as if, Lara thought, he was simply awaiting her within the memorial.

But of course, the inside of the tent was empty.

And yet, Lara felt her father's spirit all around her.

She held the jasmine close to her and whispered, "To see a world in a grain of sand . . . and a heaven in a wild flower."

"Miss you, Daddy."

She knelt down in front of the memorial.

There was a headstone outside the tent's opening, with an inscription that read:

LORD CROFT
DIED IN THE FIELD 15TH MAY 1981
LOST BUT NEVER FORGOTTEN

Never forgotten, Lara echoed in her mind. *Twenty years gone, and never forgotten.*

She placed the flowers on the ground next to the marker, and knelt next to the memorial for almost an hour, until the sun vanished over the horizon, and Hillary came to fetch her for dinner.

3. Powell was dressing for dinner when Pimms burst into the bedroom, eyes wild, and said simply: "They're here!"

Powell looked up from buttoning his shirt.

"The custom of knocking, Pimms. Are you familiar with it?"

"Yes, sir. Sorry sir, it's just that they're here, they're here. The Council."

"Really?" Powell frowned. "The Council?"

"Yes, sir. Three of them: Mr. Gareth, Mrs. King, and Mr. Ravenna. They're downstairs, in the drawing room, waiting to speak to you."

"Hmmm." That was interesting: after the meeting, he would not have been surprised by a phone call, or perhaps a request for a meeting from Gareth, but a face-to-face session with three-fifths of the High Council?

"So what shall I tell them, sir?"

"You may tell them I am dressing, and will be down

in a moment. You offered them something to drink, I assume?"

"Oh my goodness." Pimms looked horrified. "I forgot, sir. I wanted to let you know they were here, so—"

"Well, go down and see to it. Mr. Gareth prefers Courvosier: offer him the reserve. I'll be there in a moment."

Pimms nodded, and backed out of the room quickly.

Powell slipped on his suit jacket and stood before the mirror.

Why was Gareth here? On one level, that question was simple enough to answer. The distinguished gentleman had sent him. Their leader was concerned about the search for the artifact, and he wanted to express it, put a little pressure on Powell. Gareth's presence said again how important the Triangle was to the Order. But the more Powell thought about that explanation, the less he liked it. The distinguished gentleman played his cards close to the vest. He would never betray his interest so brazenly, except as a matter of misdirection, and there was no need for misdirection here. Time was running out, and everyone knew it. No, whatever the reason for Gareth's visit, it was subtle, it was devious, and it was something that Powell would not learn standing before the mirror.

So he went downstairs to the drawing room. Gareth had, of course, taken the red leather chair, where he sat with a brandy snifter. Ravenna was on the end of the couch nearest his mentor, and Mrs. King stood at the piano. All of them turned to face him as he entered, but it was Gareth who spoke first.

"Mr. Powell."

"Mr. Gareth. Sir."

"Forgive us the intrusion. I'm here on behalf of the Council, to continue the discussion of this afternoon. Regarding the Triangle."

The man's expression betrayed nothing.

"Well. As I mentioned this afternoon," Powell said, keeping his tone and his own expression neutral, "we are following a number of promising avenues. I have every confidence our research will bring us results in very short order."

He smiled, waiting for Gareth's reply. Which would give him, if not the answer as to why the man was here tonight, at least the beginnings of an insight into the distinguished gentleman's reasons for sending him.

But to his surprise, it was Mrs. King who spoke next.

"I've been looking at some of your research," she said, stepping forward. "I'm afraid I don't share your optimism."

Powell was momentarily taken aback. "Really?"

"Really," Mrs. King said, and now he noticed she had a briefcase, and from that briefcase she pulled out a handful of charts, no, they were maps, computer-generated, and from his own research team. It was all Powell could do not to scream in anger, heads were going to roll, whoever had given out this information—

"These maps are based on the patterns you've extrapolated."

"Yes."

"I have the raw data here," she said, pulling out another piece of paper, a list of hexadecimal numbers, the same one Powell himself had looked at this afternoon. "At first glance, it appears as if there is a pattern to the data. A somewhat incomplete pattern which—"

"Forgive me for interrupting, Mrs. King, but none of this information is new to me. I've noted the pattern, and the missing data, and my team is working to extrapolate the complete information."

Mrs. King pulled another piece of paper from her briefcase. "This may be new to you, Mr. Powell. Here is the complete statistical array, including the missing data."

Powell was speechless.

"You were correct in your inference, Mr. Powell." Mrs. King smiled. "I congratulate you."

"This is . . ." Powell searched for the words ". . . impossible. How could you have done this so quickly?"

Gareth cleared his throat.

"Langley," he said. "The new Crays. The situation seemed to warrant it."

And what could Powell do to that, but nod grimly. His mind was racing, wondering what the endgame was here, and knowing that he was at least one step behind. Not a comforting thought.

"And here," Mrs. King said, "are the maps based on this new, complete data. Maps that show us the location of the first tomb."

She handed him another print-out, of the Eastern Coast of the United States, with a red arrow pointing to a spot on the map not far from New York City.

"America? That's impossible." Powell peered at the map. There was something written next to the point of the arrow, one word, the name of the town where

Powell's meticulously extracted information told them they would find the Triangle.

Secaucus.

"Are you playing a joke on me?" Powell's voice came out shriller than he intended.

"The joke, Mr. Powell, is apparently on all of us," said Mrs. King.

"But who would do . . ." His voice trailed off, and he stopped for a moment, realization spreading across his face.

"Exactly," said Gareth.

Embarrassment mixed with fury, twenty years gone, and the man was still making a fool of him.

"I, for one, am incensed," said Ravenna, speaking for the first time, rage contorting his face. "Your supposed research, Mr. Powell," he shook a finger "has resulted in our having nothing on this, the most important question the Order has ever considered!"

Powell, for once in his life, was speechless.

"Mr. Powell." Gareth leaned forward and put his soft, fleshy hand over Powell's. "We have lost valuable time. I do not wish to be kept in the dark any longer. Your honest opinion, please, are we going to find the first tomb in time?"

Powell swallowed hard.

For a second, he considered confiding in the man. While Gareth and he had never been close, the man had helped push him forward for committee assignments, alerted him to opportunities that other, more senior members might have rightfully considered theirs.

He should tell him that their worst fears were true,

that the fact was the *Aegyptica* avenue of research had
been their primary focus, and with that completely dis-
credited, there was no way the Artifact would be found
in time. He would have to tell him that, in fact, because
there was nothing else to tell him, he couldn't very well
lie to the man, could he?

Wait a moment.

Of course he could.

"This is a disturbing development, of course." Powell
handed the charts back to Mrs. King. "But hardly fatal to
our efforts. Only this afternoon, I had asked Miss
Holcomb to consider other translation matrices, and in
addition," he looked over at Pimms, "my associate Pimms
had made some promising steps toward locating the device mentioned in the *Aegyptica*, and our own archives."

Gareth frowned. "The device? You actually think we
could find it?"

Powell nodded his head. "Yes, sir."

Mrs. King glared at him, and suddenly Powell realized the reason for her presence. If he had confessed to
failure, she would have killed him and taken over the
project on the spot.

"Well, good." Gareth stood. "I am glad you remain
on top of the situation, Mr. Powell. Keep me informed
of your progress, updates daily at this point, please."

"Of course, sir. Pimms will bring them to your office."

Powell saw them to the door.

When he returned, Pimms was waiting. "Naturally I
wouldn't say anything to contradict you sir, but which
device—"

"In the archives, Mr. Pimms. I'll give you a list of

records to consult." He glanced at his watch: seven fifty-three. He had planned on dinner—a potential new recruit for the Order—but there was no time for that now.

There was time only for a quick phone call to Miss Holcomb, asking her to bring the rest of her team here immediately, so that they could refocus their research.

Before it really was too late.

4. Croft Manor's Clock Tower rose two stories above and slightly to the left of the South Entrance. An engineering marvel at the time of its construction in the early 1600s, for centuries it had been used by the Manor's staff and residents to synchronize schedules and allow the household to be run in a precise, orderly fashion. The clock was no longer used for such purposes, of course, but it still remained the Manor's most visible, distinctive feature, essentially unchanged for hundreds of years, as the Manor itself—externally—remained a symbol of Elizabethan England.

Inside, of course, was a different story.

Modeling, remodeling, and modernization had taken place continuously over the course of its existence. Gaslight, indoor plumbing, phone lines, and electricity—literally miles of pipe and wire—had been routed behind walls, under the floors, in the ceilings. Paint, carpet, tile and marble surfaces had come and gone, and come, and gone again. Her grandfather had completely redone the Chapel; her father had knocked down the wall between the Bacon Room and the Muniment Room to make his Study.

Lara had performed her fair share of changes as well: closing off one end of the ballroom to transform it into an exercise chamber, and taking space from the Long Gallery to make Bryce's workstation. Those two changes in particular, she suspected, had sent the original architects spinning in their graves.

But she thought they might like what she'd done in the Observatory.

She'd kept the original mechanism, and replaced the old lens with a twenty-two–inch reflector. Bryce had hooked a computer and high-resolution imaging station to the telescope, enabling the machine to capture and analyze what the telescope was seeing.

Tonight, the telescope—and Lara, who had her right eye pressed to the eyepiece—was seeing something very special indeed.

Mercury and Venus, flickering in blue and green, approaching alignment.

"Hello?"

Lara looked down.

Hillary was crossing the darkened room, carrying something in his arms. Lara frowned.

"I'm not wearing that dress."

"I'm not carrying that dress," Hillary said.

"Then what are you doing?"

"I thought you might be cold, so I brought you a blanket."

"I'm not cold." Lara slid her chair away from the telescope, and looked up through the open glass dome into the starry night above.

"Spectacular," Hillary said.

She had to agree. "Daddy would have loved this. The alignment."

Sitting next to the telescope controls was a beautifully crafted brass orrery, an astronomically correct model of the solar system. Lara put her hand on the brass Pluto, which in turn caused all the planets to both spin and edge forward around the sun in their particular orbits.

"Alignment?" Hillary put a blanket around her shoulders. "What alignment?"

"Tonight, Mercury and Venus align with Earth. It's the first stage in the alignment of all nine planets, culminating in a full solar eclipse. It only happens once every five thousand years."

Which was, now that she thought about it, a strange confluence of events: the anniversary of her father's disappearance, and the start of a once-in-a-lifetime astronomical event.

Something tugged at her memory.

"When is the eclipse?"

Lara shook her head, and cleared it. "Not until the eighteenth. But there's plenty to look out for until then. Some strange things are going to happen."

As if on cue, out of the corner of her eye, Lara saw something flash by in the sky above. She smiled. "Speaking of which . . ."

A bolt of orange and purple suddenly appeared. Hillary looked up, and did a double-take.

"What was that?"

Before Lara could answer, another spiraling flash of light arced across the sea of stars above them. Then came another, and another.

"The Aurora Borealis." She bent back to the computer for a second and set the display to capture. "Like I said, strange things."

Hillary looked puzzled. "Aurora what?"

"The Northern Lights—only way, way south. They normally only appear over the Pole."

And Hillary, who was normally the second most cynical person she knew—number one on that list being of course, Mr. Alex West. The gall of him, to send her a card today after not a word between them for six months—looked up, positively captivated by the sky above him.

"Good heavens. It's beautiful."

Lara nodded. "It's incredible."

She turned and saw the Lights, shimmering and dancing, reflected in Hillary's eyes.

"Daddy really would have loved this."

She took Hillary's arm, then, and for the next little bit of time, the two of them stood there together, heads tilted back, watching the skies.

That night, Lara went walking in her dreams.

She rose from her bed, and, barefoot and in her pajamas, took the Grand Staircase down the Long Gallery, past her father's Study, the Library, the Chapel, out the West Entrance, and then down the steps to her father's monument.

Above her the Aurora Borealis still flashed, wisps of red and blue and orange mixing with the moon's pale rays, shining down on the marbled replica of the field tent and the small headstone before it.

A warm breeze blew. Lara smelled desert, and sand, and the expedition camp, just as it had smelled outside Al Iskandariya.

The stone tent began glowing from within, a pale golden light that drew her closer, closer, closer . . .

She reached up to touch it. The marble tent shimmered, and before her eyes, transformed into canvas, fluttering in the breeze.

Lara pulled back the flap, and entered the tent.

It was her father's tent, just as she remembered it: his sleeping bag, his trunk, his books, his boots, all just as it had been every night of the two weeks she'd spent with him in the desert. And directly in front of her, sitting on a stool, framed in the golden glow of the kerosene lamp his hand was even now adjusting—

Lara gasped, and as the breath escaped her lips, the man before her turned.

It was her father. Exactly as she remembered him: his skin, burned from the desert sun, laugh-lines tugging at the corners of his mouth, his mustache a hundred different shades of brown, his eyes the same piercing shade of blue as hers, and now their eyes met, and—

"What was that, Daddy?"

The voice came from over her father's shoulder, and even before she looked, Lara knew what she would see.

Her younger self, the seven-year-old she had been that summer, sitting cross-legged on the ground. The camera her father had given her (to keep her out of his hair, she realized now) beside her, looking to her father, as always, for the answers.

Lord Croft turned to that younger self now, and smiled.

"Just the wind, Lara. Just the wind."

The kerosene lamp flickered.

"You should be asleep, angel." Her father smiled. "Look at the time."

He pulled a pocket watch out from behind the little girl's ear, his pocket watch, the one he always carried.

"Daddy!"

Her father shook his head. "My goodness, it's the magic clock. Hidden for centuries, just behind Lara's ear."

The little girl took the watch, and popped it open.

"Mummy."

Lara's heart leaped in her chest. She'd forgotten all about that, the black-and-white cameo of her mother, inside the watch face. The image came back to her instantly, though she hadn't seen it in years and years. It was how she remembered her mother, when she pictured her.

"She looks so beautiful."

"She loved you very much." Her father sighed. "I wish you could remember her."

"That's okay, Daddy. I have you." The little girl held the pocket watch to her ear. "And time. I have time."

"Yes, you do." Her father nodded. "Rivers of time." And as he spoke, her father turned from the little girl in the dream to her, the adult Lara, watching, and his gaze pierced her.

And suddenly, it seemed to Lara, it wasn't a dream at all.

"Through all those rivers, Lara. I'll be with you."

Colored light sparkled behind him, a miniature Aurora.

And then he walked out of the tent.

No, Lara thought.

"No," the young Lara whispered, and rose, and stood at the entrance to the tent. "Daddy? Are you out there?"

The tent flaps rustled and stirred in the wind. But there was no answer.

"Daddy!!!"

Young Lara ran out of the tent, calling after her father. Only her dreaming self, now was young Lara, and as she emerged into the darkness, she found herself standing not in the garden outside Croft Manor, but in a vast desert wilderness, an ocean of sand and night and wind, and her father was gone.

He'd left her alone again, a seven-year-old girl with no one, no mother, no father, no friends, no one to help her make her way in the world.

In the night sky above her, the planets moved closer together, Mercury, and Venus, and Mars, all nine of them, growing closer, closer, like a stop-motion series of photographs, heading toward alignment, and dragging the Earth with them.

The wind howled.

Lara was back inside the tent, her grown-up self again.

"Daddy?"

Dust swirled before her.

The tent flaps whooshed shut.

Lara sat up in bed, wide-awake, sweating, disoriented, her heart hammering in her chest. Outside, the last of the Aurora's light was fading, leaving only the pure white of the moon's beam shining through her bedroom window.

Lara sank back against her pillow, her breath coming easier now. She wiped a hand across her brow, and lay there for a moment, thinking about her dream, enjoying the stillness of the night.

Hold on a moment.

She sat up in bed.

The night wasn't entirely still, after all.

Lara heard, quite distinctly, the sound of a clock ticking.

5. **A** second later, she had it: The Clock Tower.

Big clock, loud tock. Fine. Back to bed.

Lara frowned.

Except that she'd never been able to hear the Clock Tower's ticking from her bedroom before, so it made no sense she would hear it now.

It wasn't the clock by her bed ticking either, that was digital; so was her watch, and so was everyone's, now that she thought about it, digital and synchronized, thanks to Bryce.

But there was something ticking, nonetheless—a dry, reverberant, continuous sound, like a child striking two wooden blocks together in a huge, empty playroom.

Lara pushed back the covers and climbed out of bed.

Her room was at the very top of the Grand Staircase: the sound seemed to be coming from almost directly below her, someplace downstairs. She padded barefoot down the staircase, one step at a time, soundless, like a cat, till she reached the bottom of the stairs.

Now the sound was coming from behind her.

Bryce's workstation? She thought so; that seemed the most likely place for any sort of electromechanical noise to be coming from. Wouldn't that be just like him to try to get revenge on her for busting up his droid by waking her up in the middle of the night?

But as she moved along the wall next to the stairs, she realized the ticking was, in fact, coming from the paneling that lined the area beneath the stairs. Which was silly: How could a piece of wood tick? It couldn't, clearly.

But if there was something behind that wood . . .

Images of secret passageways, trapdoors, hidden store-rooms, suddenly flashed through her mind, her child-hood fantasies suddenly grown plausible. Lara rapped her knuckles on one panel, then another. Both solid: no echo. She tried another, and another, and then out of nowhere came the sudden thought: What if she was dreaming this nighttime walk, too? Wouldn't that make more sense, because the idea of a clock that could tick loud enough to be heard up a full flight of stairs was—

She stopped dead in her tracks.

She rapped, and heard an echo. And the clock tick-ing, louder than before.

She felt along the panel, looking for a way to open it. The wood bowed inward against the pressure from her hands. *Ah.* Easy enough to see what lurked behind.

Lara turned into a spin kick, slamming the heel of her foot into the wood, which splintered into a thou-sand pieces as if it had been made to come apart. She found herself staring into a hidden storeroom of some kind. Pushing aside what remained of the wooden panel, she stepped inside.

Shelving lined the walls; a musty smell filled the air. The first thing she saw was a stack of leather-bound journals, red and brown, a half-dozen or so bundled together with twine, atop a shelf. The cover of the top journal was inscribed with the words "Croft—May '81."

She cut through the twine, and began flipping through the pages. Her father's handwriting, her father's journals.

Why didn't he ever tell her about these? And how did they get here, in a hidden storeroom in Croft Manor?

The clock was still ticking.

On the ground, directly in front of her, was a single dusty crate. The ticking seemed to be coming from inside it.

Lara knelt down, running her hands over its edges, brushing dust off the shipping label, which said only: CROFT—MISCELLANEOUS.

She pulled a screwdriver off a nearby shelf, and set about prying the lid open.

Two years ago, a week after she hired Bryce, he showed up at the Manor with his things up in an old Airstream trailer, which he'd parked outside the North Entrance.

Hillary had taken one look at the trailer and given Bryce a day to get it off the grounds before he had it hauled away. Of course, the trailer still sat in exactly the same place, surrounded by an array of satellite dishes and power cables that made the North Entrance virtually impassable unless you knew exactly where to step.

Which, thankfully, Lara did.

She reached the door of the trailer and rapped her knuckles smartly against metal, several times in quick succession.

"Bryce!"

No answer.

She put her ear to the trailer door, heard mumbling.

"Bryce! Open this door!"

"Unnnh," he grunted, as he complied.

Bryce was wearing the same clothes he'd had on the day before. He looked, frankly, as if he'd spent several days in them. The inside of his trailer, however, looked worse.

It was the first time Lara had seen it in several weeks. His little bugs were everywhere, dozens of them, walking around among the fragments of broken radios, Walkmans, and other electronic gadgets from which he'd made them. The bugs never rested, of course, they were mechanical, just clambered over each other, the mattress on the floor, and the clothes that Bryce left lying around.

It was a disaster area: a mess. Lara wanted to hire a cleaning crew to box up everything inside and throw it away. She didn't understand why Bryce insisted on living in the trailer.

"Why don't you live in the house? I have eighty-three rooms."

He shook his head.

"I'm a free spirit, me."

Lara shrugged, looked at the trailer's tires, all four of which were flat. "Got it, sure. Your choice."

"So what do you want?"

"You. Now."

"Now?" Bryce raised a hand to his eyes, and squinted out into the gray mist that surrounded the trailer. "I just got to sleep."

"Now." Lara turned and started heading to the house.

"But it's all foggy out!" Bryce called after her. He wrinkled his nose. "And what's that smell?"

"Morning. It's six," Lara called over her shoulder. "That's what the world smells like in the morning. Dew on the grass, that sort of thing."

"Oh." He yawned. "Interesting."

"No dawdling, Bryce. Come."

She watched him shiver, and shut the trailer door behind him.

"This had better be good."

"Let's find out," Lara said. "Come."

They walked past the omnipresent satellite dishes, and entered the house.

6. Lara had turned on power and lights in the Tech Room before going to fetch Bryce. As they entered, he stopped in his tracks, and frowned.

"Where is that ticking sound coming from?"

Lara pointed to his workbench, on which stood a mantel clock, perhaps a foot tall, dark wooden case, white faceplate, brass numbers and workings.

"I found it."

But Bryce wasn't listening. He was walking around the ring of computer monitors, looking underneath the tables, behind chairs, his eyes creased with concern. "Where is my droid?"

"It was in the way, so I moved it."

"I was working on that droid." Bryce sounded hurt. "It's in a very delicate state."

"I'm familiar with how delicate that droid is," Lara said.

"Hmmphh." Bryce now stood over the bench, staring down at the clock. "This is what you want me to look at?"

"That's it."

Bryce stared at it for a moment, shifted his gaze to her, down at the clock again, and then back up at her. "It appears to be a clock."

Lara nodded. "I found it last night. It was ticking."

Bryce nodded. "Ah. One of those ticking clocks."

Lara was in no mood. "It was hidden in a secret room."

"Ooooh." Bryce smirked, and was on the verge of making another joke when Lara shook her head.

"Please. Don't even start."

"Lara . . ." he sighed. "It's a clock. It ticks. It tells the time." Bryce looked at the clock, then at his watch again. "It's wrong."

"It started ticking last night, during the first stage of the alignment. It woke me up."

"The alignment?"

Lara explained. As she talked, Bryce held the clock in his hands, turning it this way and that, examining it underneath the halogen lamp on his workbench.

"Interesting." He picked up a small fiber-optic, and began running it over the clock's surface. An enlarged image appeared on the tech bench CRT. "The style is Victorian, but the screws are precision-machined. A deliberate reproduction of a period piece."

"It's camouflage," Lara said.

"What?" Bryce shook his head. "Who would do such a thing? And why?"

"That's what I want you to find out."

Bryce set down the clock and stood. "I shall add this to my 'to do' list."

Lara put a hand on his shoulder, and sat him back down.

"No no no. You do this one now."

"Now? Lara, have a heart, I'm working on no sleep, the Streetfighter is still in pieces, the household clocks are—"

She held up a hand. "Stop. Bryce, this has something to do with my father, I know it does. It's important, with a capital 'I'—do you understand?"

He sighed, defeated. "All right, I'll do my best."

"Thank you, Bryce."

"You're welcome." He stretched, and yawned. "My best requires coffee. I don't suppose anyone is making any?"

Lara looked at the monitor. It was just after six.

"Hillary's in the garden. He loves making coffee."

She stood.

"And where are you going?"

"There was a journal with this," she said. "I want to take a look at it. I'll be right back."

"All right, I'll be here." Bryce picked up the fiber-optic and the clock again.

Lara could tell from the sound of his voice that he was already getting absorbed in the task. He was a good man, Bryce was. He just needed a little direction. And an occasional shower, and perhaps a trip to a gym, now and again. A good man, nonetheless.

"You're a good man, Bryce," she called over her shoulder, heading back toward the hidden storeroom and her father's journals.

Lost in his work, he didn't respond.

* * *

Ten minutes later, Bryce had the back off the clock and was running the fiber-optic through its inner workings, a dizzying assortment of gears, cogs, and flywheels, all now projected on the large Tech Room video monitor.

Lara studied the screen intently, her father's last journal—it was labeled MAY 1981—on the bench next to her. She'd barely had time to glance through it, but she had made one interesting discovery. Half of its pages—the most recent half, up to and including the day of his disappearance—were missing.

"Look" Bryce said. "Do you see how the threading works so that the little gear will only touch that larger one there every few hundred revolutions? This is incredibly precise construction."

"So you understand how it works?"

Bryce nodded. "I will soon enough."

"So what made it start ticking?"

"I don't know that yet. It looks pretty ordinary to me."

Lara frowned. "Well, keep looking."

Lara heard the door behind them open. She turned and saw Hillary, already dressed in a suit and tie, entering the room, carrying a mug in each hand.

"Good morning, Lara."

"Good morning, Hillary. And thank you."

"You're very welcome." Hillary set one of the mugs down on the bench next to her, then turned to Bryce. "I thought you might like something a little different this morning." He held the other mug out at arm's length, and a wicked smile crossed his face. "Decaf latte with nonfat milk."

"Eh?" For the first time that morning, Bryce's eyes opened wide. "Decaf? Milk?"

Lara stifled a laugh.

Hillary nodded. "Yes. Tell me what you think of it."

He set down the mug next to Bryce, who peered over the rim anxiously. Steam fogged his spectacles, and then he broke into a big grin.

"It's black. Hillary, you prankster, you." He reached for the mug, taking his hands off the fiber-optic. "Champion. Steaming sump oil. Ta."

The fiber-optic slid from its position, and the image on the screen jerked suddenly, the fiber-optic's small movements magnified a thousandfold on the monitor.

The gears and springs disappeared, and the screen filled with the image of a triangle, etched in a metal plate. Strange hieroglyphs surrounded it.

A triangle.

Deep within Lara's mind, something stirred.

"Wait!" She leaped off her chair and leaned into the screen. "What did you do?"

Bryce, coffee cup halfway to his lips, stopped suddenly. "What?" He looked around nervously, afraid to move. "What did I do?"

Lara pointed at the screen, to the triangle, and the symbols etched around it. "What's that?"

"I dunno. I just took my hands off the fiber-optic."

Lara touched the triangle's edge. "Look at that."

"What is it?" Bryce asked.

Lara frowned. "I think . . ." she began, still staring at the edge of that triangle, and her voice trailed off, as she

tried to place the image. It was familiar, not the hieroglyphs, the triangle. She knew it from somewhere . . .

"Let's see if we can get the whole image," Bryce said,
gently taking hold of the fiber-optic again, and before
Lara could stop him, his gentle movement sent the entire image lurching; the symbol was gone, the hieroglyphs were gone, and the memory Lara had been trying
to tease forward was gone as well, and they were staring
at the now-familiar panaroma of ticking clockworks.

Bryce said, "Bugger."

Lara said, "Bugger."

Hillary, who had been leaning forward along with
the two of them, simply said, "hmmm," straightened
up, and went to fetch more coffee.

An hour later, having given up on locating the image
again via the fiber-optic, Bryce was well along in the
process of taking the entire clock apart. Lara had been
watching him, mesmerized, as he'd removed tiny screw
after tiny screw from first the outer case and then the
inner workings, arranging them into a neat, geometric
pattern on the bench next to him.

"What an awful lot of work that must be, your construction there," said Hillary, who had also taken notice
of Bryce's screw arrangement.

"That's my map," Bryce replied, without looking up.
"So I know where they all came from."

"What a pity your appreciation of ordered space does
not extend to the area around your trailer," Hillary said.

Now Bryce did turn around, and glare. "Har har,
very amusing."

The clock was still ticking, although much quieter

than before; the outer casing had apparently acted as some kind of resonance chamber. The wooden casing was indeed a sort of camouflage as she suspected; the interior was of a much more modern manufacture, made within the last few decades.

Lara thought about that for a minute. Why? Why make a clock look like something it wasn't? The answer to that was obvious: to disguise its real function.

But would someone have gone to all that trouble to disguise an ordinary clock? The answer to that was just as obvious: No. Which meant that the important part of the clock was hidden, which meant . . .

"It's all camouflage."

Bryce, who had a small jeweler's screwdriver inserted a full inch into the mechanism and was using the on-screen image to guide his movements, paused for a moment.

"Did you say something?"

"I said it's all camouflage."

Bryce put down the screwdriver, and looked up, a puzzled expression on his face. "What? Camouflage?"

Lara stood. Her muscles were stiff; it had been a long night, a strange night, starting with the alignment, and the Aurora, and her dream, and now this clock. All of those things were related somehow, she was sure of it, and all of them—in some way—related to her father.

"Camouflage," Lara said. "A covering, designed to obscure the truth."

"Which is?"

"That's what we're going to find out."

Bryce pointed at the clock. "So how do we tell which part of this is camouflage?"

"Try this."

Lara picked up the clock's workings, raised them over her head, and smashed it down against the tech bench. Hillary, who had been standing a few feet back from the bench, literally jumped. Bryce's neatly arranged pile of screws flew into the air, and scattered across the room.

Lara frowned. "Hmmm." The workings were dented, but intact. She looked around the tech bench, and spotted a hammer. She picked it up, gauged its weight in her hand, and smiled. "This should do the trick."

"Lara, are you—" Bryce opened his mouth, closed it, opened it again. "I hope you know what you're doing."

"We'll find out soon enough."

Lara raised the hammer—

Bryce covered his eyes.

Hillary flinched.

—and brought it down with a satisfying *thwack*.

She did it again, and again, and again. The air was filled with cogs and wheels and springs, brass and steel and rubber, and with each blow the workings before her got smaller and smaller and smaller and she saw—

The dull gleam of silver, and turquoise, and a single, glowing ruby light.

"It was all camouflage." Hillary spoke from over her left shoulder. "Do you see, Bryce? It was camouflage."

"I see it," Bryce's head was practically leaning on her right shoulder. "Hidden within. What the hell is it?"

Lara didn't answer, just set the hammer down, and began prying away what remained of the outer mechanism. The inner clock was still ticking, connected at the ruby eye, which was in fact a raised cog, rising up out of the inner mechanism.

"It's magnificent," Hillary said.

"It's old," Bryce said.

Lara had the entire clock exposed now, the false workings stripped away. The outer faceplate was a circle superimposed upon a square, all of a dull silver, the circle divided into twelve equal sections, each marked by a hieroglyph. Its inner faceplate was another circle, this one turquoise, with a triangle superimposed on it, and the gleaming eye at the center of the triangle.

An eye inside an equilateral triangle. An eye inside a pyramid.

The All-Seeing Eye.

Bryce leaned even farther over Lara's shoulder, reaching for the clock. "I wonder what makes it tick."

"An eye in a pyramid," Hillary said. "Why is that so familiar?"

Lara heard both of them, but it was as if they were speaking from the end of a long tunnel, and moving away from her.

It wasn't the tech monitor, or the clock, or the shattered workings that lay strewn about the room that she saw now.

It was the eye in the pyramid: her father's eye, brilliant blue, framed within a triangle made of his thumbs and forefingers.

The past rose up, and surrounded her.

Interlude

"The All-Seeing Eye."

Her father stared through his fingers at Lara.

"I see all."

She giggled.

"I know all. I know," he leaned closer, and closer, and lowered his voice, "you had no peas for dinner!"

"Daddy!"

"You had no peas for dinner," her father said, in a deep voice. "And you yelled at Olivia."

"I did not yell."

Her father shook his head. "You yelled."

"How do you know?"

He peered through the triangle again. "I know all. I see all."

Lara frowned. "Olivia told you."

"Yes." Her father lowered the triangle. "Olivia told me."

Lara looked sheepish. "I didn't mean to yell. I was just mad."

The two of them were in her father's tent, which they'd been sharing all summer. Lara, who had been on the verge of falling asleep, had heard the digging team coming back from the site and lit the kerosene lamp, awaiting his arrival. "You missed dinner."

He took her into his arms, and hugged her. His face and clothes were still caked with sand. "I'm sorry, angel. But that's still no excuse for yelling."

"I know." She did know, but she was getting tired of how little she saw of her father. He'd warned her before they left that she would have to spend a lot of time by herself. She didn't mind so much, especially since he'd given her the camera, but the last few days had been simply ridiculous; he was up and gone before she was awake, and he didn't came back until she was already asleep.

It was all right at the beginning of the dig, when she could go out with him and they'd see how far the workers had gotten, but since they'd found the tomb, and started working underground all the time, where he wouldn't let her go . . .

"I see that you are no longer mad at me." Her father made the triangle with his fingers again.

"I am mad," Lara said, but her father made such a funny, fake-serious face then that she couldn't keep a smile from the edges of her lips. And then he reached out and tickled her, and it was impossible to do anything but laugh.

"No fair!" she giggled. "No fair." So she made her fingers into the shape of the triangle, and he did the same to his, again, and then they stared at each other through the shapes.

"I see all," Lara giggled.

"And I see it's bedtime." Her father stood. "After bedtime, in fact."

"Daddy, you didn't even tell me about what you did today! Did you find anything?"

He shook his head. "No. But we can talk about that tomorrow." He walked to her cot, and sat down on the edge. "It's time for you to get back to bed."

"I'm not tired."

"Lara—"

"Tell me about the Eye again, Daddy. The All-Seeing Eye."

"Ah." He reached into his pocket, and pulled out a cigar. "Wouldn't you rather have a different story tonight?"

"No."

He struck a match, lit the cigar, and puffed once. "All right, then—go on and get it."

Lara popped up off the ground and ran to her trunk. On top of all her clothes—most of which she'd never worn; she'd spent the summer in her one pair of khaki shorts and white shirts just like her father—was the volume her father had lent her before the expedition, Hagbard's *Legends of Lost Civilizations*.

Clasping the oversize volume in both arms, Lara brought it back to her father. He took the book from her and made space for her on his lap.

"From the beginning?"

Lara nodded, and he opened the book to a double-page illustration of something hurtling to the Earth. A group of primitive people gathered around the impact site, looking on in wonder and puzzlement.

"Long, long ago," her father began, "a meteor crashed to Earth."

"How long ago?"

"A very long time. Thousands and thousands of years."

"That's not very precise. You told me scientists should always strive for precision."

"Well." Croft puffed on his cigar, blowing the smoke away from Lara and toward the open tent flap. "This is not science. It's a story."

"But—"

"No more questions, please. Or we won't finish till tomorrow morning."

Her father cleared his throat, and continued. "Strange phenomena began to occur around its crater. An ancient people excavated the meteor, and found, buried at its core, a mysterious, crystallized metal.

"People came from all over to see the crater," her father said, "and what had been found within: a mysterious, odd-shaped slab of metal, an object that all tribes and their leaders had come to view as a gift from the gods." There was a picture of the crystallized metal, shining in the crater, sparks flying off it, and thousands of people, kneeling together in circle after circle after circle around the crater, lying down and bowing to the metal.

"They worshiped the metal for its magical powers:

The sick became well, the foolish became wise, and the wise became even more inspired. Such was the case with their king. Recognizing the metal's power, he ordered that it be taken from the crater, and forged into a sacred shape. For a hundred days and nights, the fires blazed, the hammers struck, the bellows roared, and at the end, the strange object from the sky had been transformed into a single, perfect triangle. And then the king himself engraved upon that triangle an emblem of its great importance, a single eye that proclaimed to all its mystical power."

Lara made the finger triangle again, her expression deadly serious. Calling on the powers of the All-Seeing Eye within that triangle herself.

"The mysterious Triangle induced great insights in its guardians, great knowledge in mathematics and science. They lived in peace with the peoples, animals, and forests that surrounded them. They attained spiritual insights that were thousands of years ahead of their time. They came to see themselves as the guardians of humanity's fate, and they built themselves a city whose like had never been seen upon this world, then or since."

Her father turned the page, and there was a picture of that city, built inside the crater where the meteor had first fallen to Earth: a wondrous construction, streets spiraling up, up, up and around a pyramid at the center, a pyramid marked with the symbol of the Eye at its apex, a pyramid that was a temple, a place of veneration, where the Triangle was kept, consulted, and worshiped—a continous source of inspiration for the legendary city around it.

"It's beautiful," Lara said, and her father smiled and ruffled her hair gently.

"Beautiful beyond words," he nodded, "They called themselves the People of the Light. The civilization they built, the culture they established, lies at the heart of humanity's lost golden age: All the gods at play from all mythological dramas, all legends from all lands, are but whispered reminiscences of this beautiful city."

Lara smiled, and the smile turned into a yawn, which she quickly covered with her hand, or her father would have stopped the story there and made her go back to sleep, leaving out the most exciting part. He turned the page, and on the left-hand side was an illustration of that same city, surrounded by a horde of barbarians, troop after troop of bearded warriors mounted on horseback, and even more soldiers on foot, carrying spears, swords, and shields, converging like ants on a feast.

"But great beauty always inspires jealousy, and thus it was in this instance. Others heard of the power of the Triangle, and wished to possess it for themselves. Barbarians from every corner of the Earth joined forces, and a great war was fought, until finally, the barbarians stood at the gates of the beautiful city. Then began a terrible siege. Food and water grew scarce; disease swept through every house; fires raged. And within the Great Pyramid, the High Priest, knew that unless a miracle was forthcoming, the People of the Light, and the gifts they had brought humanity, would perish forever."

There was a picture of the High Priest, an ancient, fierce-looking man, surrounded by fire, sweat glistening on his face, standing before the altar, hands on the Triangle.

"And as the High Priest prayed, that miracle did seem to happen, for even as fire engulfed their homes, the sun appeared to go out."

"It was an eclipse," Lara said, pointing to the sky above the High Priest, where the sun was being blotted out by the moon.

"Not just an eclipse, but an alignment of all the planets." He looked down, found his place, and started reading again. "Believing the end of the world to be upon them, their High Priest prayed desperately to the heavens. 'Let my enemies be vanquished!' he cried out. And his prayers were answered in one horrific instant, as the power of the Triangle shone forth from the Pyramid, a blinding flash of light that destroyed everything it touched.

"The High Priest came down from the Pyramid, and walked through the streets of his once-wondrous city, and saw death everywhere: death that had vanquished his enemies, down to the last soldier of the invading army. Miraculous death, for it had spared the Spiral City's defenders and inhabitants without exception. The extent of the Triangle's powers all at once came clear to him; while the planets were aligned, power beyond imagination was his.

"But it was the measure of his greatness that he realized that this power should not be held by any man, this power that could realize the human mind's every wish and turn it into terrifying reality. This was the power of gods, and meant for gods alone. The High Priest declared that the Triangle, which had come to them from the sky, had to be destroyed, lest its power be usurped by a soul of lesser purity."

Her father turned the page, and now there was a picture of the High Priest again, placing something wrapped in a golden cloth into the outstretched hand of a single horseback rider.

"But the mysterious metal resisted all attempts to burn, crush, or bend it. So instead, the High Priest ordered it cut into two smaller triangles. One half was to stay at the Temple, while the other half was to be hidden at the end of the Earth to prevent the Triangle's power from being used again. But in defiance of the High Priest, the Craftsmen who had cut the Triangle in half secretly made a highly advanced device. This device was intended to serve as a guide to find the hidden piece, and preserve the Triangle's powers for future generations."

"The magic clock," Lara said.

Her father nodded. "It was their descendants who swore a sacred oath to use the Triangle to stop time itself, and bring their ancestors back to life. But they realized the exact alignment of the planets necessary to activate the Triangle's power would not be due for another five thousand years."

Her father shut the book. "And that would prove to be just long enough for little Lara Croft to grow up and find it. Now—" He tapped Lara on the nose with his forefinger. "It's time for you to go to bed."

Lara made a face. "I'm not tired."

"Don't give me that eyebrow, young lady. With all

this in your head you should have wonderful dreams. Let's go."

Lara yawned, and climbed into bed.

Her father turned off the kerosene lamp, and as he did so, Lara remembered her question from earlier.

"What were they called again, Daddy? Those people who made the clock?"

Her father, in the middle of putting the book back in the trunk, took a long time to answer.

"Illuminati, angel."

"That's right," she said. "The Illuminati."

She closed her eyes, and drifted off.

7. Bryce was laughing.

"The Illuminati! Dear God, Lara, you can't be serious. I mean—"

She glared at him.

"You are serious." Bryce, who had been sitting quietly as Lara shared her memories of that night twenty years ago with her father, pushed to his feet. "Lara, your story was very entertaining but . . . the Illuminati?" He looked over at Hillary. "A secret society that runs the world? They're not real; they don't exist. Except in the tortured recesses of every conspiracy theorist's mind."

"Really?" Lara pointed to the symbol on the clock: the eye in the pyramid. "And this is . . . ?"

Bryce snorted, pulled out his wallet, and threw a handful of bank notes on the tech bench, notes of different sizes, colors, countries.

"Very impressive," Hillary said. "Opening an exchange bureau?"

"My suppliers often prefer to deal in certain kinds of

currency," said Bryce, pawing through the pile of notes, "and so I keep a lot of different—a-*ha!*" He pulled out an American dollar bill, and turned it over. "Here's your eye and pyramid again. Do you mean to suggest the Illuminati designed this particular currency as well?"

"You're missing the point, Bryce."

"Lara, Lara, Lara . . ." Bryce shook his head. "Let's please be realistic for a moment. This is a story your father was telling you, that's all. A good night story to help you sleep. It's ridiculous to suggest that this clock we have here—" he pointed to it "—was built by a secret society to locate the pieces of some mysterious, all-powerful Triangle."

"All right then." Lara pushed her chair back from the table and stared up at Bryce. "So what is it? Why is it ticking? How did it get in that storeroom?"

"Er." Bryce frowned. "Hmmm."

"I should think the answer to the last question, at least, is clear." Hillary was still standing, hands clasped behind his back. "Your father put it there."

"But why? Why hide it in a place where no one would find it?"

"Excuse me, Lara. That's not exactly right. He hid it in a place where only one person could find it." Hillary stared at her. "You."

Lara nodded, ran her fingers around the edge of the clock. "Yes. And he must have expected me to find it now, although I don't see how he knew—"

The clock's turquoise faceplate sprang open.

"Hello?" Bryce said, leaning over Lara's shoulder. "What have we here?"

"We have you blocking the light," Lara said.

"Sorry." Bryce moved back, just a little, enough for Lara to see what was on the other side of the faceplate: a series of turquoise rings, each of them split into twelve equal sections, and marked with a hieroglyph.

"What do those say?" Hillary asked.

"I don't know. Nine rings . . . nine planets?"

"It looks like eight rings to me," Bryce said.

Hillary leaned over. "No, it's nine." He put a hand on Bryce's shoulder. "I'll get you more coffee."

"Ha, ha."

Lara stood, and started pacing. " 'A guide to find the hidden piece'; those were my father's words."

"A guide how?" Bryce shook his head. "I don't think they had GPS satellites then. No." He shook his head again. "Never."

"Her father believed it," Hillary said. "And he was no fool."

They all stared at the clock. No one spoke for a good long time.

"Okay," Bryce said finally. "Supposing. What now?"

"What now, indeed." Lara sat back down, and contemplated the object in front of her. She'd never seen a device like this before. She had no idea how it was intended to work: as a sort of compass, a sundial, in another fashion entirely? She thought of other civilizations, other objects designed to use celestial phenomena for their own purposes: the Great Pyramid at Chichen-Itzá, Stonehenge, the Ur-Kolan at Dembrovik. She would have to investigate. There were several volumes in the Library that she could refer to as a starting point. She should begin immediately, though it would help if there were someone she could call who could give her a quick overview of—

"Ah." Lara snapped her fingers.

"What?"

"I know a man who may be able to help us." She stood up. "Hillary. I'm showering, then I'd like breakfast in the Solarium, please. Fruit salad, and a Belgian waffle. Cappuccino."

Hillary nodded. "Fifteen minutes."

"Thank you," Lara said, standing. "Bryce?"

He nodded. "Yes. Yes, I think I'll have the exact same thing, only instead of the fruit salad, kippers. And no cappuccino, just—"

Lara shook her head.

"What?" he asked.

"I'll be needing the Norton."

"Your motorbike? It's not ready. I told you that. Should only take another day or so. Half a day maybe. Without any further interruptions."

Lara shook her head. "Forget the upgrade. Half an hour."

"Half an hour?" Bryce rolled his eyes. "Dear God, Lara."

Hillary turned to go. "Your breakfast will be waiting, Mr. Bryce. When you're ready."

He groaned again. "You two."

Lara clapped him on the shoulder. "You're a good man, Bryce."

She went upstairs to shower and change.

* * *

An hour later, Lara was on the Norton, on the M-25, heading down into London. She hadn't been there in six months, a long time for her. The family had a rowhouse in St. James, but she was currently letting it to the Foundation. The rowhouse brought back bad memories. It had been the scene of a particularly nasty run-in with Alex. That was all water under the bridge, because it wasn't as if she'd be seeing him again anytime soon.

Of all the motorbikes she owned, the Norton was her favorite for highway driving: she let it out full-throttle, and weaved in and out of traffic. She wasn't in that much of a hurry, but the speed limit here was ridiculous. She pulled up even with a lorry on her right. The window rolled down, revealing a balding, overweight driver with a leering, gap-toothed smile.

"Like your leather pants, missy!" he shouted.

Lara smiled. "I like your teeth!"

He glared, and gave her the finger.

She laughed, and zoomed on past.

Forty minutes later, she had the bike parked, and was walking in the front door of Boothby's. Boothby's Auction House, the granddaddy of the auction troika, along with Christie's and Sotheby's, and her personal favorite among the three. Most of the artifacts she brought back—that were hers to sell—were sold here. And there was selling going on as she entered.

"Lot 121. A Louis XV ormolu mounted bracket," the auctioneer was saying.

A well-dressed young man offered her a catalogue as

she walked in, but Lara waved him off and found a seat in the back of the auction hall, on an aisle. A professorial-looking gentleman on her right—bow tie and blue button-down shirt—was studying his program intently. The entire auditorium, in fact, was full of button-down types: collectors, she supposed, archaeologists, lawyers, bankers, Internet moguls. Lara felt a little incongruous in her leather biker gear and shades.

She liked feeling incongruous.

She put her boots up on an empty chair in front of her. The professor next to her raised a discreet eyebrow.

Lara turned. "What?"

He reddened, and hunched down in his chair.

The auctioneer cleared her throat, and began speaking.

"This piece dates from the mid-seventeenth century and is one of the earliest extant using the ormolu process." Behind her, an elderly gentlemen hovered around the clock. He straightened, clasped his hands behind his back, and smiled. "The movement has back count wheel strike and is signed Adois Gormlee. The pendulum is hung on a silk suspension. The case is Doré bronze with a courting couple featured above the white porcelain dial. A one of a kind item, with a reserve of two million pounds sterling."

The auction started; the reserve was immediately met. Lara leaned back and watched as the bidding progressed. The clock eventually went to an imperious-looking woman seated behind her, for far too much money, which only reinforced Lara's kindly feelings toward Boothby's clientele: They wanted what they wanted, cost be damned.

Lara shifted in her seat. The movement caught the attention of the elderly man onstage, whose eyes widened in surprise. Then he smiled, and pointed discreetly to a spot offstage.

Lara returned the smile, and nodded her understanding.

"Lot number 155," the auctioneer said. "The Dagger of Xian." A curtain on the right of the stage parted, and two security guards entered, carrying a glass case through which could be seen a jewel-encrusted dagger. "An artifact such as this rarely comes on the open market, ladies and gentlemen, so if you'll bear with me for a moment, I'll briefly outline its provenance."

She didn't need to hear about the dagger's origins, though she was tempted to stay and see how much it went for. But Lara wanted her questions about the clock answered more than she wanted to see how much money would be wired into her account.

She got up and left the auditorium. The grand lobby was packed with buyers and sellers, mingling, talking money, fashion, summer houses, all the upper-crust chitchat Lara found so tiresome. Still, it was a beautiful room: huge domed skylights that flooded the room with sunlight, bouquets of flowers scattered artfully about, Carrera marble floors—

"Lara Croft."

Lara turned, and saw Alex.

Alex West. In his trademark jeans and leather jacket, looking exactly like he had that last day.

"You're looking well," Lara said.

"And you're looking . . ." He scanned her outfit, top to bottom. "Looking—"

"Don't," Lara warned.

"What?"

She glared.

"They're auctioning the dagger, you know," he said, nodding in the direction of the auditorium. "I would have thought you wanted to see that."

Lara shrugged. "This part is the icing."

"Of course." He nodded. "That was nice work, by the way. In China."

"Why, thank you, Alex."

"Still pretending to be a photojournalist? Y'know, it's cool that you still have a day job, even though it is obviously just for show. And how 'bout those Pulitzer Prizes. I mean—wow."

"They seem to impress the little people. Like yourself." She smiled. *I will not let him get under my skin. I will not let him get under my skin.* "And your day job? Still pretending to be an archaeologist, Alex?"

"Doing my best." He smiled. All of a sudden Lara remembered the good times they'd had, which made her smile.

And then she remembered Tibet, frowned, and cleared her throat.

"Well. I have to be going. Good seeing you again."

"Lara . . ." He put a hand on her arm. "Did you get my card?"

She looked down at the hand, and then up at his

face. "You'll remove that immediately, or I'll break one of your ribs. Possibly two."

Alex removed his hand. He looked hurt. "You didn't get my card?"

"I got your card. Thank you," she said grudgingly.

"You're welcome." He looked around the room. "Hey Lara, do we always have to fight like this? Perhaps we don't."

"Maybe we do."

"Why?"

"Let me see." She raised her right forefinger in the air, touched it to her lips, pretending to think. "Tibet has slipped your mind, I suppose?"

"Oh. You're talking about the, uh, prayer wheels."

"Very good Mr. West. Yes, I'm talking about the prayer wheels. You'll recall I paid you in advance?"

"That? That was a finder's fee."

Lara shook her head slowly. The nerve of the man. "No, that was a consulting fee. I didn't ask you to find anything."

"What?"

She folded her arms across her chest. "You stole my prayer wheels."

"Steal? Me? From you? No. I mean, it's not like you ever really owned them or anything."

With great effort, Lara stopped herself from punching him in the face. Alex, oblivious to her anger, went on.

"You and me babe: the same animal."

"Oh really."

Now he did pick up on something.

"Well, ah, we fall into the same category. You know, like in the Yellow Pages.

"Oh, sure. We're soul mates, Lara. We're living on the razor's edge, you and me. We're in it for the thrill, the money, the buzz, the danger . . . whatever!"

"But in your case, mainly the—"

"Money." Alex shook his head. "I knew you'd pick up on that. Damn."

"You said it."

"Hey, you're the Tomb Raider."

"Yes, I am." She jabbed a finger in his chest. "And don't forget it."

Lara spun on her heel and walked away.

"Lara!" Alex was still coming after her. "Lara!"

She stopped and let him catch up.

"Lara," he said softly.

She turned and looked him in the eye. "I think your clients need you."

Lara nodded her head in the direction of a dozen Japanese collectors, coming out of the auditorium hall and headed in Alex's direction.

"Mr. West! Mr. West!"

Alex turned, saw them, and groaned.

"You'd better run along, Mr. West," Lara said. "It seems you're wanted on the floor."

"Lara . . ."

"After all, as you once said so memorably, it's all just a business. So why don't you go do business."

He frowned. "That's not fair."

"Life's not fair, Alex," she said, as the collectors caught up and surrounded him, pulling him away.

So much for Alex West. The nerve of the man, calling her babe. That would be topic of conversation number one, the next time they met. Babe.

And then she saw the man she wanted to talk to, the elderly man who'd been up on the stage with the ormolu clock. The man who'd been one of her father's closest friends, coming through the crowd toward her.

"Mr. Wilson!"

"Lara. Lara my dear." They embraced. "You look well."

"You too."

"How is Hillary's boy? And the house?"

"They're both fine. You should come see them."

He nodded. "I should. I will. But first . . . I'm intrigued by what you told me over the phone."

Lara patted her shoulder bag. "I think you'll be even more intrigued when you see the clock."

"I don't doubt it. Let's go to my study."

Wilson led the way, expertly threading a path through the chattering crowds. Lara caught sight of Alex being peppered with questions by his clients. He saw her, too, and Lara felt his gaze following her, across the lobby floor, and into the executive elevators.

So much for Alex West.

8. Lara had known Mr. Wilson for her entire life. It wasn't too much of a stretch to say that he was more of an uncle to her than her own parents' siblings. After her father's disappearance, after her troubles at first the Wimbledon School and then Gordonstoun, the one phone conversation Lara could have with an adult that wouldn't consist of listening on her part and lecturing on the adult's was with Mr. Wilson. He listened, and encouraged her to follow her own interests. He'd convinced her reluctant relatives to let her join Professor von Croy's expedition when she was fourteen, and he'd backed her decision not to follow through on her planned engagement to the Earl of Farrington. Wilson's London apartment had been a crash pad for her on more than one difficult occasion, and his office at Boothby's was where she always brought her finds for the house to auction off.

Wilson led her down the hall now to that office.

Etched into the frosted glass door were the words:
P. WILSON—HOROLOGIST

He unlocked the door and turned on the light.

"Here we are." The office, a single large wood-paneled room, reminded her, in certain respects, of her father's own study, though instead of the archaeological relics Lord Croft had favored, the shelves of Wilson's office—his study, as he liked to call it—were lined with clocks and clock mechanisms from all ages.

Wilson shuffled over to his desk and sat down.

"Give me a moment, will you, Lara?"

"Of course." She set her helmet down on the corner of the desk as Wilson opened one of its drawers, pulled out a notebook, and flipped to the back of it. Then he took a fountain pen from the holder on the desk, and made a note.

"Keeping track of the ormolus," he said, as much to himself as to Lara. "That one went for quite a bit more than I thought it would." He put the pen back into its holder, the notebook into the drawer, sat back in his chair, and smiled at Lara. "Oh, and the dagger? That was yours, wasn't it?"

"Yes."

"You'll be happy to know that went to Lord and Lady von Biester, at twice the asking price."

Lara nodded. "Good." The von Biesters were avid collectors of Asian relics; they were also fairly close neighbors of hers, so she'd get to see the dagger again, which was always nice.

"So?" Wilson said. "What can I do for you, my dear?"

Lara slung her bag onto his desk, and opened it.

"You can tell me about this." She took the clock out and put it down directly in front of him.

Wilson's eyes widened. His mouth opened, but no sound came out. For a second, Lara thought he might be having a heart attack.

"Are you all right?"

"Good Lord." He looked up at Lara. "Where did you get this?"

"You recognize it?"

He took a handkerchief out of his pocket, and dabbed at his forehead.

"I . . ." He paused for a moment, and shook his head. "No. But it's incredible." He touched the surface with his hand gingerly, as if he were afraid of burning himself. "Incredibly ancient. Incredibly old." He pulled open his desk drawer again, and brought out a magnifying glass. "Lara. This is a very unique object."

"Yes." She spoke quietly. Wilson held the glass near the clock, and was going over every millimeter of it with such intense concentration that she was afraid to do much more than whisper for fear of distracting him.

Wilson set down the glass, and ran his finger along the outer edge. The casing sprung open, just as it had for Lara, revealing the clock's inner mechanism.

"Only one of the dials is working at the moment. It glows like the Eye. Less so, but it's getting brighter."

Wilson nodded. "Yes, I see."

"And it seems to be running backward, like it's not so much keeping time, but counting down to something."

"Yes, I see. Here. Come look." He motioned Lara closer, and gestured to an elaborate arrangement of tiny cogs at the center of the mechanism. "You see this? It reverses the direction of the action, so the outer clock face would run forward." He pointed to the workings. "Incredible detail."

Wilson pointed to three small dot symbols that orbited around the center point of the luminous dial. "And these . . ."

"I thought these looked like planets."

"I suppose. Yes. They very well could be." He frowned. "Whatever made you think of that?"

"The clock began ticking the night the first three planets aligned," Lara explained. "Which is what has me puzzled. In your experience, have you ever heard of another clock that worked like this one? A clock that begins ticking because of some astronomical event?"

Wilson shook his head. "No. Never. I can't begin to conceive how one would construct such a piece." He continued to study the clock. Lara found herself studying him. Strange, but she had the feeling he wasn't being completely honest with her, that he had recognized the clock. This was, of course, ridiculous—this was Mr. Wilson; he would have told her if he had. Yet the man was clearly affected by the piece: His eyes, she was surprised to see, had welled up with tears.

Lara put a hand on his shoulder. "Mr. Wilson. Is something the matter?"

"No. It's just . . . fascinating. Incredible. Incredibly beautiful."

"Do you see any way to get at the inner workings?" Lara asked. "It's perfectly sealed, I don't know how, or with what. I couldn't find a seam, and I didn't want to break it."

"No." Wilson nodded. "You shouldn't break a thing like this."

"Daddy hid it, Mr. Wilson. It was hidden in the house for twenty years."

"He must have thought it was very valuable."

"I suppose," Lara replied, remembering how she'd found the clock, buried toward the bottom of the crate, underneath, of all things, a Balinese death mask. "He surrounded it with other objects. Random things. Highly valuable on the open market, but to a true insider, just trinkets. Baubles." Baubles like a jeweled goblet from Constantinople, turquoise memory stones from Easter Island, a Hopi kuchina doll—a grab bag of goodies, no earthly reason to put them all in the same place.

"He never mentioned finding this to you?"

"No. His field journals made no mention of the clock, either; the last one had half its pages ripped out." She had time to wonder why on the ride down. Had her father done it himself? If so, why? Where were the missing pages—hidden in another secret storeroom back in the Manor? Was there some other clue she had missed? *Daddy*, she thought, *what are you trying to tell me?*

"He always steered his own course, your father," Wilson said, as if he were reading her mind. He had put the clock down and was now standing at a little wooden cabinet behind his desk. "He was a great man."

"He knew I would find the clock." Lara rose and came around next to Wilson. He was staring at a photo, one of a half-dozen hung on the wall behind the desk, this one of her father and a much younger Wilson at a formal dinner party; it had to be forty years old. "But I don't know what he wanted me to do with it."

"Would you like some port?" Wilson went on as if he hadn't heard Lara at all. "It's really very fine."

"No, thank you."

Wilson poured himself a glass, and drank it down.

"I can't help you, Lara," he said, so softly she almost had trouble hearing him.

"Mr. Wilson?"

He shook his head as if to clear it, and smiled.

"I mean, I have never seen anything like this. It's beyond my expertise, it truly is. It's a mystery." He looked her straight in the eye. "You should keep it yourself."

"I intend to." Lara opened her mouth to ask him if there was anyone else he could recommend she go to, which was another ridiculous thought. There were no two people in the world alive today who knew as much about clocks as Mr. Wilson, but stopped the question when she saw him shuffle unsteadily back to his chair and sit down.

He's gotten old, she realized, and wondered when that had happened. For so long, when she thought of Mr. Wilson, she thought of the elegant, refined aristocrat who used to take her around to the Natural History Museum, and the Archaeological Institute, who she had been proud to have as her escort to the Huntingdon Debutante's Ball. This Mr. Wilson was a frail old man.

And my father's contemporary, Lara reminded herself. *If Daddy were still alive, he would be exactly the same age. Time stands still for none of us.*

"It's good to see you again." Lara scooped the clock up off his desk and put it back into her bag. She bent over and gave him a kiss on the forehead.

"Yes, yes. Good to see you." He smiled weakly, and said good-bye.

The entire ride back to the Manor, she had the most eerie feeling that she would never see Mr. Wilson again, or hear his voice. It upset her, so much so that she refused to let Hillary make her dinner, and dressed both Bryce and him down for denigrating Wilson's expertise.

When the phone rang, as she was working later that evening in her office, the last person she expected it to be was the man she'd driven down to London to see earlier that afternoon.

"Lara. Hello, it's Mr. Wilson."

"Mr. Wilson. How good to hear from you again." And it was; he sounded much, much better than he had this afternoon.

"Yes. Well, ah, you see, I had a second thought about that clock."

"Really?" Lara had the *Astrophysicist's Lexicon* out on her desk, and had been e-mailing back and forth with a historian in Sydney on what the symbols on the clock might mean, but her progress had been minimal, at best.

"There is a man who may be able to help you. You see, I, ah . . . a friend of mine. I told him about the, ah, the clock and he's very intrigued. He may be able to help identify its origin."

"Excellent." Lara tried to sound excited, though part of her was thinking that Wilson knew she normally didn't like to conduct her business with strangers, and even beyond that, that the information she shared with him was confidential.

Suddenly the unease she felt earlier was back.

"At any rate, I took the liberty of setting up an appointment for you tomorrow. At eleven. I hope that's all right?"

"Fine."

Wilson gave her the address, and a name. There was a moment's pause.

"You'll call me later tomorrow, let me know what you find out. Won't you, Lara?"

"Of course I will."

"Good. Well then, take care."

"Well, thank you, Mr. Wilson. I will. Lots of love. Take care."

Lara put down the phone, and considered this for a moment. Mr. Wilson sounded worried. Who exactly was he sending her to see tomorrow?

Behind her, something exploded.

Lara reached for her guns, only her guns weren't there, and she kicked herself for not being prepared. She turned, ready to confront whoever, and saw . . .

The pot pie she'd been preparing in the microwave had exploded. The glass was covered with potato.

"Bugger."

She opened the door and pulled out the still-flaming dinner tray and dropped it onto her desk.

Hillary peeked his head around the doorframe.

"Ah. Microwave au briand. Looks delicious."

She pointed a finger. "Go. Buttle, or whatever it is you do when I'm not around."

He went. Lara sat back down, and poked a fork into

her dinner. She was suddenly very aware of her father's image, staring down from the portrait on the wall.

She steepled her fingers together, rested her chin on her hands.

"Daddy," she said quietly, staring up at her father. "What the hell is going on?"

9. Lara woke early and made preparations.

Ten o'clock found her dressed in dark slacks and pullover, driving down the M-25 in the Aston Martin, once again bound for London. She had chosen slightly more formal wear, and a slightly more formal mode of transportation to present herself to Mr. Wilson's clock expert—first impressions and all that—which had caused Hillary to raise an eyebrow when she came down to breakfast.

"Lady Croft," he said, pulling out her chair. "Two days in a row, two different outfits, neither of them shorts and a T-shirt? We're living in extraordinary times. I am tempted to wake Mr. Bryce."

"You'll know they're extraordinary when I put on that dress, Hilly."

He bowed. "I shall look forward to that day. Myself, and my bankers."

The address Wilson had given her was in Holland Park. She garaged the car in an underground facility, and made her way down Melbury Road to number 25, an imposing townhouse with an oversize front door that looked like it belonged on a much larger building.

Two video cameras, mounted discreetly above the door on either side, followed her progress up the steps. Their mountings, she noticed, were commercial-grade: thick, dull gray steel. Anyone attempting to break in would have to deal with those cameras, and they looked as if they'd been specifically designed to be difficult to deal with. Curious.

And curiouser: There was no bell to ring. No knocker on the door, either. If you weren't expected, not only were you not going to get in, you weren't even going to be acknowledged.

Lara, though, was expected. When she tried the door, she found it was unlocked. She pushed it open, and it swung wide effortlessly, though with the impression of great weight precisely balanced. A formidable door, indeed—heavier, she suspected, than even the hard oak it appeared to be. Steel-reinforced, possibly.

Who, exactly, was this man Mr. Wilson had sent her to see?

She stepped inside, and found herself looking up yet another flight of stairs, in a lobby fully as imposing as the outside front door. A young man in a black waistcoat was walking down the steps, right hand outstretched. He immediately struck her as far and away the most insubstantial thing in the room.

"Lady Croft?"

She took his hand, and nodded.

"Mr. Powell?"

"Oh, good heavens, no. No. I am his associate, Mr. Pimms."

"Mr. . . . Pimms?" Lara had a moment where she wanted to laugh, but squelched it.

The young man, whose unfashionably long hair made him seem like a courtier from a different era entirely (the 1800s, Lara thought—or perhaps, the 1980s?), smiled broadly.

"Yes. Pimms. Like the beverage." He bowed slightly. "If you'll follow me . . ."

Pimms led her through the lobby, and down a long corridor. They passed a technician hard at work on a marble bust. He was removing a greenish mold that had obscured the face. Lara stopped for a moment to watch him work.

"A painstaking process," Pimms said, noting her interest. "Very skilled, I'm told."

Lara nodded. "Who is it?"

Pimms paused a moment. "Ah, you know, I'm not actually sure." He smiled.

Lara smiled herself to be companionable, but inside her head, an old, rarely used word came to mind, one that she felt fit Pimms quite well.

Nincompoop.

They kept walking. Powell was evidently a collector of all sorts of archaeological relics, judging by the motley collection of items he had on display. A Native American headdress, a medieval longsword, and a huge stone fertility totem, whose public display Lara thought in questionable taste. Questionable, that is, until they emerged into a grand chamber that redefined the term "bad taste."

"Goodness," she said, the word escaping her lips involuntarily.

"Impressive, isn't it?" Pimms, having mistaken her meaning entirely, gestured toward a row of statues against the far wall, a half-dozen anatomically correct Masai warriors arrayed for battle. "This is our newest acquisition."

The chamber was a single huge room, a chamber that reminded her of some nineteenth-century maharajah's version of an art collection. There were pieces from all over the world, arranged willy-nilly along the walls, statues and art from North Africa, Asia, and the Americas. In the center of the room, a series of sunken cushions, a seating area surrounded by a variety of Persian rugs. No two alike.

Lara felt the overwhelming urge to visit some remote, frozen corner of the world where she could look at a plain white landscape for a while.

"What," she asked, shaking her head, "does Mr. Powell do?"

"He's a lawyer," said Pimms. "I'm his law clerk. A, ah, fairly recent appointment."

"A lawyer," Lara repeated, slightly incredulous.

"Isn't it obvious?"

She turned, and saw a tall, elegant-looking man approaching. He wore a dark green smoking jacket and a smile that she found at once utterly insincere and completely captivating. He's probably a very good lawyer, she thought to herself, picturing this man before a jury.

"Lady Croft." The man extended his hand. "My pleasure. Manfred Powell, Q.C."

"Good morning." His grip was firmer than she expected; she gave it right back to him.

"I trust you had a pleasant trip down."

Lara nodded. "I did, thank you." She let his hand go, noted with pleasure a slight wince on his part. "This is quite a place you have here, Mr. Powell."

Pimms leaned forward. "Lady Croft was wondering whose was the face in the restoration."

"The bust?"

Lara nodded.

"Pluto. Not the dog, you understand, but the King of the Underworld."

Pimms laughed. Lara didn't.

"But of course, I know you know the difference, Lady Croft." Powell led her to the cushions, and sat down. "I believe you are quite an authority on things ancient and mythological."

She sank down into place opposite him, taking off her backpack.

"Well, you know. I travel."

Powell smiled. "That's quite an understatement, Lady Croft. I've seen your pictures in the magazines. You're very good."

"Very good," Pimms chimed in. He was standing behind Powell, hands clasped together, waiting to receive commands.

"Thank you. Both of you."

"And Mr. Wilson tells me you're quite the archaeologist, as well."

"He's very sweet. And very generous with his praise."

"He's an old friend of the family, I understand."

"Yes. I've known him all my life."

"And he knew your father quite well, I believe?"

"They were great friends."

"Wonderful." Powell nodded. "I had the honor of meeting him myself once. In Venice."

Powell knew her father? Lara raised an eyebrow.

During her conversation with Powell, Pimms had disappeared. She heard his footsteps now on the carpet behind her, lighter than before. Was the man trying to sneak up on her?

Lara shifted slightly in her seat, giving herself easy access to the gun sheathed in her right boot.

"Ah, Pimms." Powell looked behind her and smiled. "Aren't you late?"

Lara turned and saw Pimms's face screwed up in an expression of confusion.

"Eh?"

"I completely forgot you had to go." Powell shook his head regretfully. "What a shame. Say good-bye to Lady Croft."

"Ah. Yes. Of course." Pimms looked disappointed. "Good-bye, Lady Croft."

"Good-bye, Mr. Pimms." He turned on his heels and left.

"Now, then," Powell leaned forward slightly. "Mr. Wilson said you had something you wished to show me."

Lara nodded. She opened the main pouch of her backpack—it wouldn't do to open the wrong compartment and show Powell her weaponry—and pulled out a stack of photographs.

"Yes," she said. "These are pictures of the object I'm hoping you can help me to identify."

Powell's face fell.

"I had hoped you would bring the clock itself. It's hard, sometimes, with just photographs."

Lara nodded. "I understand. I'll appreciate whatever help you can give me."

"Of course." There was a small table to Powell's right; he opened a drawer in it and pulled out a magnifying glass. "I'll do my best."

He flipped through the stack of photos once, his face impassive, then returned to the picture on the top. The seal, on the clock's outer casing. The eye in the pyramid.

"This is an interesting design. The All-Seeing Eye. Isn't it?"

"Yes." Lara nodded.

Powell looked at her straight on. She couldn't read him at all.

A very good lawyer, she decided. Perhaps worth hiring the next time she found herself afoul of the law.

"What a fascinating piece. It is a shame you only brought photographs. Ah, well."

He flipped the top picture over, and looked at the next with his glass, then the next, and so on. When he'd finished, he spread out a few on the table, and began examining them again.

"Are clocks your area of expertise as well?"

"Clocks?" Powell responded without looking up. "No, I wouldn't think so."

"Mr. Wilson said—"

"Ah yes, Mr. Wilson. He is, as you suggested, too generous with his praise." Powell was looking at a picture of the two dials now. "You told him, I believe, it started ticking the night of the Aurora?"

"Yes."

"Hmmm." He shook his head. "Do you know why?"

Lara hestitated for a moment.

"Lady Croft?"

Worth testing to see how little he did—or didn't know. "Have you ever heard of the 'Clock of Ages'?"

"Hmmm? No." He moved the glass to the next photo on the table: the Clock, with the outer casing open, the nine concentric rings inside visible. "But it sounds intriguing. You must tell me about it."

"It's a myth," she said carefully. "An ancient clock that is a map, and a key, actually."

"Really?" Powell's lips curled into an expression of vague amusement. "To a buried treasure, no doubt. And this is that clock, you think?"

"I don't know. I was hoping for your guidance."

"Hmmm."

Lara looked around as Powell continued to scour the photos for details. Her eye was drawn to an ivory letter opener on his desk, at its hilt was a tiny crest.

The All-Seeing Eye.

What the hell?

"You said you were a lawyer?"

"Yes." Powell still didn't look up.

"And this," she gestured to her photos, "this is a hobby?"

"This is an obsession." Powell shook his head, and then he did look up finally, and smiled. "And really my specialty. My practice centers around antiquities."

"I see." Lara managed a smile of her own. "Perhaps I'll have need of your services one day."

"I would be honored to be of service." Then he shook his head, and set down his glass. "But this . . . completely eludes me." He met her eyes then, with that straight-on gaze she found so difficult to read. "I think I have never seen anything quite so beautiful that I know so little about."

Lara didn't know how to respond to that. Was the man coming on to her? Another antiquities expert—at least as unscrupulous as Mr. West, if she was any judge of character—was the last thing she needed in her life at the moment.

"So you can tell me nothing about the Clock?"

Powell shrugged. "A wise man knows what he doesn't know."

"And admits as much?"

"Exactly." He shook his head, picked up one of the photos again. "Clock of Ages, is it? You'll have to let me know what you find out about this."

"If I do find out anything, I most certainly will." Lara gathered all the photos together, and stood. "Thank you so much for your time, Mr. Powell."

"Not at all. This has been a pleasurable torment, Lady Croft. My ignorance amuses me."

Lara managed a farewell smile and handshake. But amused was not the word for how she felt at the moment. Confusion was more to the point.

On her ride home, lost in thought, she drove right past the Surrey exit without noticing.

10. Finally home, Lara changed into more comfortable clothes and spent the early part of the afternoon clearing out the storeroom she'd discovered the night of the Aurora. It was busywork, the kind she normally hated: sorting the artifacts into piles—those to donate, to sell, to keep; going over her father's journals for any mention of the clock, and finding nothing, unfortunately. But it gave her time to think about everything that had happened in the last two days, and to come to some conclusions. The ones she'd reached so far:

One. The clock she'd found was indeed the Clock of Ages her father had told her about.

Two. People—Powell and Mr. Wilson, specifically—were lying to her. Both had recognized the Clock, and refused to say so. Why, was a matter that was still unresolved in her head, but foremost in her thinking was another thing her father had said: A secret clock is a priceless treasure. Priceless, in particular, to those who knew the powers the Clock held the key to. The descendants of the People of the Light: the fabled Illuminati. Bryce was right, they were the punch line to every conspiracy theorist's favorite joke, but on the other hand . . . there was that letter opener at Powell's. Which led her to conclusion number three, that being, there was a lot more to Mr. Powell than met the eye.

She picked the last of the boxes off the shelf, and set it down on a table in front of her.

"Knock, knock, may I come in?"

Lara turned and saw Hillary leaning through the splintered panel that served as entrance to the store-room. He held a stack of paper in one hand.

"Hello, Hilly."

"Lara." He squeezed through the opening. "I've had a little background work done on your friend Mr. Powell."

"Anything interesting?"

"Lots." He began reading from the report briefly out-lining Powell's youth. He'd been born in Dorset, schooled at Oxford. A barrister at twenty-three, and ap-pointed Queen's Counsel at the unheard-of age of thirty-six. Current occupation: counsel to several large banking firms, board member and ranking stockholder for a number of important multinational corporations.

"He's got homes in London, Venice, and Washing-ton, D.C., as well as an apartment in New York City. And some very powerful friends—you'll note the names Mr. Powell's pops up with in the society pages."

"Finances?"

"Accounts in several Swiss banks. I'm afraid our sources can't touch the information without leaving fin-gerprints."

"I don't think that will be necessary right now," Lara said. "Although—"

The lights went out.

"Bryce," Hillary said in a calm voice.

Lara pushed past him and stuck her head out the panel. "Bryce!" she yelled. "Bryce!"

"Sorry!" The shout came from the Tech Room across the hall; a second later the lights came back up.

"Could you put that report on my desk, Hilly?" Lara picked up the opened cardboard box, and slung it under one arm. "Thanks."

She crossed the hall and entered the Tech Room. Bryce was perusing the clock underneath a high-power glass.

"What happened?"

"Red wire to green wire. My mistake." He spoke without looking up. "I thought I had found a way in for one of the fiber-optics."

There was a faint smell of burnt rubber in the air, and a thick strand of what looked like blackened wire at the edge of the workbench.

"No damage to the Clock?"

"No damage to the Clock." He shook his head. "But I'm not sure I'm getting anywhere with this."

"Leave it," Lara said. She hefted the cardboard box onto another bench. "Maybe I'll try to pump Powell for some more information."

Bryce shook his head. "Mister 'my ignorance amuses me.' "

"That's what he said."

Bryce snorted. "My ignorance amuses me, too."

"Yes, I've always found your ignorance amusing. But Powell's not ignorant."

"No?"

"No." Lara pulled a pocketknife out of her shorts and sliced through the packing tape on the cardboard box. "He's not ignorant. He's lying. He knows a lot more than he's letting on. Something's up with Mr. Powell."

She reached into the box and lifted out an old but perfectly preserved record turntable.

"I wondered what had happened to this."

"What the hell is that?" Bryce asked.

Lara set the turntable down on the bench and plugged it in. The platter spun smoothly. She picked up a glass and examined the cartridge. It appeared fairly new.

"This?" Lara smiled. "This is analog, Mr. Bryce. Nonbinary, nondithered, and noncompressed. Audio at its finest."

"Eh?"

"Inspiration, Bryce. Inspiration."

She clapped him on the shoulder, and went off to find Hillary, to see if he knew where her father's record collection had ended up.

Dressed in a gray wool coat, with Italian leather gloves to protect his hands from the chill, Powell stood high above the old control room floor at Battersea Power Station number two, looked out over the railing, and frowned.

"I despair of humanity ever reaching its fullest potential, Pimms. I truly do."

He swept his arm across the expanse of the immense

area below, the cavernous old generating station that had once provided London with a large percentage of its electricity. Battersea had been an ungodly beautiful building: polished parquet floors, wrought-iron staircases, Art Deco–style tile inlays throughout, shining chrome and steel everywhere.

Now it was, to be charitable, the very definition of a disaster area: holes in the roof, puddles of water everywhere, rust, decay, refuse, structural damage . . .

Powell shook his head. "Some would say Battersea is beyond saving."

Pimms cleared his throat. "They would be wrong, sir."

"Yes, yes they would, Pimms." He nodded. "They would be wrong, now that Manfred Powell is on the scene." On the scene, and in charge of the restoration, in charge of turning the old power station into a museum to commemorate England's century of Empire. A restoration made possible by funds surreptitiously channeled through the Order and into the coffers of the Committee to Save Battersea. They owned the station now, and he had the crew working from pictures of Battersea shortly after the construction, working round-the-clock. By the time they were done, the station would once again be one of the most admired buildings in London. Or he would know the reason why.

The comm unit on his belt buzzed once, softly. His company was here.

Powell turned away from the railing and headed for the staircase, crooking a finger at Pimms to indicate that he should follow.

"I wonder what Mr. Scott thinks of the way our fair

England has treated the gem he provided her? Allowed to fall into disrepair, bid out for use as a theme park, gutted and then left to rot? How can a people allow this to happen to their architectural treasures?"

"It is a crime," Pimms said.

"You're bloody well right it's a crime," Powell said. "And the villain, I suggest to you, Pimms, is the fine men and women of Parliament. A Parliament that is unable to preserve its country's past, much less provide for its future. Is this any way to run a world, Pimms?"

"I—"

Powell wagged a finger. "The question was rhetorical. The answer is 'Of course not.' "

"Of course not," Pimms said obediently.

Powell nodded. "Which is why the Illuminati are necessary. It is our job to preserve the past; our task to plan for the future. Humanity is at a critical stage in its history, Pimms. We must step forward and provide the leadership that the world needs."

Powell led Pimms through a door from the control room and out onto one of the scaffoldings on the building's exterior. On the ground below, carefully threading its way down the alley to the main construction site entrance, was a black taxicab. The cab stopped, and discharged a passenger. An old man in a brown trenchcoat, carrying a brown satchel. Wilson: on schedule, looking about furtively, clearly wondering if he'd come to the right part of town.

"He looks nervous."

"Yes." Powell pursed his lips. "As well he should be." They continued to descend the scaffolding. As they reached the ground, Richards, who was in charge of the renovation, approached with a clipboard.

"No Carrera, Mr. Powell," he said. "But good news: We can get a different grade of the marble from one of the local suppliers. At half the price."

"No Carrera?" Powell frowned. "That is not good news, Mr. Richards. You called Venice?"

The man nodded. "I did, sir. Yes, sir."

"You mentioned my name?"

In the harsh lights generated by the arc welders, Powell saw Richards's face color.

"Uh, no, sir."

"Mention my name." He picked up the clipboard, and signed it. "I want Carrera for this station." He handed the clipboard back to Richards as Wilson approached.

"Ah, Mr. Wilson."

"Mr. Powell. It's good to see you again. You're looking well."

"And you." But Powell was lying. Up close, the strain was clearly telling on the old man. There were dark circles under his eyes; Powell thought the man might have been drinking. Which wouldn't do at all. Powell wanted him at ease.

"Thank you for coming. I realize it's quite late."

"No, no." Wilson shook his head. "I know how important this is."

"This is quite a busy area, Mr. Wilson." Powell held out his hand, and Pimms handed him a construction worker's hard hat. "You should wear this."

Wilson placed it on his head; it tilted awkwardly. Powell smiled, reached up, and adjusted it for him.

"You brought all your notes on the Clock? And your original photographs?"

Wilson patted his satchel. "They're in my case."

"May I?" Without waiting for his reply, Powell nodded to Pimms, who took the satchel and opened it, holding it out at arm's length. Inside, as promised, was a stack of paper and photographs: images of the Clock, Powell saw.

"Good," he said. "Thank you."

Pimms snapped the case shut. Powell indicated the path before them to Mr. Wilson. "Let's walk."

The power station complex was surrounded by a warren of alleyways, access roads, and cobblestoned streets. Powell led the group outside and along one of the smaller pathways, noting that Wilson was still ill-at-ease. The man took each step slowly and carefully, like a closet drunk afraid to reveal himself. Perhaps a little humor to relax him?

They stood now in the shadow of the immense main building. High above, workers on a gantry were welding huge sheets of steel over the holes in the complex walls.

"We own this building now," Powell said matter-of-factly.

"You do?" Wilson shook his head, caught himself. "I mean, we do?"

Powell raised an eyebrow. Interesting slip, that "you." He made note of it. "Yes, we do. I'm thinking of living here. Just me and my Abyssinian cat. What do you think?"

Wilson looked confused. "Ah . . ."

Powell waved him off. "Just kidding."

At that second, sparks showered down from the

gantry above—silver and blue flashing against the night sky. Powell was reminded of the Aurora the previous evening.

"Two nights in a row of celestial spectacle, Pimms. Extraordinary times we're living in, wouldn't you say?"

"Yes, sir."

"And you, Mr. Wilson? How do you feel about what is happening?"

Wilson frowned. "I don't take your meaning."

Powell stopped in his tracks, and turned to face the older man. "The alignment, Mr. Wilson. A chance for the Order to emerge from the shadows at last, and take our place as the world's rightful leaders. How do you feel about what is to come?"

"I am excited, of course."

"Of course." Powell clasped his hands behind his back, and kept walking. "And yet there are those who would oppose such actions on our part. Out of a misguided fear of our motives. I'm sure you understand."

They continued on down the street in silence, as sparks hissed above. To his left, Powell heard the sounds of distant laughter and music. The Thames was but a few hundred meters away. He glanced to his left and saw the river, and on it one of those God-awful tour boats, lit up like a Christmas tree.

They moved on, around a corner. The music and laughter faded away; the four chimneys of Battersea loomed above.

"I fear Lady Croft may turn out to be one of those misguided souls, Mr. Wilson. But of course you know her far better than I. Like an honorary uncle, she said of you. Lady Croft, that is."

"She said that?"

"She did."

Wilson swallowed, visibly moved. Powell was not pleased to see it.

"She must mean a lot to you."

"She does. I've known her all her life. Since she was a little girl."

"But thankfully, you betrayed her." Powell stopped walking, and turned to face Wilson. "What a relief."

A huge spot, set up to provide light for the welders above, shone behind the older man.

"Well, ah, I don't think . . ." Wilson cleared his throat. "I . . . I mean . . ."

"Sending her to us," Powell said, his tone cutting. "To me. That was a betrayal and you know it."

"I had hoped that was not necessarily a . . . betrayal. I had hoped you and Lara—Lady Croft, I mean . . . could . . ."

Powell shook his head in disgust. The man was bleating. Powell hated bleating.

"Trust me, it was most definitely a betrayal. But that's all right, that's a good thing. And yet, Mr. Wilson," he folded his hands over his chest, "you worry me. I can feel your conflict over this. I can't help wondering what you may have told Lady Croft. About the Clock. About me. About the Order."

As he spoke, Powell leaned forward, so that he and Wilson were barely a foot apart as he finished. The older man was visibly quaking.

"I would never breach my oath." Wilson set his jaw. "Never."

"Not even for your lovable pseudo-niece?"

Wilson lowered his head. "Not even for her."

Powell smiled. "Good."

The two men stood facing each other. Powell took the older man's measure, noting how fast his chest rose, up and down, up and down, his nostrils flaring, his breath making steam in the chill night air. *Perhaps he hasn't told her yet,* Powell thought. *But he will. He most certainly will.*

He touched the comm unit on his belt, once. Then Powell held out his hand, offering it to Wilson.

"Shake."

A beat, then Wilson took his hand and shook it. His index finger extended toward Powell's wrist briefly: Powell's made the same movement.

"Kneel please, Brother Wilson."

Wilson knelt, bowing his head. He knew what was expected of him. *The man has been one of us for a long time,* Powell thought.

"Brother Powell," Wilson began, his tone suddenly, strangely, formal. "I kneel before you, our brethren and the Eye That Sees All in humiliation and disgrace. I vow to pledge my allegiance anew."

As Wilson spoke, Powell saw a figure emerge from behind one of the many shadows cast by the immense power station. This was Mr. Julius, captain of what Powell liked to think of as his own little strike force, though of course they were all initiates of the Order to one degree or another. Julius had come now in response to Powell's touch of the comm unit, but the man was never more than a few seconds away from him at all times.

"Judge me," finished Wilson, still kneeling, head still bowed, eyes closed.

Julius handed Powell a scabbard. Powell drew a sword from it, as Pimms inhaled sharply.

Then in one fluid, precise blow, he raised the sword, and swung it, keeping his eye on the target: just above the vertebrae at the base of Wilson's neck, a half-inch space between the bones, to allow the blade to pass through cleanly and—

Snikt.

The head rolled to the ground. The headless body slumped over.

Powell took a step backward, and in one practiced motion, resheathed the sword and handed it back to Julius.

"Well. That felt good."

He smiled at Julius, and turned to Pimms, who was suddenly sweating.

Powell grinned.

"I know. Right now you're feeling strangely but vividly alive. Takes a little getting used to. But trust me—these are the best of times. Bag the head, would you?"

Julius handed Pimms a canvas bag.

Pimms turned white as a sheet.

"Bag it?"

"Bag it." Powell nodded. "And then bring his satchel to me at the office. And Julius—"

The team leader stepped forward.

"Mr. Powell?"

"You may begin the operation."

Julius smiled. "Yes, sir. You'll be at your office, I take it?"

"Yes, indeed. Waiting with bated breath."

Julius nodded, and then melted away as quickly and silently as he had arrived.

Powell looked up at the twinkling stars above, inhaled the night air, and felt completely, totally, at peace with himself.

11. **W**hen she was younger, Lara had gone through a phase of hating everything that Croft Manor represented: all that hidebound, stuffy tradition. She had painted her room black, bought a boa constrictor for a pet, taken up with some of the more déclassé gang elements from the village. Now, she'd more or less made her peace with who she was and where she'd come from. But still, she had those moments of wanting to thumb her nose at the portraits staring down at her from what seemed like every spare inch of wall space, which is where the bungee-jumping came in.

However, as she stood on the middle landing of the Grand Staircase in Croft Manor, dressed in her pajamas, she wasn't thinking about the bungee-jumping. The thoughts that occupied her mind were the same ones she'd had for the last two days, ever since the Aurora, her discovery of the hidden storeroom underneath the stairs, and her puzzling conversations with Wilson and Powell. She thought of her father, and the stories he'd told her so long ago, about the all-powerful Eye, and the Illuminati.

And now that she was thinking about Mr. Wilson . . .

Strange that he hadn't returned her calls. Two of them this afternoon, another just an hour ago. Lara had half a mind to go to his apartment right now and make sure he was all right.

Perhaps she would do that, even though she was already dressed for bed. But first—

"Hilly?"

"A minute," he called back. "I'm just hooking up the second set of speakers."

She heard a needle drop onto a phonograph record: a second later, the sound of Bach's *Concerto No. 5* came wafting through the hall. A few seconds after that, she heard Hillary's footsteps descending toward her room.

"Thanks, Hilly." She spoke without turning, gathering herself. Time to put the events of the day behind her. Already she could feel the music working its magic on her. It was soothing, relaxing. One of her father's favorite pieces, she recalled; she hadn't heard it in years.

"Is there anything else you need?"

Lara shook her head. "No, thank you. Go on to bed."

"I will. Don't you stay up too late."

"I'll try not to." She heard him head back upstairs, and stood there for a moment, looking down the stairwell, at the polished marble floor thirty feet below her.

Lara took a deep breath, and dove headfirst over the railing.

As she fell, she was aware of the music and the

ground growing ever closer, but foremost in her mind, strangely enough, were her father's words from long ago:

A secret clock is a priceless treasure, he had said.

The floor loomed before her.

A foot away from a messy end, the two bungee cords attached to the harness around her waist reached their farthest extension, and stopped her. They held her suspended in midair for a split second. That was long enough for Lara to execute a perfect double flip, and snap back up, past the middle landing she had jumped from, past the huge crystal chandelier, and all the way to the top of the Great Hall.

The music soared. She spun, did a flip, a backflip, and dove again.

A secret clock is a priceless treasure.

That is why her father had hidden it. Because everyone aware of its value—anyone who knew the story of the Triangle's power—would do almost anything to obtain the Clock.

Lara fell, spun, and rose again.

Moonlight lit the staircase and the vestibule. Lara twisted in midair, a corkscrew, spinning once, twice, and then rising. She needed this, needed to get her blood flowing again; she'd been cooped up too long in the house, in London, in civilization. She was starting to feel like Lady Croft: Might as well have a bloody tea party tomorrow for the ladies in the village for all the life she was living. If her father could see her now . . .

A priceless treasure, he had said.

Priceless to none more than the Illuminati. Once

they uncoverd its whereabouts, they would stop at nothing to obtain it.

Lara spun again. She fell past the huge window that graced the Grand Staircase, and as she finished her turn, for a fleeting moment she took in the huge skylight above the Great Hall.

Outside she glimpsed movement: shadows. She spun, keeping them in sight as she rose: black-suited figures, night goggles, weapons slung over their shoulders, backpacks, a good dozen of them. A thin beam of red light shot across the floor below her and was immediately joined by another, and then another, and another: laser sights, crisscrossing the entryway.

Invasion.

Lara fell again. In the Tech Room, she saw the motion detectors activate a steel cage scything down over the Clock. She rose into the air; she reached out and grabbed the huge crystal chandelier by its support line. The crystal rattled. Lara steadied herself, and the chandelier. Then she began spinning it, swinging it around in an ever-widening circle, a circle that took her with it. Down below, the floor was alive with shadows, the distorted reflections of her midnight intruders.

The chandelier was whipping around like a giant slingshot now—faster and faster, in a wider and wider circle. Lara hung from it, her body almost parallel to the ground. Her feet brushed the marble railing of the middle landing.

She let go of the chandelier, and started running.

Still suspended by her bungee cords, the centrifugal force let her run at a ninety-degree angle to the ground, up and around the inside of the balcony, going higher and higher until she was at the upper level.

Then she reached down and unclipped the bungee cords.

She flipped again, in midair, and landed on her feet in the upper corridor.

She needed her guns; they were on the other side of the stairwell. Hugging the ground, staying on her toes, she began to move. As she did so, she realized she hadn't once questioned who the intruders were, or what they were after.

The Illuminati, come calling for their precious Clock.

Laser sights skittered and danced on the walls of the stairwell behind her. The voices were coming closer. Time to move.

She raced down the long passageway leading off the landing, hugging the wall. She heard a weapon being cocked. As she ran past a closet door, she threw it open; silent rounds *chunked* into the doorframe, splintering the wood, sending plaster flying into the air.

She heard footsteps ahead of her too. Damn. They must have come up the other side of the landing as well. They were, in fact, everywhere in the house. She could hear them trooping down the Entrance Hall, throwing open doors, drawers, and closets. An explosion sounded, then another: *What the hell?*

A black-suited figure turned the corner just ahead of her.

Lara's mind raced: forward roll, somersault into a flying kick, knock him out, take his gun, but then . . . ? There were too many to do a frontal assault; she needed to take them down one at a time and she needed her own guns—not just the Colts in her bedroom, but the heavy weaponry down in the Equipment room. How was she going to get down the two flights without—

Ahh.

She raced back down the corridor the way she'd come, and took a hard right down a short corridor. Footsteps sounded behind her again. She passed a linen closet on the left, the King James Bedroom on the right. The hall dead-ended in front of her. The two doors, and then nothing.

No way out; the invaders would turn the corner and see that. Lara smiled.

She was exactly where she wanted to be.

Powell was relaxing in his bedroom, lying facedown on a tatami mat. He had a small comm screen folded open in front of him: Julius's face filled the LCD display. The man wore night goggles and a black turtleneck. Barely visible in the picture behind him was a huge English manor house.

"We're in, sir," Julius said. "We have targeted the objective."

Powell reached a hand forward and depressed a button next to the screen. "Excellent, Julius. Contact me once you've secured it."

Julius nodded. Powell flicked the screen off, and exhaled a sigh of satisfaction.

He doubted that Lady Croft was enjoying the evening as much as he was.

* * *

Lara's wristwatch beeped. She pressed it once, silencing it. Not that a little electronic noise would give her away, but . . . better safe than sorry.

Now she heard only the muffled noises of explosions, of weapons firing, and the heavy thrum of an old turbine engine. It needed to be oiled: Hillary was slipping. But then, when was the last time they'd used the dumbwaiter?

That was where Lara was now, hunched over into a little ball, squeezed into a space meant for two serving trays, heading down through the bowels of Croft Manor. For the moment, the intruders had no idea of her whereabouts. She doubted that would last long. The way they had come after her so precisely when they first broke in, they must have some kind of heat-sensing equipment. They'd be able to find her no matter where she—

Her heart stopped in her chest. Hillary. And Bryce.

They'd be after them as well.

The dumbwaiter came to a stop. Lara pushed open the doors, and squeezed out into the darkness. The stone floor was cold; she wished for something more than slippers. She paused for a moment, letting her muscles uncramp, her eyes adjust to the darkness. She knew the room she was in intimately, but had never entered it from the dumbwaiter before.

She reached along the wall, found the light switch, and flicked it on.

Harsh light flooded the room, reflected off the hood of the Aston Martin, the chrome of the Streetfighter, the windshield of the Land Rover, her entire neatly parked collection of vehicles. The light also glinted off a row of display cases on the opposite wall. The cases were glass—bulletproof, shatterproof, glass—and held her weapons. The antiques—the Brownings, Messerschmitts, and Lugers in one case; the semiautomatics—the Uzis, Kalishnikovs, the NTGs in another; the grenade launchers, the chemical drops, and the really good stuff (as Bryce liked to call it) in a third.

Lara sprinted across the room, reaching for the key pad on the second case so she could punch in the unlock code, get her weapons, and check on Hilly and Bryce. Then she could begin teaching these intruders a thing or two about the proper way to enter an English country home.

She entered the first number, and the equipment room door blew off the hinges.

Lara barely had time to step back from the case before the invaders were through the door and firing, three of them—damn those heat sensors—and she backpedaled away and started to run. The bullets shattered the case alongside her and she leaped, and rolled behind a massive steel equipment chest just as the shelves where she kept all her communications gear literally exploded with bullets. Pieces of equipment went flying past her, and at her, and onto the floor next to her.

One of them happened to be a comm link, complete with headset.

Bryce's new favorite. Hooked up to cameras throughout the house, it allowed you to see everywhere, talk to anyone . . . supposedly. Base stations in the Tech Room on the main floor of the house, and in Bryce's trailer.

Bryce's trailer.

Lara picked up the comm link and put it on.

"Bryce! Bryce! Come in!"

Static.

"Bryce!"

Gunfire punched into the metal chest. Lara peered around the corner of the chest and saw a green canvas bag sitting on the ground about five feet away. Army surplus, courtesy of an old friend, Major Tom Severino, USMC. She hadn't gotten around to unpacking it yet. Good thing: The contents of that bag were about to come in mighty handy.

She reached out to grab it and nearly got her arm shot off.

"Bryce! I'm in the equipment room!"

More static. She didn't want to think about what that could mean, except to conclude that she was on her own, at least for the moment, so she'd have to make do.

She picked up the back half of a walkie-talkie that had been shredded by gunfire, and tossed it halfway across the room. As it fell, gunfire exploded in its wake.

Lara jumped out, grabbed the green canvas bag, and rolled back behind the metal chest. She quickly opened the bag, and pulled out a C-S gas-cartridge launcher. The bag had half a dozen gas cartridges in it as well.

Perfect. That ought to even up the odds a little bit.

The lights went out.

Oh, hell and damnation! Only one reason for them to switch out the lights: They had night-vision goggles. Night-vision goggles and heat sensors: She was dead where she sat on the cold stone, dead in her pajamas and—

"Lara?"

"Bryce." *Thank God.*

"You seem to be in a bit of a tight spot."

"Switch your cameras to night vision, Bryce." The security cameras all had infra-red lenses as well as standard optical ones. "You have to be my eyes."

"Switching. Are you armed?"

"After a fashion." She racked home one of the gas cartridges. "How's Hilly?"

"Better than you. I've got him on-screen now." Bryce chuckled.

"What?"

"You ought to see him. He's got that ridiculous dressing gown on with a Kevlar vest over it, and that old shotgun of his."

"Good."

"Are those C-S cartridges you have?" Bryce asked.

"You can see better than I can."

"And do you have a mask?"

She turned and glared in the direction she remembered the security camera being in. "I'm improvising. They're stealing my bloody Clock, aren't they?"

"You've got that right. A good half-dozen of them in the Tech Room, using a torch to burn their way in. Five minutes, tops, they're through, they're in, they've got it."

"Well, you don't have to sound so bloody cheerful about it. All right." Lara took a deep breath. "Let's deal with them one room at a time. Talk to me."

"Right. Three bad guys, all with night vision. Number one, standing by the Aston Martin."

The Aston Martin. Lara fixed its position in her

head. He was close, maybe ten feet away, about 150 degrees clockwise from her position—

A fusillade of gunfire slammed into the metal chest.

"He's firing, by the way."

"You're such a help." In one fluid motion, Lara spun, raised the launcher above the metal chest, and fired. The cartridge whooshed as it left the launcher. She heard it impact—hard—on something, and then a second *smack*, a sound like a sack of flour slamming into the wall.

"Bingo. One clay pigeon down, two to go." Bryce sounded happy, but there was no time for that. Out there in the room, where the gas cartridge had exploded, Lara knew tear gas was beginning to fill the air. And as Bryce had pointed out, she didn't have a mask.

"Next. Quickly, please." She reached into the bag, pulled out another cartridge, and racked it into the launcher.

"Number two, crouching, by the TVR."

Lara fixed his position in her head, then rose again quickly, set the launcher on the chest, and fired. The cartridge whooshed—

Glass shattered.

What?

"Oh, bugger. Sorry. I reparked the TVR."

Gunfire exploded again around Lara. She didn't have time to think, just dove around to the other end of the metal chest.

"You drove my TVR?"

"Well, I just ran it into the village for—"

"Later, Bryce. Where is number two now?"

"Right." He cleared his throat. "Number two is moving to the Lotus—which is, uh, in the same spot. He's standing . . ."

Lara had dragged the green canvas bag along with her: she racked another cartridge, and coughed. Damn. The gas. Have to finish this up quickly.

She turned, raised the launcher and fired. This time, the *whoosh* of the cartridge was followed by a satisfying *smack*.

"That's two. Three is on the move; this one's clever." He was silent for a moment.

"Bryce?"

"Sorry. Can't pick him out."

Damn.

Lara coughed again; her eyes started to water. Number three was going to wait her out; he must have guessed she didn't have a mask. He was going to lie low until she started coughing and wheezing and getting sick, and then he was going to just walk over and put a bullet right in her brain.

She coughed again.

"The hell with that."

"Say again, Lara."

She ignored Bryce, squinted into the darkness. There—hanging on the wall behind her. More gadgets. Not Bryce's. These were the key fobs—remote controls—to all the cars.

She stood and ran to a new position, grabbing the fobs on the way. As she ran, she started pressing buttons, one by one, as many as she could. The noise, after so much relative silence, was deafening. Radios blared. Engines roared.

"Oh, good show," Bryce said. "That's got him moving."

Lara crouched down again, gasped for breath, and coughed.

"Where?"

"Number three is hiding betweeen the MacLaren and your father's old Lea Francis. I think he's a little freaked by all the noise."

"Hiding?" Lara coughed again, harder this time. There was a burning in the back of her throat she couldn't get rid of.

"He's pretty pissed off—I think he might run his keys down the side of the MacLaren."

Lara blinked through her tears, squinted, looked down at the key fobs in her hand. There: the one for the MacLaren.

She leaned out and pressed it.

The headlights on the MacLaren blazed.

"Dammit!" That was Bryce: his night vision must have shorted out—that meant so had number three's night goggles.

Lara got to her feet, and coughed again. A telltale signal of her position. Number three fired, but he couldn't find her. He shot wildly, blindly, and kept missing. He was blind. Lara wasn't. She could see just fine now.

She spun, and kicked at his head.

"Three is down," Bryce said.

But Lara didn't care about that; she was already reaching through the shattered glass of the weapons case and grabbing her twin .45s and running for the door that led back to the main part of the house—and the Tech Room, and the Clock.

"Bryce! Are they still there?" She coughed as she ran, trying to clear her lungs.

"Can't see. They've laid down smoke cover. Careful."

She tore down the corridor as fast as she could. Bryce was right about the smoke; it was getting heavier as she got closer to the Tech Room, but she couldn't worry about that right now. She could only worry about the Clock, and then she was through the Tech Room door and she saw—

The smoke thinning.

The cut metal bars of the security cage.

The empty pedestal where the Clock had been.

"Dammit!"

Lara spun on her heel and ran out of the room. Maybe she could still catch them, maybe—

Footsteps. Behind her. One man.

Lara spun, tightening the triggers on both her guns as—

Hillary flinched.

Lara gasped.

She twisted her arms, her wrists, so that the barrels of both guns fired up and into the ceiling. Plaster imploded: a light sprinkling of dust, like a little cloud of snow, fell to the ground.

"Oh." Bryce's voice came over the headset. "That was a close one."

Hillary, who was indeed wearing a dressing gown and Kevlar vest, as Bryce had told her, uncocked his shotgun, and wiped his brow.

"I think they've all gone." His voice came out as a strangulated whisper.

Lara lowered her guns. "They got what they came for."

Hillary sat right down on the floor.

"Excuse me a moment, while I'm sick."

"Sorry about that." Lara holstered her guns.

"You don't look well either."

"Tear gas." Lara shook her head. "It'll pass."

Which it would. But what wouldn't go away quite so quickly, she suspected, was the sick feeling in her stomach.

Her father had trusted her with the Clock—something he considered of all-consuming importance.

And she had let him down.

12. Powell usually began every morning with a vigorous massage and a shower, but today he was in a more contemplative mood. So much good fortune, so unexpectedly, with the promise of so much more to come . . . it was worth simply basking in the moment.

He drew back the office drapes, unrolled his tatami mat, and knelt down on it.

It was just after dawn. The early morning sun caught the brushed steel of the orrery on his desk. As the orrery spun, the gleaming reflections from each of the planets shot out like miniature lightning flashes, causing a flickering, strobelike effect.

He watched the miniature worlds for a moment, then closed his eyes, and prepared the first prayer in his head. But he couldn't concentrate on the ritual. All he could concentrate on was the simple fact that, at long last, the Clock was his.

Praise be to the All-Knowing, though if the truth be

told, he reflected, the All-Knowing had much less to do with it than Julius's thorough planning and preparation. That man was worth a dozen Pimms. If only, Powell thought wistfully, Julius could be given some of the social graces he lacked at present, then . . .

There was a knock on the door.

Powell opened his eyes.

"Go away."

The door swung wide, and—speak of the devil— Pimms stepped in.

"Good morning, sir. I'm sorry for interrupting, but . . ." Pimms voice trailed off. "Goodness."

He was staring at the desk, at the orrery, and at what stood next to it.

"Is that the Clock?" Pimms asked.

Powell rolled his eyes. "No, it's a fish I caught. It's a bouquet of fresh flowers."

"I see." Pimms frowned. "Sir?"

"Of course it's the Clock." Powell got to his feet in one fluid motion. "Lady Croft was kind enough to let us borrow it."

"Really?"

Powell rolled his eyes.

"Ah." Pimms pursed his lips. "Did . . . is, ah, Lady Croft, ah . . . dead?"

"No. Still in the game."

"Wonderful. Good, I mean."

Pimms's all-too-obvious interest amused him. Powell picked his tea off the desk and sipped from it. You could hardly blame the man, of course; there was a lot about Lady Croft to be interested in.

"Girl's clearly got a lot of spunk, wouldn't you say, Pimms?"

"Yes. Well. She's very . . . ah . . ." Pimms reddened.

"She taught Julius and his men a thing or two about home invasion. I'm sure we'll see her again."

"You think so?"

"I do. I suspect we may even need to hire her, Pimms." There was clearly more to Lady Croft than first met the eye. Or rather, more to her besides what met the eye. A great deal of her father in that girl, it seemed to him.

Pimms was still staring at the Clock. "May I?" He held out his hand as if to touch it.

"Look with your eyes," Powell said sharply. Miss Holcomb had spent two hours examining it closely, but as yet she'd been unable to say for certain exactly how the mechanism functioned, or what touching the knobs at the Clock's four corners would do. Knowing Pimms, he would find, and hit, the self-destruct button.

"Of course. I'm sorry." Pimms knelt down, and got his head as close to the Clock's glowing eye as was humanly possible. "It's very beautiful. Ingenious. What makes it glow?"

"A previously revoked law of nature: $e=mc^2$. Perhaps you've heard of it?"

Pimms nodded. "Yes, but—"

"Ah, Pimms. You'll force me to explain, won't you?"

"Sir?"

"Never mind." The opportunity for quiet meditation over, Powell decided to get back to work. Just a few last calculations to do, anyway.

He stood up, crossed the office, and hung his robe on a hook next to the cherrywood filing cabinet. Underneath the robe, he wore his customary dark suit and turtleneck. He settled into his chair, and carefully opened the Clock so that its inner mechanism was fully revealed.

"The puzzle, Pimms, is that there is no apparent energy involved in the operation of this Clock. It works, all on its own." He pointed to the sweeping dials on the inner three faces. "Like magic."

"Magic. Really? Like in the old stories?"

"That's right. Just like in the old stories." Powell woke his laptop; the astronomical charts Miss Holcomb had provided were set up in one window on his screen, and a function calculator on another. On his desk were a compass and sextant; he made a reading off the Clock's innermost ring, and began taking measurements.

"That's incredible." Pimms pointed to the Clock. "So this is going to lead us to the first tomb?"

"Once I finish here," Powell said, "we will have the tomb's exact location."

"What are you going to tell the High Council?"

"That we figured it out," Powell tapped his laptop with the sextant, "with our very expensive supercomputers."

Pimms frowned. "We did?"

"Pimms." Powell sighed, shook his head. "Pimms, Pimms, Pimms." He shut his laptop. "No. We did not figure it out with our supercomputers. We failed utterly. But we are not about to admit it."

"No? I mean . . . No. Of course not."

"So what are we going to tell the Council?"

"Ummm." Pimms opened his mouth, shut it, and opened it again. "That . . . we figured it out with our computers?"

Powell smiled encouragingly. "That's the spirit, man." He stood up and clapped Pimms on the shoulder. "You're getting the hang of it. Lies, and half-truths. Excellent." He laughed. Pimms laughed. Powell raised a warning finger. "Except, of course, when dealing with me."

"Right." Pimms swallowed hard. His eyes were focused on the scabbard that lay on an angle across the desk.

Fear, Powell thought. *Far and away the best motivator.*

"Good man." Powell turned and walked to the window. "Miss Holcomb will be coming by soon for the Clock. She's made arrangements at Oxford for the use of a scanning microscope. You'll supply her with any monies she needs."

"Of course."

Powell took in the awakening streets outside. It was a glorious day—a glorious moment. The Clock was his.

"Croft had it all these years." He spoke aloud without thinking, shaking his head in wonderment. The man would have let the alignment pass without using it, he knew that, felt it in his soul. The fool.

"Lara Croft?" Pimms asked.

"No, you fool. Lord Croft. I doubted its existence . . . but he felt it in his bones."

"He was a great man," Pimms said.

Powell gave him a withering glare. "And how would you know?"

"Oh, eh . . . Mrs. King told me some stories—"

"Please." Powell shook his head. "Yes, he was a great man. But then again, I'm alive, and he's not."

Lara hadn't even bothered trying to clean up after the invasion, and had forbidden Hillary from doing anything, either.

"We'll get TDM down from London," she said. "They'll clear away all the trash. Then we can work on fixing up the place."

Hillary—whose room had suffered minimal damage—had gone up to bed willingly. Bryce was another matter entirely.

"I'm going to modify the bugs." He was sitting at the workbench in the devastated Tech Room, with a monocle in his right eye, a fiber-optic in his right hand, and a half-dozen of his little creatures in various stages of deconstruction on the bench before him. "I think I can get them to handle the cleanup."

Lara left him to it, and headed upstairs to get dressed. She needed to hit something: She chose the gym. Two hours later she was covered in sweat, and feeling angry.

Mr. Powell—for she was convinced that he was behind the break-in; it was the only explanation that made even a lick of sense—*Mr. Powell,* she said to herself, *I want my Clock back.*

She showered and had breakfast. Out in the lobby, she found Hillary with a pen and paper, taking notes on the damage. Bryce was sitting on the ruined staircase, looking dejected. He looked up when he saw Lara and shook his head.

"The bugs," he said. "They're rejecting my definition of trash."

"Is it, perhaps, too liberal a definition?" Lara asked.

Bryce glared.

Someone knocked on the door. Lara opened it. A UPS courier, with an ungodly big smile for this time of the morning, stood there.

"Sorry miss, I tried your doorbell, but it must be—" His jaw went slack.

"Broken? There's a lot of that going around, as you can see." Lara took the envelope from him, the pen from Hillary, and signed in the spot that said "received by."

The UPS man's eyes, meanwhile, were taking a one hundred-eighty–degree tour around the lobby. "What the—"

"I woke up one morning, and I just hated everything." She handed him back the envelope.

He stared at her as if she were speaking Swahili.

"You take your copy," Lara said helpfully, "and hand the envelope back to me."

"Right. Thanks." He did so. "Cheers."

He left without looking back.

"Who's 'Stribling, Clive, and Winterset,' then?" Bryce was peering over her shoulder at the envelope. "Sounds like a bunch of lawyers."

"They are a bunch of lawyers." Lara turned the envelope over, and ripped at the seal. "My lawyers."

"Oh. Shut my face again."

"Well, you are very nosy." Hillary peered over her shoulder now. "What's in the envelope?"

"Another envelope." Lara pulled it out; a typewritten letter was attached to it with a paper clip. The letter was on Stribling, Clive, and Winterset stationery. It read:

> As per instructions of our Client, Lord Croft, this envelope to be delivered to his daughter, Lara, on the 6th day of July 2001, if, and only if, Client should predecease this date.

A chill ran up Lara's spine. She sat down heavily, taking Bryce's place at the foot of the ruined staircase.

"Lara?" Hillary was leaning over her, concern etched on his features. "What is it?"

"It's a letter from my father."

"Your father?"

She nodded. "Written before he died and delivered today—as per his instructions."

"Bloody hell," Bryce said.

"Holy shit." Hillary clapped a hand over his mouth the second the words were out. "Excuse me."

Lara looked down at the envelope; the flap was sealed in red wax, her father's seal, the "C" he had always used. She turned it over. The single word "Lara" was inscribed, in his perfect copperplate hand, on the front.

Tears filled her eyes.

"Are you all right?" Hillary asked.

"Tell you the truth," she said. "I'm not sure."

She pulled out her pocketknife and slit through the seal. Her hands, Lara was surprised to note, were trembling.

She put away the knife and pulled out the letter. It was on her father's stationery. It was in her father's hand.

> To see a World in a Grain of Sand,
> And a Heaven in a Wild Flower,
> Hold Infinity in the palm of your hand,
> And Eternity in an hour.

"Well?" Bryce asked.

She read it out loud.

They were all silent for a moment. The letter dangled from her hand.

"Blake, isn't it?" Hillary asked.

Lara nodded. "He always used to read me that poem."

She'd wondered why then; she wondered why now. What was her father trying to tell her?

"Is it a code, you think?" Bryce asked.

Lara shook her head, and tried to reason it through. First the Clock, then this. The two were related, they had to be. Related to the alignment, clearly. Related to the Triangle. And if a secret clock was a priceless treasure . . .

"I think," she said, standing up. "I think . . ."

Bryce and Hillary looked at her. "Yes?"

She pushed past them, and headed for the Library.

Fifteen minutes later, she was perched on the ladder, next to the literature stacks, holding the first edition of *William Blake: Poetry*, in her hands. She hadn't seen this book in years; her father used to have it out on his desk all the time. The illustrations in it were incredible:

gods and demi-gods and all manner of apocalyptic visions, matched in intensity only by Blake's own verse.

She flipped through the pages till she came to "Auguries of Innocence," the poem whose first two lines were the sum total of her father's letter, and there they were again: "To see a World in a Grain of Sand" . . . She'd been expecting a clue of some kind, but there was nothing. Nothing. Now what?

Lara closed the book and climbed down off the ladder. She sat down at her father's desk, the morning sun beating through the windows behind her, and carefully laid the book down.

She opened it, and a chill went down her spine.

She'd been holding the book upside down, and had opened it to the endpapers—which were embossed with the eye in the triangle. The All-Seeing Eye.

Lara flipped to "Auguries of Innocence" again, and started skimming. The poem was several pages long. She came to the last few lines, and read them out loud.

"*We are led to believe a lie, when we see not thro the eye . . .*"

Her voice trailed off. Next to the text, in faint black ink, there was a drawing: the eye in the triangle again.

Lara flipped to the back of the book.

The Eye in the Triangle.

She took out her pocketknife again, and delicately sliced open the book's handmade binding.

Underneath the old leather, there was a carefully folded sheaf of papers. Lara gently pulled them apart, and flattened them out on the desk.

The top piece of paper was a letter from her father—a real letter this time. His writing covered the entire piece of paper, in a hand more delicate and much smaller than she was used to seeing from him.

My darling daughter, if you are reading this letter, then I am no longer with you.

Heart hammering in her chest, Lara read on.

Interlude

♄
♇
☇
⊕
♈
♀
♊
⚇

The paper was thin: the ink tended to blot. Croft had to write much more slowly and carefully than he was accustomed to.

I believe I have deduced the secret location of the Tomb of the Dancing Light, where the first half of the Triangle is hidden. I may be wrong, but God willing, I am not. However, I cannot test my theory as each piece of the Triangle is hidden not only in space but also in time. And the Clock is more than just a guide, it is the key that can open time itself.

The power of the Triangle is real, Lara. If its two pieces are reunited, its possessor will wield a god-like power which I have come to believe would be ruinous to Humankind. The Clock I told you about is the key to the location of its pieces, its precise lat-

itude and longitude. In a few days, I leave for a long journey, which I hope will lead me to the Clock. If I do not find it, I fear there are others who will. And these are dangerous men.

"Daddy!"

Lord Croft, sitting at his desk, looked up.

Lara was standing in front of the still-spinning globe, hands on hips, frowning.

"I'm sorry, Lara. Did you find it yet?"

She smiled. "I found it ages ago, but you were still writing, Daddy. So I was just spinning it."

"Ah, yes." He nodded. "Keep things moving. I'll be right with you."

"All right." She went back to spinning the globe. "But we don't have all day, you know. We still have to wrap presents."

Croft's heart almost stopped. Good Lord, it was Christmas Eve. He'd completely forgotten. He picked up the bell on his desk and tinkled it. A minute later, the door to his study opened, and Hillary walked in.

"I see the entire family is hard at work," he said.

"I'm finding Cambodia," Lara announced.

Hillary raised an eyebrow. "You don't say?"

Croft motioned him over to the desk. Hillary bent low; Croft whispered in his ear.

"It's Christmas Eve, Hillary."

He nodded. "I am aware of that, sir."

Croft glanced over at Lara, who was watching them suspiciously.

"I've completely forgotten to pick up Lara's new bicycle. It's all ready down at Grosvenor's. Do you think you could . . ."

"Of course, sir." Hillary straightened, and cleared his throat. "I'll send Mrs. Dooley for those vegetables right away. I know the young lady loves her vegetables." He spoke very loudly. Lara looked straight at him and frowned.

"I don't like vegetables at all," she declared.

"I daresay you'll find these to your taste, miss." He looked at Croft and smiled. Croft smiled back. "If there's nothing else, sir . . ."

"No, Hillary, that's all. And thank you."

Hillary bowed and left the room.

Good old Hillary. Croft watched him go and wondered what would happen to the house without him. He dreaded finding out, but find out he must, and all too soon: The old man had just celebrated his sixtieth birthday.

Croft picked up his cigar from the ashtray and frowned; he'd set it down so long ago it had gone out.

"I'll get the matches for you, Daddy." He looked up. Lara had the drawer of a side table open and was scrounging around inside of it.

"No, no, angel." He shook his head, set down the cigar. "Not now. Besides, haven't I told you you're too young to play with such things?" More than told her; it was the one time he could remember actually yelling at his daughter. He'd smelled smoke, walked into the Library, and found her frantically trying to snuff out a small fire in the trashcan. She'd been playing with matches, and accidentally dropped a lit one in there. One more minute . . .

He shook his head. "Now, please. One more minute, Lara. I'll be right with you."

She made a show of sighing heavily, and went back to spinning the globe. He went back to writing.

> *Whatever happens to me, whether I get the Clock for you or not, you must be in the Tomb of the Dancing Light at the exact moment of the planetary alignment. Even in this letter I only dare reveal the merest clue to its whereabouts, so high are the stakes involved in this enterprise.*

The stakes. Croft shook his head. To call them high was an outrageous understatement. If the Illuminati were allowed to get their hands on the power of the Triangle . . .

He wrote for a moment longer, then set down his pen.

On the mantel behind him was a vase full of white blossoms. Croft picked one, and stood up.

"All right, young lady. I'm ready for my geography lesson."

Lara looked up excitedly. "Okay, Daddy." She put a hand on the globe, bringing it to a stop. He came and knelt down next to her, holding the flower behind his back.

"This is Eurasia," she said, outlining the shape of the continent with her index finger. "A lot of people think it's two separate continents, Europe and Asia, but it's not, not really. It's just that people in Europe like to think they're important enough to have their own continent. Especially the French people."

"Really?" Croft suppressed a smile. "And who told you that?"

"Hillary." She frowned, and squinted, and finally pointed her finger at a spot on the globe. "There it is. The Khmer Kingdom."

"Cambodia. Very good, angel. Now here, let me show you something else."

He wrapped one hand around hers, and guided her fingers carefully to a point in the upper left-hand corner of the country.

"Unexplored."

Lara's eyes shone with excitement. "You mean no one's ever been there? Really?"

"Not when they made this globe, no. But now . . ." He shook his head. "I'm afraid there aren't very many unexplored places left in this world, angel. You've inherited a very boring planet."

"An intelligent person is never bored, Daddy. Isn't that what you always tell me?"

He smiled. "You're right, of course."

Lara pointed to the "unexplored" area again. "So what is there?"

"Ah. I'm glad you asked."

Croft pulled the flower out from behind his back.

Lara gasped. "Oh."

"You like it?" He held the flower under her nose.

"It smells so lovely." She shut her eyes and breathed in the scent. Croft could smell it himself, a delicate sweetness that reminded him of warmer climates, different times. "What is it?"

"This is Poet's jasmine—white jasmine. It's a very rare flower. I have a few vines in the greenhouse."

"It's beautiful."

"This jasmine only likes to grow where it's warm. In the warmer parts of Western China, along the Himalayas. And along the Khmer Trail it only grows on a thirty-mile stretch, in a place no human has seen for a thousand years."

"Jasmine," she repeated. "A thousand years."

"That's right, angel. Jasmine. Along the Khmer Trail. You'll remember that, won't you? You'll remember it, when the time comes?"

She nodded. "Yes, Daddy. Jasmine. I'll remember."

"Good." Croft took his daughter in his arms and hugged her, his eyes filling with tears.

For some reason, he felt like he was saying good-bye.

13. Lara was in Bryce's trailer. Her father's letter lay next to a scanner Bryce had hooked up to his Sony V10. The letter, and the elaborate diagrams her father had drawn on the accompanying sheets of paper, as well, thankfully, as images of the clock, were all in the computer. Digital files for them to manipulate, study, reorder. Lara had the keyboard, and was typing away furiously, doing just that. Bryce had a Vaio on his lap, and was reading the text of the letter out loud, off its screen.

" 'I have told one and only one person the secret, and I hope you will remember the scent of jasmine, for that person is you.' " Bryce stopped reading, and looked up. "And you remember?"

"Exactly."

"Clever of you."

"I'm a clever girl." Lara heard a skittering sound, and looked down. One of Bryce's little insects was clambering over her boots; she kicked it away.

"Hey!"

"It was crawling up my leg."

"He," Bryce corrected. "*He* was crawling up your leg."

"It. Don't anthropomorphize, Bryce."

"So you don't need the Clock, after all," Bryce said. "You know where to go."

Lara nodded. "After a fashion. But thirty miles is a mighty long stretch of trail. Besides, 'The Triangle is hidden not only in space but in time,' my father wrote. Remember?"

"I remember. But how can you hide something in time? I don't understand."

"Neither do I. But the People of the Light did, and that's what matters. There." She punched a last sequence of numbers in. "I think I've got it."

Bryce set down the Vaio, and joined her at the V10's screen. She had a model of the solar system in the main window.

"Very pretty," he said. "Pretty planets, all in a row."

"This is exactly how they looked, just before the alignment."

"Okay . . ."

"So." Lara held her hands poised over the keyboard again. "We think the three dots on each dial of the Clock represent planets, and the Clock is ticking backward, right?"

"Actually we don't just think that anymore, thanks to your father's notes," Bryce said. "We know it. We know—"

Lara glared. "A simple 'yes' would suffice."

"Oh. Sorry. Then, 'yes, we know the Clock is ticking backward.' "

"Thank you." She punched in a sequence of numbers. On the computer screen, the planets started to move.

"The first three planets to align were Pluto, Neptune, and Uranus."

The models on the screen lined up.

"And when those three aligned, our Clock started ticking. The first dial. Right?"

"Right."

"Now . . ."

Lara brought up a new window, the scanned image of the Clock dials. She focused in on the first.

"The three planetary dots provide a basic star map. If we extrapolate along the path of alignment, we have one axis of our location: a guide to latitude. Now, I'm sure these symbols . . ."

She clicked on the image of the dials, zooming in on a detail of the runic markings around each.

". . . are the key to the other axis: a measurement of longitude. We can get the exact position of the tomb off of this."

"And so can Powell."

"I'm afraid so."

"And he's probably got top-secret Illuminati supergeniuses, dozens of them, working on the solution."

"And we've got you."

"Me? You're the languages expert."

"This is a numbers problem." She punched in some more keys, and row after row of hexadecimal code appeared. "That's up your alley, isn't it?"

Bryce sighed. "Couldn't we just follow Mr. Powell wherever he goes?"

"He'll be well-guarded, I assure you. Besides, the idea is to get there first. Surprise and all that."

"All right." Bryce leaned forward. "Let me see if I get this. There are three stages of the alignment."

Lara nodded. She held up three fingers, then ticked one off. "My father said the Triangle was divided in two. Now, there are two more stages in the alignment. So let's look at the second stage. Here's the solar system, as of today, seventeen twenty-eight Greenwich Meridian Time. Now . . ." she typed again, "let's just speed everything up."

On-screen, the planets spun, whirled, and hurried along in their orbits.

"And here goes Saturn, Jupiter, and Mars," Lara said, watching as those three worlds approached perfect alignment. "And my guess is they're going to line up just at the exact second the second dial of our ticking clock reaches zero. Watch the readout here." She pointed to the lower left-hand corner of the screen, where a digital timer was counting down. "I set it up to mirror the movement of the second dial."

The planets aligned.

The digital clock read zero.

"Bingo." Bryce said. "So how much time is that— from now, until the second stage?"

Lara looked back at her notes. "About two days."

"Forty-eight hours before you have to be in Cambodia, ready to save the world. Do you think Mr. Powell will be there?"

"I know he will. Him, and a few dozen of his black-clad assistants."

"You'd better pack a lot of ammunition."

"I'm not going to outgun them, Bryce." She tapped the side of her head. "I'm going to outsmart them. I've had a lot more experience at the tomb-raiding game than Mr. Powell or any of his friends."

"Outsmart them? Really? So you won't be bringing your guns?"

She smiled. "My Colts are an integral part of the tomb-raiding experience."

There was a knock on the trailer door. Hillary stuck his head in.

"TDM is done cleaning inside. I thought you'd want to know." He peered around the trailer, and made a face. "Should I send them in here?"

"Careful," Bryce said, "or I'll let the bugs loose on you."

Hillary blanched.

"He's lying." Lara stood and stretched. "Let's leave Bryce to his numbers, Hilly. I need to pack a bag."

"Oh." Hillary frowned.

"What?"

"The laundry room, I'm sad to say, did not survive the recent . . . ah . . . renovations."

Lara shrugged. "I don't need a lot of clothes."

"You don't have a lot of clothes." He brightened. "I think the dress may have survived."

"Ha-ha." Lara said. "I'll check storage. I should have a few more things there."

"I think it's a lovely dress," Bryce called out.

She stopped at the door, and turned back to him. "You, Mr. Genius. Fewer wisecracks, more calculations. I need an exact address for this tomb."

Powell had maintained a residence in London for over thirty years. Yet in all that time, this was the first occasion he'd had to visit Whitechapel Street.

"Disgusting." He looked at the uncollected trash along the avenue, the deserted warehouses, and frowned. "It looks like New York City."

"It's very popular among the *artistes*, sir," Pimms offered. He was chauffeuring: Powell was in the back, surrounded by the afternoon papers. Jakarta was exploding again; there was a meeting of the regional committee this evening at the Fitzroy. He was skipping, but he planned to send Miss Holcomb in his place so that he could brief her; he'd been boning up on the latest himself.

"And here's number twenty-five and a half." Pimms pulled the car over to the curb. He came around and opened Powell's door.

"See if you can find us a good restaurant around here for luncheon." Powell climbed out, the *Times* rolled up in his right hand. "Not Asian. And we'll want to go straight to the airport afterward."

"You're certain he'll accept?"

Powell smiled. "He'll accept. Here." He handed Pimms the paper. "Read up on Indonesia. You can help me prepare Miss Holcomb's brief."

Powell turned to face the building. The ground floor was a solid wall of concrete, with two inset steel doors. The one on his left had the number 25 stenciled above

the door. On the door itself was a sign that said
BUCKET'S CONFECTIONERS. The one on the right had a
big 1/2 drawn on it, in green fluorescent paint.

"Charming." Powell rang the buzzer.

"Hello." A tinny voice sounded from the intercom
plate.

"Hello, I'm looking for Mr. West."

"Bugger off."

"Hello?"

"No salesmen."

Powell frowned. "I can assure you, I am not a sales-
man."

There was no response.

Powell rang the buzzer again.

"*Bugger off!!!*"

"The next time you say that," Powell said, slowly and
calmly, "I shall break down your door and chop your
head off."

A pause.

"Who the hell is this?"

"My name is Manfred Powell, and I wish to talk to
Alex West about a job. Is this Mr. West?"

"A job? Why didn't you say so?" A loud buzz
sounded; the door sprung open. Powell stepped inside.

He was at the bottom of a long, concrete staircase.
The steps were crumbling away: the steel handrail
was rusted. He put on his gloves and gingerly climbed
to the top, touching the rail as infrequently as possible. A formidable-looking steel door swung open, revealing an unshaven, rather dissolute-looking young

man in blue sweatpants, a white T-shirt, and a black ski cap.

"Christ, what a night. My cousin's bachelor party." He rubbed his eyes. "You're Powell."

"I am."

"What's this about a job?"

Powell stood silently, waiting. Eventually, West got it.

"Oh, oh right, come in, come in." He swung the door wider. Powell stepped in, past him. "Excuse my manners. Or lack thereof."

West's apartment was a single, cavernous room. The only recognizable piece of furniture was a four-poster bed shoved next to the floor-to-ceiling windows. Every remaining inch of space was occupied by relics of various sorts: sculptures, decorative jewelry, totems, artwork.

"Mr. West. This is actually quite nice. I'm surprised."

"Eh? This? Nice?"

"Your collection. Very impressive." Next to Powell was a big slab of granite, resting on four pillars of milk crates. The granite was covered with shards of pottery: One of the bigger pieces had writing on it.

Powell picked up the shard, and turned it over in his hand.

"Canaanite?"

"Assyrian. Close, though." West managed a smile. "You an archaeologist, Mr. Powell?"

"Hardly. But I am interested in exploration. As a matter of fact, at the moment, I have a dig going in Cambodia."

"Really?"

"Well." Powell smiled. "Almost. Actually, I'm looking for someone to help with the operation."

"Cambodia, eh?" West yawned. "Sorry. You want coffee? There's some in the fridge I could heat up."

Powell shuddered. Reheated coffee? "No. No, thank you. But help yourself, please."

West went to the far wall, took a mug out of the refrigerator, and put it into the microwave. "So, Cambodia. I haven't been there in, oh, two years, I think. Did an environmental impact study: Tonle Sap, maybe you've heard of it?"

Powell shook his head. He continued to tour the room as they talked.

Alex continued. "Big dam; helluva big dam. Make a lake out of half the country, I think. Lose a lot of valuable archaeological sites. Greenpeace hired me to write about the potential damage."

On another makeshift table, Powell found a stack of snapshots, and picked them up.

"Greenpeace? You're not an environmentalist, are you, Mr. West?"

"Oh, no." The microwave dinged. West took out his coffee. "I'm a capitalist."

"Good. I detest people with noble motives." Powell flipped through the pictures: Here was West, in Egypt, posing with his arms around a group of diggers, the Pyramids in the background. And here he was buried to his neck in a mound of sand, in front of him a line of camels. More of Egypt, a lot more.

And then he came to another series of shots: ice, and snow, and people in mountain-climbing gear. And here . . .

West, arm-in-arm, with Lady Croft. Huge, snow-covered mountains loomed behind them.

Powell held the picture up so that West could see it. "Is this Everest?"

"Everest, no. Tibet, yes."

"And this is Lara Croft, isn't it? Lady Croft?"

For the first time that morning, West's eyes opened all the way. "You know Lara?"

"Only slightly. I do expect to be seeing her again, very soon."

"Huh. Well, tell her I said hello." West sipped his coffee and made a face. "On second thought, maybe you'd better not mention my name. Jeapordize your relationship, I'm afraid."

"You and Lady Croft had a falling out?"

West smiled, and set down his cup. "So. Let's talk about Cambodia. I don't mind telling you I'm interested, depending on the time commitment, and the money. Especially the money."

"There's plenty of money," Powell said. "But the time commitment will be commensurately steep. And immediate."

"Immediate?"

"Immediate." Powell looked at his watch. "As in jetting from Heathrow in one hundred-twenty minutes. If we hurry, we have time for lunch."

"Lunch." West laughed. "That's a good one."

"Perhaps you could suggest a place?"

"Are you serious?"

"Mr. West, I am the most serious man you're likely to ever meet in your life."

West shook his head. "Well, I'm sorry, Mr. Powell. This afternoon, in about a hundred-twenty minutes, is my cousin's wedding. And I'm afraid I just can't skip out on that. The family would never forgive me."

"Oh." Powell shook his head. "Is there nothing I can say that will change your mind?"

"No, I'm afraid not."

"Well, I hope you don't mind if I try." He set down the pictures, and clasped his hands behind his back. "Mr. West, have you ever heard of the Clock of Ages?"

West laughed again. "The Clock of Ages? That's a good one. I'd say it's a toss-up between that and the Holy Grail as to which one causes more wild-goose chases. Though I suppose you'd have to throw in the Ark there too, because since that movie . . ."

West continued talking. Powell reached into his pocket, pulled out the Clock, and set it down next to the pottery shards on the granite table.

In mid-sentence, his mouth still open wide, West suddenly stopped making noise.

He looked down at the Clock, up at Powell, and then back down at the Clock again.

"This Clock," Powell said, "is the key to a far greater treasure. One I need your help to recover."

West swallowed hard, and found his voice again. "My help?"

"That's right, Mr. West." Powell picked the Clock off the desk again, and put it back into his pocket. "Now, shall we discuss the job further? Or are you still planning on attending your family function?" He leaned closer. "I could give Lady Croft a call, I suppose. I've heard she's quite capable."

West's eyes, which had been round as saucers, suddenly regained their focus. "Oh, no, Mr. Powell." He shook his head. "I'm your man."

"Good. Now then . . . lunch? I'm famished."

West nodded. "We want the Aquarium, down on St. Katherine Dock." He walked quickly to the refrigerator, opened it, and put his coffee cup back in. "I'll go get my gear."

14. Bryce worked twenty-six hours straight to nail down the exact location of the tomb. Lara spent the first half-hour of that time gathering her clothes, and packing. Then she and Hillary inventoried the damage to the house, and made lunch, after which she went and knocked on the trailer door.

"How's it going?" she asked, leaning her head in.

Bryce looked up at her, and grunted. "I'm thinking evil thoughts about you, Lara Croft."

"As long as you're thinking." She shut the door and returned to the house. She went to the Library and brushed up on her Khmer. She went for a run around the grounds. She made tea. She went and knocked on the trailer door again.

"Grrrr," said Bryce.

"Grrrr yourself."

She changed the oil and rotated the tires on the Land Rover. She went for another run. Things got so bad she even called Alex West, to see if he had any interest in coming out for dinner—she really should patch things up with him, especially after he'd taken the time to send that card the other day. Though there was no question about it, they could never really be friends again.

Alex's mother answered the phone. She was looking for Alex, too. They exchanged pleasantries.

"If you happen to see my son," his mother said, "tell him he's out of the family."

At midnight, she stopped by the trailer again. Bryce was slumped over the keyboard, head in hands, still staring at the screen. She left without saying a word, and went to her bedroom.

She fell asleep rereading her father's letter.

She woke at four and looked out the window. The light in the trailer was still on; she saw Bryce pacing. Rent a Lear Jet to Phnom Penh, Land Rover to the foothills of the Dangrok Mountains: those had been her rough travel plans. But there wasn't time for that now. She'd have to take air transport all the way to the Khmer Trail. She'd still need the Land Rover, though. Which meant she needed a favor.

Lara got up, dressed, and went downstairs to make a phone call.

Being quite honest with herself, Lara was the most competitive person she knew. Everything she did, every game she played, she played to win.

John Shugrave was exactly the same way.

He was a mercenary, ran a team of mercenaries who, for a price, would go anywhere, do anything. "The

Marines for hire," Shugrave claimed. He did have a few former Marines in the group, along with a Mossad agent, a woman who'd been with MI-5, and a bearded wildman who (translation provided by Shugrave) claimed to have personally destroyed two dozen Russian tanks during the Afghani uprising. An eclectic group: Lara met them while she was training for her first major expedition on behalf of Natla Technologies.

Her ship was anchored off the coast of Cyprus when a major storm came up. Hillary was by himself, aboard the boat; she was below, working on her scuba technique and reflexive breathing. The storm snapped the boat's communication antennae. Hillary lost contact with her. A passing ship rescued him. Assuming the worst, he called in help for her, at the highest levels he could reach (it was the last expedition she ever took him on—the man was a chronic worrier).

They sent in Shugrave, who went down with two men from his team, both former U.S. Navy Seals. But it was Shugrave himself who found Lara, safe in an underground cave, waiting out the storm.

"I'm here to rescue you," he said, rising up out of the water.

She raised an eyebrow. "From what?"

The storm, meanwhile, had risen in intensity. Shugrave received word that both of them should wait it out in the cave. They passed the time until it was safe to go, playing chess, using seashells.

Lara won.

They bet on who could hold their breath the longest underwater.

Lara won.

Then they arm-wrestled. Shugrave won—not without some difficulty—righty.

Lefty, they went to a draw. They went again. Another draw.

Lara put her hand down for a third go, and Shugrave waved her off. Then he offered her a job. She declined.

When they got back to shore, he took her out to dinner, and proposed. She declined that, too, which didn't seem to upset him too much. "I was just trying to show you I'm an old-fashioned kind of guy," he said, as dessert was being served. "That my heart's in the right place."

"Please—no discussions of your anatomy, sir," she replied. "I'm an old-fashioned kind of girl."

They went to a bar and met Shugrave's team. Then they played darts. Lara won. They stayed up late, playing other games, some of them competitive, others requiring a more cooperative spirit. Lara left the next morning for a meeting with Jaqueline Natla. Shugrave went to Somalia. They'd seen each other once since then, for breakfast in the Tokyo airport.

He answered the phone on the first ring.

"Shugrave."

"Croft."

"You're up late."

"Early, actually. I need a favor, John."

She explained.

"Not a problem. I'll send Tookie to Heathrow—give him an hour and a half. I'd come myself, but I'm in Mexico City."

"Really?" Lara had dialed his Los Angeles number. "What are you doing there?"

Shugrave laughed. "Actually, I'm not in Mexico City at all. I can't tell you where I am."

"Of course you can't."

"In fact, we've been on for twenty-five seconds now, so I have to hang up."

And he did. Lara listened to the dial tone for a second, and then hung up herself.

She turned around, and Bryce was standing there, waving a piece of paper.

"I want overtime for this one," he said.

Instead of more money, Bryce got Hillary's French toast, as did Lara, who wolfed hers down in no time at all. She brought her suitcase down to the Main Hall, and then, Bryce and Hillary in tow, went through the equipment room, picking up one item after another: ropes, computers, pitons, and of course, her guns, which she immediately holstered with a satisfying *thwack*.

She went to her father's Library and got the Blake first edition. She had her father's notes, and his letter, in her hand. After a moment's hesitation, she folded them back into the lining of the Blake.

"A little light reading?" Hillary asked when she came out.

"A little inspiration." Bryce was sitting in a red leather chair in the Hall, snoring soundly. She whacked him on the head with the book.

"Wake up and say good-bye."

He opened one eye. "Good-bye."

"Good-bye." She put the Blake into her backpack.

Bryce opened the other eye, and stood up.

"You're going."

"That's what I said."

"I was asleep." He yawned, and looked at his watch. "How the hell are you going to get to Cambodia in fifteen hours?"

She slung her backpack over her shoulder.

"Oh, I'll be calling in a favor."

"What kind of favor?" Hillary asked.

"That's a secret." Lara slipped on her sunglasses. "I could tell you, I suppose. But then I'd have to kill you."

"Don't tell me," Bryce said. "I'm asleep." He sat back down in the chair.

"I'd like to know," Hillary said. "For my own peace of mind."

"You worry too much." She picked up one of her bags. Hillary picked up the other. They walked out the South Entrance to the main drive, and loaded up the Land Rover.

"Wish me luck," Lara said, climbing in.

Hillary nodded. "Luck."

She started the engine, and drove off.

Shugrave was, of course, as good as his word. Tookie met her at the cargo terminal at Heathrow. She drove the Land Rover right up into the belly of the C-130 transport. They took off immediately.

The flight took ten hours; they were refueled in midair. Lara slept virtually the entire time, figuring it might be her last chance for a while. When they flew over the Dangroks, she showed Tookie and the navigator the map Bryce had printed out for her.

"I want to go here," she said, pointing a half-mile due north of the tomb's location.

"Here's better," Tookie said, pointing another quarter-klick west on the map, to a hill that rose a few hundred feet above the surrounding terrain. Lara saw that he was right, as usual. That hill would give her a better vantage point. So the hill it was.

Twenty minutes later she and the Land Rover were down on the ground. Lara folded up her parachute and switched on her comm link.

"Bryce?"

"No, ah, this is Hillary. Lara? How are you? Everything all right? Anyone I can call?"

She heard snoring in the background. "Wake up Bryce and put him on, Hilly. Thank you."

May was monsoon season in Cambodia; the rains had just come, and the air was wet and thick. A steambath. Lara wiped her brow, reached into her backpack and pulled out her binoculars—the new ones Bryce was so proud of: high-powered zoom, infrared lenses, knobs whose functions she was just beginning to guess at.

The air was thick with the smells of the jungle. The slope directly beneath her was dotted with banks of purple hyacinths, orange and yellow tiger lilies: rhododendrons, and lush vegetation that stretched out into a green carpet beneath, extending into the distance as far as she could see. To her right, she glimpsed matching blue and red ribbons: the blue, a river, mostly hidden by the jungle, but visible for a few hundred-odd yards at a stretch, and the red, reddish-brown actually, a single-lane road stamped out of the rich clay soil.

A mile or so directly ahead of her, the green gave way suddenly to a clump of brown: Ants swarmed over the clump. People, actually. Lots of people.

Lara raised the binoculars to her eyes.

The clump of brown was a huge hole in the ground, a massive excavation. Hundreds of workers, brown-skinned men stripped to the waist, hauling ropes with all their might. The ropes were tied to huge metal bolts. The bolts were sunk into giant blocks of sandstone, which they were pulling up from the ground, leaving behind a black empty hole.

The tomb.

"Lara?"

"Bryce."

"You're there."

"I'm here. Can you see?"

"I can as soon as you activate the video feed. Hit the red button. Ah, that's it."

Now Bryce and Hillary, back in the Manor, were seeing what she saw. On the side of the tomb, a huge as-para—a sculpture, the largest such Lara had ever seen, representing the Khmer ideal of female beauty—lay broken into two pieces. And looming high above it, three stone heads Lara didn't recognize at all. Unusual. She was familiar with Cambodian sculptural motifs. Von Croy had made sure of that, during that long-ago summer she'd spent with him at Angkor Wat. She could tell Funan from Angkor, Champa influences from the Javanese. She knew Vishnu, Krishna, and the

Ramayana, the Hindu epic whose climactic scenes were illustrated in bas-relief throughout Angkor. She could tell at a glance the asparas, the Nagas, and the singhas. Not this beast, though: It looked more Indian, in fact, than Cambodian, though it did, in certain respects, resemble some of the Asuras—the demon gods. Ravana, perhaps, though the lord of the underworld was more commonly depicted with twenty-one heads. Still . . .

Its formidable, fearsome appearance was clearly intended to convey a warning. Abandon hope, all ye who enter. And who was planning to enter?

She panned around the site. Her eyes came to rest on a man, standing next to a Land Rover—the standard model, not the souped-up 12-cylinder, reinforced chassis, aluminum-alloy interior, high-performance transmission version she had at her disposal. The man was using an astrolabe, looking up at the sky, and then down at the hood of the Land Rover, on which rested, Lara saw now, the clock. The Clock of Ages. Her clock.

The man wore black trousers, black shirt, a green vest, and, naturally, a black hat.

"Mr. Powell." She grinned. "How unsurprising. And you've brought my clock. Excellent."

Powell frowned at the astrolabe and then held it up for another man to look at, a man whose face was momentarily hidden by the astrolabe. Then Powell lowered the instrument, and Lara could see the newcomer quite clearly.

For a minute, she was speechless.

"Alex West. You greedy, greedy boy."

West smiled at Powell. The two men shared a laugh.

"No scruples," Lara growled, and lowered her binoculars.

Her earpiece crackled.

"Did you say Alex West?"

"Just hired by the bad guys. And you don't have to sound so smug about it." Bryce had never liked Alex, ever since he'd heard about the prayer wheels.

"Oh, bloody hell. I can hear a gauntlet being thrown down. Clang-a-lang!"

"Clang-a-lang? Bryce, are you smoking?"

She picked up the binoculars. Alex was holding the clock. He had the face open, and was looking down at it, and then up at the sky.

"I just know how much you love competition," Bryce said. "This is going to be a replay of the prayer wheels extravaganza, I know it."

"Bryce." Lara put a warning edge in her voice.

Heedless, he kept talking. "Clang-a-lang is the sound a gauntlet would make if you threw it down as a challenge, in olden times."

"Bryce." Lara turned the binoculars on herself now, and raised a warning finger. "Do you see me smiling?"

"No."

"No, that's right. So stow it. Haven't you got work to do?"

He sighed heavily. "Yes, your majesty."

"I expect the place to be shipshape and Bristol fashion when I return from my adventures. Take your assignments from Hillary."

"Captain Bligh?" Bryce sounded unhappy. "He'll

have me swabbing the decks. Trimming the jib. Etcetera."

"Your jib could stand a little trimming."

She turned the binoculars on Alex again. Her ex-friend was bent over, shouldering his way into the straps of what looked like a very heavy knapsack.

"What do you think he has in there? An ex-girlfriend, perhaps?"

"Bryce, get to work. I'll check in later."

Down the binoculars. Off went the flying suit.

She strapped on her Colts, returned the binocs to their place in her backpack, and strapped that on as well. She adjusted her headset, and looked down at her watch, which she'd set to count down to the next phase of the alignment. To the appearance of the first piece of the Triangle.

Seventy-two minutes, and counting.

She turned for the Land Rover, and at that moment, spied a flash of white in the bushes around her.

Jasmine. She pulled a sprig, and inhaled deeply.

"Daddy, stay close. I need you now."

Up above, the sky exploded in a flash of color. The Aurora.

She hopped into the Land Rover, and gunned it down the hill, heading for the tomb.

15.

Powell stared at the face of the clock, at the second dial, which had started to glow. Then he looked at the chronograph in his other hand.

"Seventy-two minutes." He frowned, and glared in the direction of the straining laborers, near the tomb's entrance. "We need to work more quickly."

"You mean we need them to work more quickly." West, who'd picked up the pack of his equipment he'd brought in from London, now set it down again. "Perhaps we should set an example. Get our hands dirty."

"Ridiculous," Powell said. He waved to Julius, who was standing a respectful distance back, on the other side of the Land Rover. "We'll pick out two workers at random and kill them. That will motivate the others."

West laughed. "Motivate them right back to their villages, I suspect."

Julius slipped a clip into his submachine gun, and took a step forward.

"Wait a minute." West looked at Powell, then at

Julius, then back at Powell. The smile disappeared from his face. "You're kidding, right?"

"Mr. West. As I said earlier, I am the most serious man you're likely to ever meet in your life."

"Wait, wait, wait," West said. "These fellows trust me. Give me a minute, at least."

"Sixty seconds." Powell made a face. "Go ahead. Be my guest."

West ran to the supply truck and snatched up an armful of canteens. He filled them with water and headed over to the workers. Progress stopped entirely for a moment as they crowded around him.

Bah. More time wasted. Fear, not cooperation, was the way to increase production. After this was over, Powell resolved to bring West to Venice, run through a few historical examples, perhaps a few modern ones as well, show the man the error of his beliefs.

The workers were beginning to straggle back into line. Powell picked up his megaphone.

"We now have seventy-one minutes. Faster and better, please." He spoke in Mandarin. West had managed to import some Chinese-speaking workers, who seemed to have some familiarity with archaeological protocol. One of the workers at the head of the line, a snaggle-toothed scarecrow of a man, grinned and waved at him. A half-dozen others followed suit. West waved, too.

"Pimms!" Powell shouted, reverting to English. "Get them working!"

Pimms, who was standing on top of the mound of earth they'd excavated from atop the stones yesterday, gave Powell a thumbs-up. He reached into his pocket, pulled out a piece of paper, and began reading from it—in Mandarin—into his own megaphone.

"Please hurry. The train is leaving platform insert number here."

The laborers stared up at Pimms. They looked first confused, then amused. West, who was still wandering among them, giving out water, picked up his own megaphone.

"Can you believe that jerk?" He spoke in Mandarin as well. "Anyway, guys, let's kick it up a notch. Hour and a half, two tops, and we're outta here. All done, back to the village for beer and some meat on a stick."

One of the workers shouted something; Powell couldn't quite hear what he was saying.

"You want Guinness?" West laughed, still talking through the megaphone. "That's up to Mr. Powell. What do you say, Mr. Powell? Guinness for the lads?"

Powell responded in English through his own megaphone. "Mr. West, tell them I'll buy a brewery for the village if they get us into the tomb in the next five minutes. Otherwise, it's rat poison for the lot of them."

"I'll tell them," West called back, in English as well. "Sort of." He put down the megaphone then, and spoke to the workers. Whatever he said caused them to let out a cheer, and pick up their ropes again. West picked up a rope of his own and joined in with them.

Powell watched them for a moment as they strained at the ropes, then looked down at the chronograph.

Sixty-eight minutes.

Up in the sky, the Aurora flashed, much brighter than before, much brighter than it had been during the first alignment. The electrified particles emitted by the sun, which caused the Aurora, were further energized during the alignment. And as more planets fell into line, approaching the final, total solar eclipse, the Aurora would increase in intensity on a logarithmic scale. Which made for a wonderful light show, but—

A huge *whump* sounded, and the ground literally shook.

Powell looked up to see a big, black hole where the stones had been.

The way to the tomb was clear.

"What'd I tell you, what'd I tell you." West was jogging back to him, picking up his pack, and talking at the same time. "A little cooperation, a little elbow grease, and there you have it. There you have it."

"Stop jabbering, Mr. West." Powell picked up the clock and chronograph. Motioning Julius and his team forward, he set off at a brisk pace for the entrance. "We now have sixty-seven minutes."

"Plenty of time," West said, following. "Plenty of time."

Pimms scrambled down off his perch, hard hat in hand, and joined them. As they approached the tomb, the crowd of laborers parted to let them pass. They were all staring.

"What are they looking at?" Pimms asked.

"Us. They think we're stupid." West nodded grimly to the men as he passed.

"What for? For digging the hole?" One of the workers removed his hat as Pimms passed.

"And going into it."

"Good-bye. Sayonara." The worker's English was heavily accented; he was shaking his head as he spoke.

"Bye-bye." Pimms responded cheerfully. "That one seems friendly."

"That's good-bye, as in you're not coming back." West added. "As in you poor crazy shmuck."

Powell saw that a great many of the workers had turned their backs to the tomb entirely, as if they were afraid to even look at the hole. Odd, he hadn't even considered it until now. The People of the Light, the ones who had hidden the Triangle: Of course, they would have arranged for it to be protected somehow. How, that was the question. Best to be prepared for anything.

"Julius!" he called ahead. "Keep your weapons at the ready!" Powell turned back to West. "What do they think is in there?"

"I'll find out." West walked over to the worker who had spoken to Pimms, and started jabbering away in Khmer.

Pimms fell back into line, till he was walking next to Powell.

"Ah . . . still no sign of Lady Croft?"

"Not yet," Powell said.

"Did someone say Croft?" West turned and grinned. "As in Lara?"

"Ah . . . yes." Pimms frowned. "You know Lady Croft?"

West ignored him, looking at Powell. "You think Lara has an interest in this tomb?"

"I know she does," Powell said.

"Thinking you should have hired her, perhaps?" West asked, teasing. "Buyer's remorse?"

"Of course not. Very glad to have you, Mr. West. Charmed, in fact. Particularly by the canteen stunt."

West nodded. "Lara's work is good, you know, but she's overrated. She's in it for the glory, which can cloud her judgment. I work for money."

"Fortunately." Up ahead, Julius, who was leading the way into the tomb, disappeared from sight.

West paused at the tomb's entrance. "The God-Who-Sees-All, by the way."

Powell turned to him. "Eh?"

"That fellow," West said, pointing at the worker he'd been talking to. "That's what he expects us to run into down there. The God-Who-Sees-All."

"Really?" Powell smiled. "The God-Who-Sees-All, and the All-Seeing Eye. Come, gentlemen. Let us see if they're related. Onward. Into the Belly of the Beast."

He walked forward, into the darkness.

Stunt driver. Closed course. Do not try this at home. Lara had seen all the commercials, and the warnings, and ignored each and every one of them. Instead, she had taken her Volvo out onto the old Manor hunting grounds, and practiced: the cones, the wet roads, the three-sixties, the Knievel-like jumps.

Therefore, when the sliver of road she was jouncing along at 80 kph disappeared into the monsoon-swollen river, she was completely unfazed. She shot up what had been the riverbank, and into the jungle proper. After all, she reasoned, the foliage along the river was bush, and a few flimsy bamboo shoots. And the Land

Rover did have that reinforced chassis. And if she ran into any bigger trees . . .

Well, that was precisely why she'd honed those reflexes, wasn't it?

Bushes and flowers shot past, slapping at the Rover: flashes of green and purple and violet. A flock of cranes rose into the air. Mud splashed; water shot into the air.

Lara slammed on the brakes.

Twenty feet in front of her was a stand of huge teak trees: massive, ancient, powerful, leafy branches reaching high toward the sky, their roots reaching down into brown earth, and blocks of gray sandstone. The stone was everywhere, traces of gray peaking through the green carpet fanning out before her. Gray peeked through the foliage, too. As she looked closer, she began to make out the outlines of what must have once been a huge complex—nothing on the scale of Angkor Wat, but a real find. This significant site, now, sad to say, was in very poor shape indeed—no Groslier to rescue this complex from the elements. Just her and Alex West. Greedy, greedy, greedy Alex West.

Lara hopped out of the Land Rover, pulled off her backpack, and slid out the Blake first edition. She unfolded her father's notes, studied them for a moment, and then the complex of buildings. The buildings, and then the map her father had drawn.

Right around here, if she was reading things right, was where the back door to the tomb would be. If, that is, the tomb had a back door. Her father's notes didn't say anything about that.

She refolded the notes, and returned the Blake to her backpack. Then she surveyed the ruins.

"Hmmm." She folded her arms, and looked about. Where to begin? She could use a little inspiration.

Color flashed.

Lara spun around.

A little native girl, in a bright saffron dress, was playing alone among a tangle of massive tree roots. Her face was hidden by a screen of low-hanging foliage.

"Hey . . ." Lara took a step forward, pushing aside the branches.

The girl was gone.

Someone giggled. Lara turned, and behind her, saw the girl dart behind a huge, winding tree root. Lara smiled, and came around the root's other side.

"Now, miss . . ."

The girl wasn't there. Impossible. Where else could she be?

Ah. Lara smiled, and looked up.

The tree's branches were empty.

In the distance, she heard a scrambling noise.

The girl was standing a hundred yards away, clear across the ruin.

Weird.

"Hey!" Lara shouted. "How did you—"

The girl smiled, and suddenly her features changed, flickering in the dappled sunlight. She looked like an old woman, a very old, wrinkled, nut-brown, Cambodian woman who, as Lara squinted at her for a better look, took a single, nimble step behind a wall of crumbling stone, and was gone.

Beyond weird. Edging over, in fact, into impossible.

Lara hadn't been expecting to see impossible things for—

She looked down at her watch.

—another forty-one minutes. Until the alignment.

What was all this, then?

She heard another giggle behind her. The little girl was standing by the Land Rover.

"All right," Lara said. "If this is hide-and-seek, you win."

No response. Lara took a step closer. The little girl didn't move.

"Who are you?" Lara pointed at herself. "My name is Lara." She spoke in Khmer. "What's your name?"

The little girl smiled and held up a cluster of jasmine blooms.

Lara's mind reeled.

"Those digging men," the little girl said in Khmer, "they are fools. The God-Who-Sees-All will swallow them alive."

Lara took a deep breath. "Why?"

"Didn't you see? They tore his lover away from him."

"His lover?"

"You remember." The little girl smiled, and her features changed again, and suddenly, she was the image of the aspara, the sculpture Lara had seen broken and tossed to the side of the tomb. The god's lover, presumably.

"The aspara."

The little girl nodded. In the sky above, the Aurora flashed again. Lara considered. The little girl and the old woman; the God-Who-Sees-All and his lover; the alignment. The tomb.

"Is there another way in?" Lara asked. "To the tomb."

"For you, yes." The little girl nodded, and suddenly her features changed again, she was the old woman from before. "Approach him with a steady hand and a clear eye, and he will let you into his heart."

Lara nodded. Steady hand. Clear eye. Right.

What the hell was that supposed to mean?

She opened her mouth to speak, and then she was looking again at the little girl, not the old woman.

"He will let you into his heart," the girl said. "But he may not let you out again."

She smiled, and pointed behind her.

Lara turned and saw three jasmine blossoms.

Poet's jasmine—as her father had promised.

When she turned back around—the little girl, the old woman, the aspara whoever-she/it had been—was gone.

16.

All right. Deep breath. Steady.

Lara stared at the place the little girl had been, her mind full of questions for which there could be no possible, conceivable, rational answer. So either she'd just been seriously hallucinating, or . . .

The old Sherlock Holmes saw came to mind: When you eliminate the improbable, whatever else remains, however impossible, must be the truth.

Improbable that a little girl could turn into an old woman. So that wasn't a little girl. That wasn't a living, breathing, human being at all.

So . . .

Lara looked back at the jasmine flowers she had pointed to, and it was as if she were hearing her father's voice again.

"Jasmine. Along the Khmer Trail, it only grows on a thirty-mile stretch, in a place no human has seen for a thousand years."

And suddenly, Lara was a little girl, in her father's

study, standing next to the globe, holding the beautiful white flower under her nose, inhaling its scent, and seeing the slow back-and-forth, back-and-forth, of her father's pocket watch.

"Jasmine," she heard him say. "You'll remember that, won't you? You'll remember it, when the time comes?" And then her own voice. "Yes, Daddy. Jasmine. I'll remember. I'll remember."

Lara stepped forward, and knelt down next to the three flowers. All right. What now?

She looked around, then down. Then she shrugged, and picked one of the three blossoms. Then the second. Then the third.

The third bloom, oddly enough, seemed to have a root. She tugged at it. The root was deep. She tugged harder. The ground around the root crumbled, revealing a hole. Lara reached into her backpack, and pulled out one of the chemical light flares. An eerie greenish glow filled the hole. It wasn't just a hole, she could see now. It was in fact, a passageway. Leading down, down, down, into an inky blackness.

Holding the light flare out before her, Lara jumped.

"Hanuman," West said. He tapped the statue on the forehead, and grinned. "The monkey god."

"Monkey god?" Powell, standing next to him, shook his head. Actually, the statues—there were six of them, all in a row—looked like monkey soldiers to him. They all wore helmets and very fierce expressions, and had been posed with long metal swords in their hands. "What on earth is there to worship about a monkey?"

"They're quite likeable little creatures," West said. "In their own milieu. And our close relatives, don't forget."

"Your close relatives, perhaps." Powell ran a finger along the edge of one of the swords, and flinched. That metal was sharp—he could have cut himself. "Mine are mostly in Switzerland."

Pimms, who'd been exploring the other side of the tomb, came around to join them now.

"What the heck are those?"

"Monkeys," West replied.

"Of course, very effective." Pimms said. "Dangerous-looking creatures. Thank goodness they're not real. Thank goodness."

"This, on the other hand," West pulled out a jewel from one of the statue's eye sockets, "seems real enough."

And indeed it did. A ruby, Powell judged. Worth a small fortune. He debated telling West to put it back, but why bother? Being honest with himself, Powell knew he was probably going to end up killing the man anyway.

Pimms dabbed at his brow with a handkerchief. "Quite a place in here, I'd say. Quite a find."

"Pimms," Powell said. "Are you quite all right?"

"Oh, yes, fine. Fine and dandy." But the man looked overwhelmed, dazed, completely out-of-sorts. Powell could hardly blame him for that. The tomb was an overwhelming piece of work, breathtaking, one might say, if you were inclined to those sort of feelings.

The focus of the tomb was a nightmare-maker in and of itself. Even in the darkness, the statue was the first thing they'd seen on entering the tomb, its outlines and size slowly becoming visible in the reflected light from the high-power torches Julius and his team held. It was a godlike statue, all shining gold, sitting cross-legged, easily twenty feet tall, maybe thirty, upon a raised platform at the far end of the tomb. The statue held ten-foot-long swords in each of its hands, each of its six hands, Powell had slowly realized. It had six arms, six swords, and three heads. Three heads.

"That's the same statue from outside," Powell realized. "The God-Who-Sees-All."

"I'd have much better peripheral vision with three heads as well," West said.

"It's very big," Pimms said. "Very big."

There was a giant green urn of some sort on the statue's lap. Steps led up to the statue, steps covered with thousands of half-melted candles.

They'd entered the chamber at the top of a sloping ramp that flattened as it entered the tomb. As they walked farther in, the size and layout of the place was easier to comprehend. It was constructed in the shape of a giant ellipse, an egg, with the statue at one end, their entrance at the other. A stone gallery, almost like a balcony, circled the tomb above their heads. Giant tree roots dangled down from the walls, disappearing off into the ceiling high above.

Twenty feet down the stone ramp they came to a raised crystal dome, three or four feet high. Light shone through it from beneath.

"I wonder how it does that," West said. He knelt down next to the circle, eyes narrowed in concentration. "Looks like mercury. A whole pool of it, underneath the dome." He stood up. "Right. Those swords," he said, pointing across to the giant golden statue. "We need them." It was only then that Powell saw that the ramp ended just after the raised dome. There was a gap of maybe seven or eight feet, empty space, no bridge, between the statue and them.

At the base of the statue was another metal plate, stamped into the floor. A triangle inside a circle. And inside the triangle, an eye.

The All-Seeing Eye.

"Why?" Powell asked. "What are the swords for?"

West walked around the bump in the ramp, holding a torch he'd taken from one of Julius's men, and now Powell saw two things, that there were runes along the edge of the dome—runes that West had been reading—and he saw that the ramp widened before it ended, forming a larger circle around the dome. Capstones were set at six equilateral points along the edge of that circle. Each had a rectangular slot in them, an inch or two wide, slightly longer across. West pointed to one of the slots.

"The runes say they go here. The swords."

"Well, let's get them." Powell looked down at his chronograph. Thirteen minutes to alignment. He turned. "Julius. Go back to the surface, please, and get something so we can reach that platform. Time, needless to say, is of the essence."

Julius was jogging away on the word "needless," waving one of his men along with him. While they waited for him to return, West set up torches around the tomb so they could get an even better look at it. There were recessed alcoves scattered all around the circumference of the great room. Powell and West did a quick survey of their contents. In one, they found a series of bas-reliefs twenty feet long; in another, a shimmering curtain of water. Several of the alcoves held identical sets of six monkey soldiers—West's relatives.

Powell moved on to explore the next alcove. Behind him, West and Pimms were still talking.

"Pimms."

"Yes?"

"Do you think you could find your way back to the surface?"

"Well, ah, we marked the way, didn't we? With those little things, blue flare thingies, so . . . probably. Yes. I hope so."

West's voice got even quieter.

"Good. Then go."

"Go?"

"Back to the surface. Lickety-split, chop-chop."

"Well . . . I don't think I can, just yet. I mean, Mr. Powell—"

"Pimms. Buddy. Seriously consider returning to the surface. Now."

Powell looked down at his chronograph. Eleven minutes.

Footsteps sounded.

Julius and his man emerged into the chamber, a few terrified natives along with them. They were carrying two bamboo ladders.

"Excellent work, Julius. Bring them right over here, that's it."

The ladders were just long enough to reach from the ramp to the statue's platform. "Mr. West. Tempus fugit!" Powell cried. "Let's get those swords."

Tempus fugit. Lara, hidden in the shadows of one of the roots she'd shimmied down, agreed. Time flies. She glanced at her watch.

Ten minutes to alignment.

She was high above the others, looking down on them as they stretched the ladders across from the ramp they were standing on to the golden statue. Powell's men swarmed across, with Alex in the lead.

"Okay, guys," he said when they were all across. "Let's strip this baby down!"

They started pulling the swords out of the statue's hands.

What on Earth?

The swords looked heavy; it took two men to carry each. Lara watched as they made their way carefully down the steps, across the ladder, and inserted each sword into a raised slot on the stone platform.

"Excellent, excellent." That was Powell. "Easy, Julius. Easy, Alston. That's it. We have only minutes left." Powell was holding the Clock of Ages in one hand and a chronograph in the other. "Remember, what we are looking for is hidden not only in space, but also in time."

Lara edged her way along the gallery, moving a little closer, then stopped.

That part of the gallery where she'd entered had been a crumbling ruin: the sandstone pried apart by roots, only small bits of the original structure still remaining. Where she stood now, the gallery was intact. She bent low, cupping the flare in her hand so as to better direct its light. The stone here was covered with runes. They looked similar to the ones from the photos of her clock, twisted, funhouse-mirror versions of the runes she was now so familiar with. These new runes formed a single, recurring message—a few lines, at most, repeated around the length of the tomb. What that message was, however . . .

She had no idea.

"What do we do now?" Pimms's voice echoed across the chamber to her.

"The Clock is the key," Powell replied. "You'll see."

She looked down. Powell's men—Alex included—stood around him in a circle. Two men were just now levering the last of the six swords into place. And Lara could see that the glowing crystal dome in the floor was, in fact, shaped like an eye.

Powell held the Clock over it. He seemed to be reading off the inner face, staring in great concentration at its surface. *Ah.* Lara had it. He was translating.

She studied the funhouse-mirror runes. What could they be? Why have two different sets of symbols, why make it difficult to . . .

Ah.

She pulled out her knife, and held its shining surface next to the runes. They reflected onto the metal surface, perfectly legible.

Funhouse mirror indeed.

Lara put the knife away, and began translating, in virtual lockstep with Powell below her.

"We are led to believe . . ."

"A lie," Lara whispered, finishing the translation for him. "When we see not through the Eye."

The Blake? What could that mean?

"Three minutes to alignment," Alex called out.

Powell's men sunk the last sword into place.

"When we see not through the eye," Powell finally finished. Then he stood over the crystal dome and positioned the clock above the eyehole.

"Forty-five, forty-four, forty-three . . ."

Powell nodded. "Stay with me, Mr. West. The timing must be exact."

"Forty-one, no shit, forty-nine . . ."

Powell looked up for a split second. West smiled at him. Powell was not in the mood; he had his mouth half-open, intending to order Julius to shoot the man, when he realized there would be plenty of time for that afterward. All the time in the world, in fact. And then some.

"That was childish." Powell glared at West. "Don't do it again, or this tomb will have a new tenant when we seal it back up."

Thirty seconds, more or less, he thought. And the first piece will be mine.

"Mr. Powell!"

That was Lara Croft's voice. Impossible.

But when he raised his eyes from the clock, there she was, standing on the other side of the tomb, above them, in the gallery.

She moved into the light. "You're making a big mistake!"

Gunfire sprayed across the tomb. Lara disappeared into the darkness.

"Cease fire! Hold your fire!" God, that was the last thing they needed right now, for a stray bullet to hit the clock. "West, keep counting. Lady Croft!"

"Mr. Powell. And Mr. West." She stepped into the light. "Alex. You've learned your numbers. How marvelous."

"Thirty-one — Hey, Lara —"

"Here on a tourist visa?"

"Twenty-nine — no, I'm working — twenty-seven . . ."

"Lady Croft." Enough of this. "Is there some good reason why I just saved your life?"

"That's not the true eye."

Impossible. "This is the eye."

"And I know where the true eye is."

"This is the true eye," Powell said, shaking his head. Lara shook hers back.

"It really isn't, you know. It's actually a mirror image."

Powell looked at West, who was still counting. "Twenty, nineteen . . ."

Was he imagining things, or did he see a flicker of doubt in the man's expression?

"Lady Croft. I believe you are trying to cheat me out of my little ray of sunshine."

"Why would I try and cheat you out of anything now? I need you to get the piece so I can steal it from you later."

In the middle of his count, West actually snickered. The sound made Powell furious.

"You're bluffing." He turned to Julius. "Make a mental note: Kill Miss Croft if she attempts any such thing."

Julius nodded. "Sixteen, fifteen . . ." West was still counting. Powell looked down at the top of the crystal dome, at the waiting eye, ready to receive the Clock.

"Well, we can do it my way, or we can all come back in time for the next alignment." Croft sounded philosophical about the whole thing. "You're welcome to try and kill me then."

Powell looked down at the clock dial. The three planets were approaching perfect alignment. "It'll be another five thousand years," Lara said, "but . . ."

His mind raced. He looked up at Croft, at the god-statue across from him, the urn on its lap. He noticed a small crystal dome embedded in the side of the urn, facing out, like a bull's-eye.

Was that the eye?

"Eleven. Ten."

He looked at the eye in the crystal dome beneath him. Was that it? Was it the eye in the flagstone, at the foot of the idol?

Damn it all to hell. He threw the Clock across the tomb at Lara: a perfect strike.

She caught it, jumped to her left, and then she was gone.

For a second, Powell couldn't speak. Bile rose in his

throat. He would kill her. Then he would resuscitate her, and kill her again.

Lara reappeared, halfway across the gallery, next to an exact mirror of the eye in the crystal dome.

"Eight," West said.

"Oh, God," Pimms said.

"Quiet," Powell hissed.

She placed the Clock in the eye.

The platform they stood on started rumbling, moving, shaking itself furiously. The whole tomb seemed to be vibrating. Powell caught sight of something wobbling in the darkness, just about where Lara was standing—a hewn tree trunk suspended by two ropes at either end, hanging at gallery height, directly opposite the golden statue. One end of the log was sharpened to a metal-tipped point, the exact size of the bull's-eye on the side of the statue's urn. The log was held in place by a metal eye-hook, jutting out from its blunt end to overlap a similar eye-hook protruding from the gallery: a metal pin was thrust into both. A thick chain snaked down from the pin, through a series of pulleys, and disappeared into the ground.

"Five."

Gears rumbled; metal clanked on metal. A lever rose up out of the stone platform, next to Powell. He pulled it.

The log swung free.

Lara Croft jumped down onto it. What was she trying to do?

"Shoot her!" Powell yelled.

They shot. Bullets dug into the log, wood chips flying. But the angle was all wrong, she was on top of it, running down the top of the log, and now she sliced the front rope, and the front end of the log, the spiked end, lurched downward.

"Dammit." Powell screamed. That was quite enough of this nonsense.

He grabbed a rifle, racked a new cartridge into place, and swung it around.

Lady Croft's angelic face was fixed firmly in his sights.

17.

Always do the unexpected. Rule number one, in Lara's book, which meant not standing next to the Clock, waiting for the first piece of the Triangle to appear. Powell's guns would be trained on her the whole time, and what chance would she have of getting the piece then?

No, she had to keep the man guessing. So when she saw the log before her swing, she decided that was as good a time as any to make her move. Now, hanging suspended in midair, gripping onto the single remaining rope that held the log up, she was planning her next one. Let go of the rope, land on that fat bastard with the gun next to Powell, use him as a shield against the others—including the greedy Mr. West, and—

Below, Powell grabbed a rifle and aimed it at her.

Then he spun the barrel, and shot out the front of the urn, on the statue's lap.

Water gushed out: Lara looked down and saw, inside the urn, cubes of a yellow, metallic substance. Gold? No.

"It's phosphorus," she realized, still clinging to the log. Which meant the second the water sank low enough and air hit those cubes—

"One." Alex said.

Air hit the cubes.

They burst into bright, glowing incandescence. Light exploded in the tomb: Lara turned her face away for a split second, so that it was only out of the corner of her eye that she saw the crystal dome next to Powell shatter, and a column of silver liquid come shooting upward. A column of mercury, was that possible?

She turned back and studied the column head-on: it was mercury, without a doubt. Reflections from its shining surface bounced a kaleidoscope of rippling patterns around the tomb, a light show the equal of any New Year's fireworks celebration Lara had ever seen.

At the top of the column, something shimmered.

"All very lovely," she heard Pimms say. "Very . . . er lovely, indeed. But where's the piece of the Triangle?"

"It's coming," Powell said. "I feel it in my bones, Pimms. Remember, it's not just hidden in space, but also in time. It will appear for just one ah . . ." Powell took a step forward, toward the column of mercury.

"There it is!" Pimms shouted. "The Triangle!"

It was there: the shimmering at the top of the silver liquid was growing in intensity. Lara could see the piece taking shape.

She let go of the rope.

Powell reached for the Triangle.

Lara somersaulted in midair, shot past him, and snatched it.

The column of mercury collapsed in a spectacular splash. Streams of it filled every conceivable crack in the floor, a liquid plant, with mercury roots, stretching outward at a hyperaccelerated rate.

Lara landed in a crouch on the dais, directly opposite Powell. She had the Triangle in one hand and a .45 in the other. The gun was pointed at his head.

"See?" she said. "I had to wait for you to find it before I could steal it."

"Nicely done, Lady Croft." Powell, instead of being angry, was looking at her, nodding his head, and smiling. That was worse than mere anger; the look in his eyes made her skin crawl. "It seems I underestimated you. I promise it won't happen again."

"I'm going all warm and fuzzy inside."

Powell nodded up at the log. "That was very impressive. I think we could use someone of your abilities."

"No one uses me, Mr. Powell."

"You don't seem to have many other options at the moment." He smiled. "My men, you see. They quite outnumber you."

Lara saw. There were a good dozen of them gathered around her, submachine guns at the ready. She saw, but what really held her attention was something else entirely.

The mercury that had spilled out from the dome, and splashed onto the floor of the tomb . . .

. . . was now running up the walls.

Not normal behavior for that element: not normal behavior for any element, as far as she knew.

"So, Lady Croft." Powell folded his arms across his chest and gave her that creepy smile again. "Just what do you think you're going to do now?"

The mercury reached the top of the walls. Within the alcoves, it began dripping down onto the heads of the statues inside. The monkey soldiers.

Lara, quite suddenly, had a very bad feeling about what was going to happen next.

"What am I going to do?" She holstered her gun, and stepped backward. "I'm going to walk out of here. And I'd advise you to do the same."

"Why, precisely, would I do that?"

She heard creaking sounds all around them. Powell's men glanced about nervously. What? Where?

"It's the only hope you have of getting out of here. Alive."

Powell looked puzzled for a moment, then grinned. "Such drama! Wonderful!" He clapped, and laughed. Alex didn't. He was seeing what Lara saw.

"Uh, Powell. I think she might be right, actually . . ."

Powell turned away from her, and spun toward Alex, furious. "Don't be—"

Lara had the distinct pleasure of seeing Powell's jaw drop wide open.

A monkey soldier, one of the statues, had stepped in between Powell and Alex, and was now eye-to-eye with the older man.

"—ridiculous." Powell finished his sentence, and stared up at the soldier. "Remarkable."

Retreat, thought Lara, and tucked the Triangle into her belt.

She heard the crack of stone echoing throughout the tomb. In the alcoves, in the gallery above, on the floor below—

—The monkey soldiers were all coming to life.

"Holy mother of God." Pimms said, stumbling backward.

The monkey soldier next to Powell raised its sword.

In a perfectly synchronized movement, every monkey soldier in the tomb raised its sword. It made quite an impressive sight.

Then the lead monkey soldier swung at Powell, who at the last possible second, ducked out of the way, and all hell broke loose.

Lara flung herself sideways off the platform, simultaneously drawing her guns, targeting the monkey soldier nearest her, and firing as she fell. The bullets shattered its sword, and its arm. So these weren't indestructible soldiers. Thank God for the small things.

On the platform, Powell's men had formed a circle around him and Pimms, firing their AK-47s at a furious clip. Alex was doing his part.

At that moment, a monkey soldier detached itself from the group attacking Powell, and turned toward Alex, drawing its sword as it approached him from the rear. What was this?

"Look man, I'm really sorry," Alex was saying. "You want this back?"

He reached into his pocket, and held out a stone to

the soldier. No, not a stone. A jewel. The soldier reached for it . . .

Alex blasted its head from its shoulders. "Sucker." As the head fell, Lara saw that it was missing an eye.

"Alex West!" she yelled out. "You're an ass!"

He turned and smiled. "I believe the correct title is 'Tomb Raider,' thank you very much."

Lara glared. "You're no Tomb—"

She heard a whooshing sound to her left, and ducked.

A sword went whizzing over her head. She drew her .45s and shot the soldier's arm off. Powell's men, she saw, were mopping up the last of the monkey soldiers.

"Could I have a look at that?" Alex smiled, and pointed at the Triangle in her belt.

"I'll take a picture and send it to you," Lara said. It was time for her to go.

She turned and ran, zig-zagging her way over collapsed chunks of masonry from the gallery above, the occasional bit of broken monkey soldier, firing her guns, racing toward the tomb entrance.

"Stop her!" Powell shouted. "She has the piece!"

A fallen column, as thick around as a redwood, lay in her path. Too high to jump, too big to blast. She leaped down, onto the floor of the tomb, and then back up on the other side, two of Powell's men in pursuit.

Two more stood in front of her.

Damn.

The ground rumbled again.

"Christ, what now?" Powell yelled, looking around. "What now?"

On the dais opposite them, the six-armed golden statue was climbing to its feet. Rising higher and higher above them. Stone cracked as it stood, like stiff, atrophied muscles angry at being forced into use again.

The thing looked limber enough as it strode down from the dais and in one smooth motion, bent at the waist, reached for, and unsheathed the six massive swords surrounding the crystal dome, taking one in each hand. It stood upright again, thirty, forty feet tall, easily, and swiveled its three heads around, surveying the chamber.

Powell's guards, meanwhile, were emptying round after round into it at a dizzying rate. Bullets tore into the statue, sending bits of gold and stone and jewels flying into the air like wood chips out of a sawmill, but the creature didn't seem to notice. It was looking for something.

One set of eyes settled on Lara. The three heads froze in place.

The two legs strode right for her, the chamber thundering with each step.

"What?" Lara shouted. "What do you want?"

She raised her .45s and started blasting away at the thing. Her ammunition took out bigger chunks of stone than the AK-47s, but it made no difference to the statue. It was the size of a tractor-trailer; it took the shots and just kept coming, massive swords swish-swish-swishing through the air in front of it.

The .45 in her right hand let out a feeble click; the clip was empty.

Lara slapped a button on the strap of her backpack. A bandolier tree slid out and hung suspended from the bottom of the pack, clips lined up in rows on both sides of the tree. Still firing with her left hand, she reached her right hand behind, and snapped the new clip into the gun.

Nice design, Bryce. She made a mental note to thank him when she got back to the Manor.

Movement to her right.

Lara turned. Two monkey soldiers charged toward her, swords held high. She swiveled her guns, but they were too close, so she ducked, and rolled—

One of the statue's giant swords came whooshing down, decapitating both soldiers with a single blow.

She ran, the statue following. Lara couldn't recall when she'd been pursued with such fervor—possibly by the Earl of Farrington, but his motives were much more transparent. So why was golden boy so keen on getting to her? What did she have that—

She felt the piece of the Triangle, tucked safely in her belt.

"Alex!" she shouted. "You wanted a look at this?"

Halfway across the chamber, at the foot of the dais the statue had risen from, West lowered his gun.

"What?"

"Here. It's all yours!"

She tossed the Triangle piece to Alex. He caught it, looking quite confused.

"Croft?" He turned the piece over in his hand. "What the hell?"

The statue turned, almost in mid-stride, and started after him, stone feet cracking the floor underneath as it ran.

Alex's eyes widened. "Shit!" He raised his gun again and fired rapidly. Lara joined in, pumping round after round into the statue's back as it raced toward Alex. With a little breathing room, Lara was able to focus and concentrate her fire. She targeted one of the statue's shoulders, gouging out huge chunks of stone.

An arm fell to the floor and shattered. One down, five to go.

The creature reached Alex. He ducked behind one of the columns supporting the gallery. Just in time. A sword sliced the air where he'd been.

The statue slammed into the column, cracking it in half.

The whole tomb shook. Dust fell from the ceiling.

"I've changed my mind!" Alex shouted. He had the Triangle in one hand. "You keep it!"

The piece came sailing back across the room. The statue turned to watch its flight.

"Grab it! Grab it!" That was Powell, who'd been watching from the dais above her, yelling at his guards. They seemed reluctant to move.

Lara holstered a gun and grabbed the Triangle. The statue came bounding back across the chamber. She circled the floor, so that Powell and his men were between her and the statue.

"Come and get it!" she shouted, holding the Triangle in the air before securing it under her belt again.

The creature leaped right for her, swords flashing, barreling over the platform as it came.

Blood and screams filled the air; Powell and his men went down. No, not Powell.

She had a split second to register that, and then she had to concentrate on the statue. It was gaining on her, and she was firing with both guns and doing some damage now, yes indeed. The statue was like a skeleton of stone, a shadow of its former self, though it still had strength enough to use those swords.

It raised one now.

Lara targeted that arm and fired, once, twice, and the elbow exploded in a shower of stone shards. The arm fell to the floor.

Two down.

The thing kept coming, but now it was like target practice, and though she was still backing up, she felt in control, taking aim at another arm with one gun now, as she reached behind her to reload the second—

The bandolier was empty.

The statue charged.

Rule number one, Lara thought, and she charged, too.

"Croft!" She heard Alex yell. "Are you out of your mind?"

Five feet away from impact, she slid, kicking out with her legs. She caught the statue in what would have been a very sensitive area for a living creature, but in this instance was only a balance point, a fulcrum, and she kicked out just hard enough to knock it off its stride. A huge chunk of rock fell from between its legs.

"Man." Alex shook his head. "That was cold."

It wobbled, and slammed into the side of the tomb, shattering another column.

The tomb rumbled again.

Dust fell on her head.

Lara looked up. The gallery was collapsing. She rolled out from under the statue, and hurled herself out of the way, just as a small mountain's worth of stone came crashing down on the statue, and that was it for golden boy; he was rubble. Powell was shouting and pointing at her as she ran toward the tomb entrance, but it was blocked by the last few monkey soldiers, who looked as though they still wanted to fight. She didn't have time for that. She leaped onto a pile of masonry, and jumped across to another. As the monkeys turned to track her, she turned and jumped toward them, and before they could even lift their swords, she was on them, using their shoulders like stepping-stones, racing over them, and launching herself through the chamber door onto the entrance ramp and out of the tomb.

She shot past dwindling blue flares, placed every few hundred feet along the passageway, and spotted light—actual, honest-to-goodness daylight—and then she was out of the tunnel and into the sun, looking at the surprised faces of the workers and some of Powell's men, who, true to their unthinking goonish nature, started to fire at her. They were too slow, and the jungle was too close, and then she was in the bushes, pushing past them, through them, the leaves slapping at her and—

Hold on a minute.

Where, actually, was she going?

The binocs and comm piece were in her pack, so

she reached down to her belt and pulled out the mini cellphone, unfolding it as she ran, hitting the speed dial.

"Bryce! Bryce! Wake up!"

She heard something—actually, several some-things—crashing through the bushes behind her. She'd wanted to get to the Land Rover—she would have bet good money on her chances to escape from or fight off anything short of an armored division in that vehicle—but looking up at the sun, she estimated she was running in almost the opposite direction from where she'd left it.

A voice came through from the other end of the phone.

"Ah, hello, Brycey can't come to the phone at the moment, but if you leave a message, he'll get back to you as soon as possible. Beeep."

She grinned. "Very funny. Ho-ho—"

Gunfire shredded the air around her.

She ducked and swerved off to her right, lowering her head and staying as close to the ground as she could manage.

"Lara? Was that gunfire? Are you all right?"

"Yes, yes, and yes. Right now I'm running blind, though, and I need directions. Coming east from the tomb. Any thoughts?"

More gunfire. Back where she had been.

"Turning on the computer, give me a moment. Here we go, ah, where are we . . . ?"

"Cambodia," Lara offered. "Remember?"

A shout, behind her. Lara glimpsed Powell's men,

pushing through the bushes. And Alex. And Pimms, pointing at her.

She took off again, full speed.

"There's a river!" That was Hillary, shouting in the background.

"Ah, the blue stripe. Yes, a river." Bryce echoed. "Ah, northeast about thirty degrees from . . . no, no, hold on . . ."

Bullets whizzed over her head. "You're putting me on hold?"

But now, as she ran, she heard a rushing sound, and she knew what that was, so without even an "over and out," she pressed the end-call button on the cellphone, stuffed it back into her belt, and shot forward with renewed energy.

Sorry, boys, she said to herself, thinking of Bryce and, in particular, Hilly, sitting in the Tech Room, wondering what was happening, *but I'll have to call you back.*

She burst through a last bit of jungle, and into a clearing. A patch of dirt, and just beyond . . .

A cliff. The rushing sound, the sound of water, came from just beyond that. Freedom.

She heard brush being forced aside, and then a voice.

"I'll shoot!"

Lara grinned.

She knew that voice. It was Alex. She could hear him panting.

"Lara. Give it up. The other guys will kill you."

She still didn't turn around. Instead, she tightened the straps on her backpack.

"They might. You won't."

"Don't be so all-fired sure about that. This job is important to me. Very important."

She turned then, and smiled.

"Not as important as I am."

He blushed.

She jumped.

18. "Yes, Mr. Gareth. No, Mr. Gareth. No, sir. Yes, sir. No, sir. One second, sir." Powell covered the mouthpiece of the phone with his left hand. "Pimms, stop staring, or I will surely send you back into that tomb to gather the ammunition we dropped."

Pimms stopped staring. He was standing next to Powell, who was standing next to his Land Rover, the secure satellite phone in hand. The dish was on the hood. Gareth had called on behalf of the Council, and Powell pictured the "distinguished gentlemen" behind him, nodding approvingly. The Council wanted to know if they'd found the piece. That was five minutes ago. He was just finishing up his rant now.

"Yes, we will track her, though I'm confident Lady Croft will come to us. One piece is no good without the other." A burst of chatter erupted from the other end of the phone. "No. It is not conceivable she would simply allow the alignment to pass without using the piece.

She is a Croft, sir. You know what that means." Powell nodded. "Yes, sir. Good-bye, sir."

He slammed down the phone, and rubbed the bridge of his nose between thumb and forefinger.

"I'm tense," he announced. "Very, very tense."

He heard footsteps shuffling away from him. Smart. Powell had the urge to grab a gun and start shooting people indiscriminately. Nothing like the power of life and death to overcome feelings of impotence.

He opened his eyes. Pimms was staring at him solicitously.

"Can I get you a drink, sir? Something to relax you?"

Powell shook his head. "No. The only thing that will relax me is the feel of that Triangle in my hand. Do you have that? No? Then leave me alone."

Of course, he had lied to Gareth. It was entirely possible that Lady Croft would simply take the first half of the Triangle and head to Bora Bora until the alignment was over. That couldn't be allowed to happen. He had to force her to bring it to him. He needed leverage.

West was sitting on the ground, leaning up against one of the stones they'd pulled from the ground earlier. He'd been very quiet since returning from his unsuccessful chase of Lady Croft.

Powell crooked a finger at him.

"Mr. West, come here, please."

West stood, and came.

Powell put an arm around his shoulders.

"I want you to tell me everything you know about Lady Croft. Who, for instance, is she closest to? Who is important to her? Who, in your estimation, would she sacrifice for?"

"Er." West shifted uncomfortably. "That's, ah, personal information, Mr. Powell. Very personal."

"Yes." Powell took hold of West by the shoulders, and spun him around so that they were looking at each other, eye-to-eye. "Exactly."

The water was warm.

The sun was warmer.

And the river was peaceful.

After her jump, Lara had surfaced, grabbed hold of a large branch, and let the current take her. It was a strong current, but not too strong; hanging onto the branch was like being pulled along by a slow-moving speedboat. Like the prep run before a water-skiing event. She lay on her back, watching the big cliff, and little Alex, as they receded into the distance.

The river flowed on. Lara went with it, the Triangle safely tucked into her belt. The sky darkened, and the rains came, heavy for a few minutes. The river flowed faster. Then the downpour slowed, and stopped, and the sun came back out.

The cliffs on either side of the river disappeared, replaced by jungle, and then farmland. In the distance she saw rice paddies, and farmers, men and women alike, some wearing hats, some stripped to the waist, all bent over, tending to their crop.

An old, toothless man in a canoe paddled by without seeing her, squinting into the river. A fishing net hung half-in, half-out of his boat.

The current slowed. Lara rolled over, and saw, fast approaching, a hut, propped up on stilts, leaning out over the river. And a second, and a third and a fourth, on either bank. Off in the distance, on a hill to her right, was a beautiful, golden building. A temple.

Lara let go of the branch, swam to the bank, and emerged near a group of children, who were playing at the water's edge; they saw her and burst into laughter.

"What is so funny?" Lara asked, mock-serious, hands on hips.

The children shrieked with laughter again, and ran.

Farther down the bank, she saw a young man in a saffron robe kneeling in the sand. His head was shaven; he was chanting. Lara waited until he finished, then cleared her throat.

"Excuse me," she said in Khmer. "My phone is wet. Do you know where I can make an international call?"

The monk looked up at her and blinked.

"Telephone." He smiled. "Sure. You come with me."

Half an hour later, she was in dry clothes—actually, a cast-off sari—and standing on the rooftop of the temple she'd glimpsed from the river. The temple was part of a larger complex of buildings, the Buddhist equivalent of a monastery, ringed by a wall. Standing next to her was the monks' leader, an elderly, somewhat frail-looking man in his late sixties. A younger monk was holding a small satellite dish out in front of him and pointing it due west.

Lara was holding the monastery's satellite phone. She'd just dialed Bryce's number, in the trailer.

"You have a circuit?" the old monk asked.

"I have a circuit." Lara nodded. The phone was ringing. "No answer yet, though."

"Hello?"

"Bryce." Lara smiled. "It's me. I'm okay."

"Ah. Thank goodness. Hillary and I were . . . after we lost contact—"

"How is Hilly?"

"I put him to sleep with a bottle of Glenfiddich a few hours ago. He'll be much relieved when he awakens. Did you get the clock back?"

"No. But I got the first piece." She felt a twinge in her arm. Despite the tender care she had received, it was still bleeding. It was just a gash from a ricocheting bullet, or chunk of monkey soldier, but it hurt like the Dickens.

"That's marvelous news. Bee-ooo-ti-ful. Smashing." Bryce sounded giddy. Come to think of it, that was how she felt, too.

"Yep. So I think I'm on level pegging with Mr. Powell."

"Won't he just want to kill you now?"

"No, no. Piece of the Triangle first, kill me later. And that's going to be his big mistake."

"Killing you?"

"No, silly. I won't ever let him kill me. His problem is that he needs the piece I have. One is no good without the other." The monk was staring at her and nodding, as if he understood the significance of what she was saying. That wasn't possible, of course, since he spoke Pidgin English at best, and had no idea what she meant with all this talk of clocks, and triangles, and killing. Still . . .

She had this funny feeling there was more to the little man than met the eye.

"Anyway, until Powell gets my piece of the Triangle, I'm his new best friend. He'll do anything for me."

The satellite phone beeped. Call waiting? Maybe it was her ride home. Shugrave had access to the Echelon network; he could scan every call coming in or out of Cambodia. Maybe it was him, or Tookie. She had told them she'd check in.

"Got to go, Bryce. Call you later."

"But—"

She clicked over to the other call. "Lara in Cambodia."

"Lady Croft." Not Tookie. Not Shugrave. Powell. "I've been scanning all London calls, hoping to find you. And now, here you are. Checking in on the home front, I see. And how is Bryce? And your butler ... Hillary? Are they standing your absence?"

"They're managing, I should think," Lara said, as icily as she could. "Not that it's any of your concern."

"I have many concerns, Lady Croft. Currently, your two friends are not high on my list."

"Keep it that way."

Powell went on as if he hadn't heard her. "What is currently high on my list is the first piece of the Triangle. You do still have it, don't you?"

"I do."

"Good. Undamaged, I trust?"

"The Triangle's fine, Mr. Powell."

"And you—how are you?"

"Alive."

Powell laughed. "And kicking, I hope."

"Not at the moment," Lara said. "I've run out of teeth to smash. But later, who knows?"

"Who knows, indeed."

"And yourself, Mr. Powell? How are you feeling this afternoon?"

"Superlative."

"Okay. 'Bye then."

She waited a moment. The phone rang again.

"Get to the point," she said, picking it up.

"Of course. I digress. You have my half of the Triangle."

"You have my father's clock."

"Ahh. Quite so. Listen, my dear, without each other we are quite useless at this point."

Lara waited.

"And we are living," Powell continued, "in interesting times. So, my dear, we should reevaluate our positions. Like it or not, you and I are in business together. We should have a business meeting. We should meet."

"You mean you would like another opportunity to try to kill me."

"Oh, that's harsh. But perhaps. Wait and see. Come to Venice. *Via Doloroso*. I'll be waiting."

The line went dead.

"Arsehole."

The monk looked at her. "Something the matter?"

She clicked back over to Bryce.

"Okay, I'm back."

"Who was that before?"

"Powell. He wants to deal."

"Of course he does. He needs the first piece of the Triangle. And you need him. He has the clock. That's the only way to find the second tomb. Unless your father's left you any more secret messages . . ."

"Not that I know of." Lara thought a moment. "Bryce, do we really need Powell? Is it possible to calculate the location of the second tomb, using the pictures you have of the clock?"

"Been there, done that. Short answer is no. My calculations were based on your translation of the runes as applied to the active dial. Each dot, representing a planet, in position, assigned a numeric value, and then projected onto their actual astronomic positions. Where they intersected, *voilà*, the tomb. Now you've got a second series of planets, and I have no way of knowing the zero reference, and on top of that, you've got to allow for the possibility that the second phase of the alignment caused some sort of realignment of the initial operators, and . . ."

She let him talk, letting her mind work as he did so. She was going to have to go to Venice and deal with Powell. Use him to find the second piece, and then . . .

What were her intentions, actually? Use the power of the Triangle for herself? Her father had warned against that: absolute power, corrupting absolutely, he had basically said in his letter. And if his assessment of the Triangle's powers was right, whoever held the complete Triangle at the moment of alignment would possess power beyond imagination. Power over space and time.

On the other end of the line, Bryce was just finishing up.

"There's a remote chance, I suppose, I could do it with a Cray, if I had a Cray. Doubtful, although I suppose it might be worth tying into Langley for just a moment and—"

"No," she said quickly. "No. There'll be none of

that." Last time Bryce had tied into Langley, it hadn't been just two days of brown-nosing; it had been a full week of ass-kissing in Washington, D.C., and she was never, ever, ever doing that again. "All right, then. How long till the last phase of the alignment?"

"Sixty-six hours, fifty-three minutes, twenty-eight seconds. So what's your plan?"

"Simplicity itself." She smiled. "Mr. Powell is going to tell me where the second tomb is."

"He is?"

"Well, unless he gets my half of the Triangle and kills me. Which he will not."

"I don't understand."

"You don't have to." And then she told him what he had to do, and hung up the phone.

"*Ar Kun.*" She smiled at the monks. Thank you.

He shook his head. "Phone drive me crazy. Tiny voices."

Lara laughed. "Necessary evil, I'm afraid."

"You think? Really?" He clapped his hands, and another monk took away the satellite dish and phone. Then he took her arm.

"Come. Dinner."

"I'm not hungry." She had things to do: for one, unload the contents of her backpack, and try to get the binocs and the comm unit dried out. The cellphone as well, and whoops! she'd forgotten all about the Blake. "I have to go back to my room."

"No. You must eat."

"Really, I—"

"Ah. Please." He shook his head and smiled. "Food is also necessary evil."

Her stomach rumbled in agreement. She let the old monk lead her off the roof, back into the monastery.

The necessary evil in this instance was *an sam chruk*, pork, tofu, and rice.

"Personal favorite of the Buddha," the monk who prepared the meal informed her. His name was Anam Don Pre, and he spoke English. "Minus the pork, of course."

Lara wolfed down two bowls of it, surprising herself with her appetite. As she was finishing her second bowl of the *an sam chruk*, the first monk appeared.

"Better?" he asked.

"Better." She patted her stomach. "Thank you."

She'd taken her meal in a small building within the temple complex. The old monk now brought her back to the temple itself. Inside, her clothes and her backpack were in a corner, lying on the stone floor, drying.

He knelt down, lotus-style. She sat in similar fashion, opposite him. At the front of the temple, on a raised dais, was a golden Buddha. Two arms, not six. No swords, thank goodness.

Dozens of candles, large and small, lit and unlit, covered the altar. Monks came and went as she watched, carrying matches, faces glowing with serenity in the candlelight.

Another monk brought them each a steaming mug of tea.

"First food. Now drink." The old monk nodded. "Then rest."

Lara took a sip of the tea: green tea. It warmed her from within, soothed her. A good night's sleep would feel wonderful; she could practically taste it. A mattress, a pillow, clean sheets. But . . .

Sixty-six hours, fifty-three minutes, twenty-eight seconds until the final alignment. Somewhat less now.

"No rest for the wicked." She shook her head. "Not yet, at least."

"You got what you came for?" the old man asked.

"Yes." Lara felt the Triangle underneath the sari, against her skin, held in place by the elastic band of her underwear.

He let out a long sigh. "Too bad."

Lara stared at him. "What?"

"Too bad for the world."

"The world is safe now." She frowned. How on earth could he possibly know what she'd been doing?

"Mmmm. A little bit safer, perhaps." In the dim candlelight, the air around the old monk seemed to . . . shimmer. "You have the piece, not Powell."

No. Lara shook her head, trying not to think of the vision she'd had before entering the tomb. The little girl, the old woman, her father—

"Your father."

She looked up, openmouthed.

"He said you would never give up."

"Wait." Lara found her voice at last. "You knew my father?"

He closed his eyes.

"Excuse me?" She frowned. "Hello?"

No response. She reached out and touched him

lightly, on the arm. For a moment, it appeared that he was not breathing.

His eyes shot open.

Lara dropped her mug, which fell to the floor.

But didn't land. Instead, it simply hung in space, inches from shattering on the stone floor, a splash of tea caught in midair as if it had been flash-frozen.

The candles were no longer flickering. The flames were a single, steady tongue of fire. The temple was utterly, completely silent.

The monk's face shimmered, shifted, features becoming indeterminate.

Her father's face appeared.

"Soon you'll have discovered all my secrets."

That was her father's voice.

"Daddy?"

"Secrets not even your mother knew."

"Secrets?" Lara shook her head again. She was lost, completely at sea. She looked down, and gasped.

Still in the lotus position, she was now floating six feet off the ground.

So was her father/the monk, a few feet opposite her.

"When your mother died, when you were a baby, I suddenly saw my life through new eyes. Your clear, child's eyes, Lara. And what I saw was . . ." He shook his head. "Judge me with your heart, angel."

"I don't understand . . ."

"You must get the Clock back, Lara. And destroy it. Or in five thousand years' time the descendants of Powell will come along, find the pieces, and reform the Triangle."

"But why can't I—"

"Destroy the Clock, Lara. Don't be tempted by its power, like I was. You must be stronger. Focus. Eyes on the prize."

"You? You were tempted, Daddy?"

Lord Croft lowered his head. "I was. Be strong, angel. And remember, I am always with you."

Now her father's face and the monk's were somehow blending together, the air shimmering around them.

"One thought fills immensity . . ."

Below her, the cup smashed on the temple floor.

She looked up, and now it was the old monk looking at her, kindly and wise and gentle.

"We will help you," he said.

For some reason, her eyes filled with tears. "You will help me? You will?"

"You need a little help. The world is in your hands. Lara. Angel." The monk's voice seemed to change again on those last two words, back into her father's. Impossible.

Lara shook her head. "I don't know what to say."

"Then finish your tea. The words will come to you, later. Now, drink."

"But my tea—"

Lara almost jumped in surprise. The mug was steaming in her hand.

And she was sitting on the floor of the temple again.

"Drink." The monk was sitting directly opposite her, as if nothing out of the ordinary had occurred. He offered a smile. "It tastes quite bad, but it's good for you." He nodded, indicating with his eyes the bandage on her arm.

Strange. It felt—

She pulled away the cloth, and saw it was completely healed.

"Food. Drink. Now rest." The monk stood, and held out his hand. "Come."

She went.

19. "Wow." West's eyes widened as they entered the Council hall. "This is—" He looked up, and down, and all around. "Wow."

"Yes, isn't it." Powell set down his laptop and the clock on one of the two long conference tables. He spread out the printouts and pictures Miss Holcomb had given him as well. "This is the second tomb. It's in a very remote little corner of the world—you'll note the ice floes in the photos here—but what's more relevant is the null magnetic field that surrounds the entire area. A dead zone, if you will. None of our electrical equipment will work, which means we will be dependent upon . . ." His voice trailed off as he became aware that West wasn't listening at all, was in fact still standing with his hands on his hips, staring at the huge, floor-to-ceiling mural behind the High Council's podium.

"That's not a Titian, is it?" West asked, pointing. "It can't be. He never did anything that big . . . did he?"

"Titian, yes." Powell said. "We have several others.

Perhaps you'd like a guided tour? Here. Let me just put these charts away, and we can get started. No rush. We have all the time in the world."

"Sorry." West said. "Let's get to work."

Powell wasn't mollified. "You are wasting my time. And my money. I am paying your usurious rates, Mr. West, because I expect you to be at my beck and call for the next two and a half days. Constantly. Without fail. Is that clear?"

"Yes."

"And another thing. You are entitled to your emotions, but they are not to interfere with the work I am paying you for. Is that clear?"

"Yes," West nodded. "All clear. Perfectly clear."

"Good. Now, as I was saying, the second tomb—"

"The Tomb of Ten Thousand Shadows."

Powell looked up. "Where did you hear that phrase?"

"Around." West smiled. "Actually, I've been doing a little research. Since I discovered I was working for the Illuminati, I thought it might be worthwhile boning up a bit on their history."

"Excellent. I'm impressed, Mr. West."

"You'll get your money's worth from me."

"Good."

They continued their discussions about how the dead zone would impact their exploration of the tomb. West told Powell where he expected the second piece of the Triangle might be, based on the history he'd been reading. Powell, in turn, gave West more background from the Illuminati's own archives. They put the two together, discussed scenarios.

The massive door to the conference room opened, and Pimms poked his head around it.

"May I interrupt?"

Powell waved him in. "You've secured our transportation?"

"I have, sir. Yes, sir. Two Chinooks."

"Excellent." But Pimms didn't look happy. "Is something wrong, Pimms?"

"Not exactly wrong, sir. Just a complication."

"Which is . . ."

"Mr. Gareth, sir. He'll be accompanying us. And so will," Pimms swallowed. "*Himself.* The distinguished gentleman."

Powell felt the blood rush to his face. "What?"

"Mr. Gareth and the—"

Powell waved him off. "Never mind. I heard you."

He got to his feet, and began pacing. Pimms, for once in his sniveling little life, had spoken straight to the point. This was, indeed, a complication. One that certainly gave him less latitude in dealing with any problems and/or opportunities that might arise once they reached the second tomb, and the final phase of the alignment occurred.

But there was no sense in letting anyone else know that.

"The distinguished gentleman?" West was smiling. "Sounds ominous. Who is he?"

"The leader of our organization."

"I thought you were the leader," West said.

"No, no, no." Powell sat again. "Just a cog, in the larger organization."

"A very important cog," Pimms offered.

"Thank you, Pimms." Powell smiled. "Now, Mr. West. We were—"

"A very, very important cog, actually," Pimms said. "Why, to carry the metaphor further, the wheel itself would—"

"Thank you, Pimms, that will be all."

Pimms bowed, and left.

"Now." Powell leaned forward in his chair. "Another important scenario we must discuss: Lady Croft."

West nodded. "Yes. You think she'll bring the first piece here?"

"I know she will. I expect her momentarily, in fact," Powell said. "I also expect her to try and gum up the works again, so to speak."

West smiled. "That's Lara, all right."

"Yes, it is, isn't it?" Powell didn't smile back. "I don't want her to gum up the works, Mr. West. I have a feeling you can help me to ensure she doesn't."

"Oh." West looked a little nervous. "What, you mean distract her at an opportune moment, something like that?"

"Something like that," Powell said. "Mr. West, you seem to me the one person who may be capable of distracting Lady Croft. Or catching her by surprise."

"Well. Heh." He shrugged. "My boyish charm, I suppose."

"Don't make a joke of this, Mr. West." Powell stared directly into the man's eyes. "Remember, you're dealing with a very serious man, and I very seriously expect to be holding both pieces of the Triangle in my hand at the moment of alignment. Should something occur to prevent that happening, I would be very—"

He made a fist of his right hand, and slammed it down on the table: the Clock jumped, the charts shook, West started in his chair.

"very—"

He slammed it again.

"—very—"

A third time.

"—angry."

The force of his blows had rattled the clock clear across the table: He picked it up and put it back in the center. Then he sat silent, glaring at West. Neither of them spoke for a good ten seconds.

"Yes." West cleared his throat. "Yes, I can see that."

"I would lash out in all directions, Mr. West. And should it be Lady Croft who denies me the Triangle, I suspect I would lash out in yours."

"But—"

Powell plowed on. "Because you have the power to stop her, Mr. West. I firmly believe that. And if you don't, I will take it as a sign that you are not as committed to my cause as you should be. Given who is paying you, at the moment."

"Mr. Powell." West, give the man credit, looked him right back in the eye. "I'll get you that second half of the Triangle. I'll put it right in your hand. That's what you're paying me for. That's what I'm going to do."

"And Lady Croft?"

"She can help me do that," West said. "Or she can get out of my way."

Powell nodded. "Good." He started to stand up. "I've given you a room at the *penzione*—" He snapped his fingers. "Ah. I almost forgot." He reached into his pocket, and brought out the clipping he'd had Pimms pull. "Your cousin's wedding announcement, Mr. West. I thought you might be interested in seeing it . . . since you had to, unfortunately, miss the affair."

West looked the clipping over with interest. "Why, this is—" He looked up and smiled. "Very nice of you, Mr. Powell. Thank you. I am interested in it."

"Good." Powell smiled. "It's from the *Dispatch*, as well. I thought you might appreciate the local flavor."

"The *Dispatch*? That's all the way out in Keenesborough, where my parents are. You didn't have to go to all that trouble to find . . ."

West was silent for a moment.

"I think we understand each other, don't we, Mr. West?" Powell clapped him on the shoulder. "Good. I'm so glad."

He crossed the room and opened the doors. "Pimms. I think Mr. West is ready to see his room now."

West was indeed. He strode past Powell without looking back.

"Have a good night's rest," Powell called after him. "We start bright and early tomorrow."

Lara watched Powell slamming his fist down on the table, yelling at Alex, and smiled.

"My, aren't we getting grumpy?" She shook her head. "Remember, boys, there's no 'I' in team."

Lying flat out on the roof opposite them, Lara lowered the binoculars, and spoke into her comm piece.

"Bryce."

"Present."

"I need those plans."

"Uh, still working on that. According to city records, that very large, impressive building you're staring at doesn't even exist."

Lara nodded. That fit: A building that didn't exist for a group that didn't officially exist either. But this building undoubtedly belonged to the Illuminati. Dead giveaway: the gargoyles holding a triangle with an eye in it. Beautiful building: huge courtyard out back, all very impressive, and very neatly tucked away in the middle of the city. A very beautiful city, Venice. She didn't think she'd be back here so soon, after that business with Bartoli. She wouldn't be back here at all, if Bryce hadn't been able to track down Tookie and send him to the monastery. That was ten hours ago: she'd awakened from a sound sleep to find the old monk standing over her, and Tookie behind him, chowing down on a bowl of *an sam chruk*.

"Love this stuff," he'd said. "Come on, Croft, shake your tailfeathers. Your chariot awaits."

Tookie dropped her in Amman, where Bryce had arranged a waiting Lear. A few hours flight into Venice, and here she was, on the other side of the street from the address Powell had given her, looking for a way to sneak, undetected, into the Illuminati building. Sneak in, find the Clock, and destroy it. Sneak out, and let Powell get the second piece of the Triangle, for all the good it would do him. She'd hide the first piece in a hole so deep British Petroleum's best engineers wouldn't be able to dig it out. Without leaving any clues behind for Powell's descendants, or anyone else. Mission accomplished, end of story.

But without a way in, without the building's plans . . .

She heard a noise behind her, and turned. Two men in business suits. One of them was built like an Arnold Schwarzenegger; the other was a few inches over five feet and looked very familiar. The Arnold had a gun.

"You gotta lotta nerve, show your face around here, Croft." The short man spoke. Lara stared at him for a moment longer, and then she had it.

"You're Bartoli's brother."

The little man nodded. "That's right. But I ain't here to talk. I'm here to give you what you give my brother."

"No thanks. I'm busy now." Lara pointed over her shoulder, at the building across the street. "See?"

Both men looked. Idiots. She drew her .45 and shot the big man once in the arm. He dropped his gun.

"Go away," she said. "Immediately."

He snarled and charged.

"Have it your way." She spun-kicked, and he went flying off the roof, his scream cut short as he splashed into the canal.

Bartoli's brother was staring at her.

She clocked him in the jaw.

"Never let me see you again," she said, addressing the prone, glassy-eyed person, "or I will be forced to take drastic action."

Just then, coming from the street below the other side of the building, she heard the sound of a metal gate swinging open. She ran to the edge, and got there in time to see Alex walking off down the street, arms swinging rapidly in that pissed-off manner she recalled all too well.

She grabbed a rope and rappelled down the side of the building after him.

He took two right turns, ending up on a small alleyway, where he paused for a moment and studied a piece of paper. Then he took out a key, walked up to a red doorway, and stepped inside.

She ducked into a doorway and activated the comm link. "Bryce."

"Not yet on those plans. I'm sorry, I'm incompetent. I'll have a letter of resignation on your desk in the morning."

In the building Alex had just entered, lights went on.

"I'll look it over when I get home, I promise. In the meantime, Hillary pulled some information for me on Powell. Can you get it?"

"I'll certainly try. Looking for anything in particular?"

"He owned a residence in Venice: I want the address."

"Hold, please."

Lara held. It was a cloudy night. In the sky above, lightning flashed behind clouds. Or maybe not lightning: maybe the Aurora, again. She looked at her watch: thirty-two hours, ten minutes, forty-eight seconds till the final phase of the alignment.

Bryce came back on with the address of Powell's residence; it was the building Alex had just entered.

"Damn." She was surprised at how angry she was. "Bastard."

Alex's face appeared at a second-floor window for a second. She had an overwhelming urge to shoot his nose off.

"I'm sorry," Bryce said. "If you'd let me use Langley, I'd have the plans in a minute, I know I would."

"Bryce . . ." She almost told him that she'd been talking about Alex, but the words, for some reason, caught in her throat. Lara had been hoping that the argument she'd seen Alex and Powell having meant the two of them weren't a team anymore, but clearly that wasn't the case. So she was going to have to go it alone, as usual (unless you counted whatever was happening with her father as being genuine and dependable, which she did not).

"I wish you'd let me help," Bryce said, in an altogether serious tone of voice she was not accustomed to hearing from him. "Since the last time we tied in to Langley, I've totally redone the scrambling procedures. There is no way in the world anyone can trace the hookup back to me. Or you. It's fail-safe. I could be using that computer all the time, I promise you."

All of a sudden, an idea struck her. It was either a very good idea, or a very bad one; she couldn't quite tell which at the moment.

"Bryce, you really want to help?"

"I really do," he said, still very serious. "I really, really do."

"It could be dangerous."

"I understand. I'm prepared."

"All right, then," Lara said. "Here's what you can do."

By the time she explained her idea, and they finished discussing it, Bryce sounded significantly less excited. But he agreed to assist her.

She clicked off the comm piece, and concentrated on Mr. West. Lights were going on all over the building now; the man was making himself right at home. Probably opening a bottle of wine, getting out the cheese and crackers, and turning on the football matches. Bastard. She wanted a few words with him.

She crossed the street, and stood at the red door. The lock was a Gianfreddi: on a 1–10 scale of pickability, about an eight. It took her thirty seconds. Then she was inside.

The building was an apartment house. Good God, on top of all his other faults, was Powell a landlord as well? Illuminati, lawyer, landlord: all in all, the most reprehensible human being she'd ever known.

She'd fixed Alex's location in her head from the outside, and took the stairs two at a time till she came to the door she judged was his. She put an ear to it, and heard the sound of rushing water. A shower. Good. She could make as much noise as she wanted rifling through the place.

The lock was a no-name, an old-style skeleton key. Zero on that pickability scale. In ten seconds she was inside.

The apartment was an old-style *penzione*, furniture in garish, faded patterns, small kitchen, icebox, and stove. She tossed it quickly. Nothing.

Then Lara pushed open the bathroom door, and stepped in.

The room was filled with steam, and the sound of Alex's off-key singing. Thompson Twins, "Hold Me Now."

"Hold my poor and tired heart . . ."

She stifled a smile. Alex's awful taste in music was legendary.

His pants were hanging on a hook, on the back of the bathroom door. She went through them, hoping for some kind of card key that might let her into the Illuminati building. Nothing. Damn.

Alex started singing Soft Cell. She decided to leave him a message on the steamed-up bathroom mirror, a single, seven letter word, which conveyed her opinion of him far better than any combination of four letter words would have done.

TRAITOR.

She was going to leave then, but as she walked back into Alex's bedroom, an idea suddenly came to her.

When he came out of the shower, quite naked, she was sitting on his bed waiting for him.

"Lara!"

She smiled up at him. "Alex."

She had to give him credit, he was doing his best to seem completely nonplussed by the situation.

"Got your message," he said, nodding in the direction of the bathroom. "So you think I'm a greedy, unscrupulous sellout who'll do anything for money?"

"You said it."

He grinned. "The money part is true, I guess."

He threw away the towel and started walking toward her.

"And while we're on the subject, I believe you still have something of mine."

"Not yours. You mean Mr. Powell's beloved piece of the Triangle."

"Of course. Mr. Powell's."

Lara shook her head. "Such loyalty," she said sarcastically.

Alex shrugged. "Possession is nine-tenths of the law."

He stood over her, and then—quite suddenly—reached underneath his pillow and produced a small handgun.

Lara supposed she should act surprised, but considering that she knew the gun was under there, having thoroughly searched the room moments earlier, the most she could muster was a raised eyebrow.

"Ah, the 'finders keepers, losers weepers' rule."

"Something like that."

Alex was standing right before her now, quite naked.

"Oho. Man with a gun. I suppose you intend to frisk me."

She stood up. Now they were toe-to-toe.

"Frisk you?" Alex grinned. "Not a bad suggestion. Even though you've probably already hidden the piece somewhere else, frisking you is never a total waste of time."

Lara grinned. "Have at it then."

She turned, and Alex rummaged through her backpack.

"Nothing here."

"No, I wouldn't expect so," Lara smiled. Of course, if he'd checked a few moments earlier . . .

Alex walked around behind her, slipped the backpack off her shoulders, and patted down her back.

"Not carrying any concealed weapons there, either."

"No." Lara turned around, and nodded at his gun. "Wouldn't it be easier to search with both hands?"

He smiled, and tossed his weapon down on the bed.

He stood close behind her a second. She felt his breath on the back of her neck.

"Find what you're looking for yet?"

"Not yet," she heard him say.

"Ah well, maybe another time." Lara turned round again, so that they were facing each other.

Alex blushed, and turned away.

Lara tossed him a towel.

Before he turned around again, she was gone.

20. Powell was in the distinguished gentleman's office, where he'd been trying—albeit surreptitiously—to convince the older man not to accompany them to the second tomb.

"The dead zone may be medically hazardous," he confided. "I've had the Chinook equipped to deal with potential casualties." Or—

"The blizzard is almost certainly not going to hit the area full force. Besides, the cold-weather gear is rated to twenty below. Although the wind chill . . ." Or—

"The real danger may come when the two pieces are put together, Miss Holcomb thinks. The person holding the assembled Triangle will be subjected to an unimaginable array of energies. According to her theory, at least."

The man was having none of it.

"The Order's most important moment in millennia, Mr. Powell. I am looking forward to it." The sun was just now setting. He stood at the window of his office, looking out on one of the canals.

His office was two floors above the Council Hall, a floor above Powell's. It had a green carpet, deep maroon walls, and floor-to-ceiling bookshelves. Two Titians, a Rembrandt, and a Picasso. It contained not a single concession to modern technology: no computer, no phone, no fax, no typewriter. If you wanted an audience, you had to see Him in person. Most of the times that you wanted to see Him, in Powell's experience, he had already summoned you anyway.

"In less than a day, we will finally have the power to bring about the earthly paradise our founders imagined. No more war, no more starvation, suffering, or disease. Utopia on Earth, Mr. Powell. Imagine it."

Powell imagined. It looked deathly dull to him.

"The Order owes you a great debt of gratitude, Mr. Powell. You have served well."

Powell bowed his head. "I am honored."

There was a knock on the door.

"Come."

Gareth walked in, Pimms a step behind.

"Excuse me, sir," Gareth said. "Pimms wanted to see Mr. Powell."

Powell looked at his aide. "Well, what is it?"

Pimms, as usual, looked nervous. "That package from England you were expecting, sir? It's here."

"Package, from England." Powell frowned. "I'm not expecting any—"

Ah.

"Lady Croft, you mean?"

Pimms turned bright red. "Yes, that's the one. I put it

in the Council Hall. Uh, her, in the Council Hall. She's waiting."

"Thank you, Pimms. I'll be down shortly."

Pimms bowed to the distinguished gentleman and Gareth, blushed again, and left.

"Interesting fellow," Lowery said.

"He keeps me amused. And he has his uses: quite good at reminding me about things."

"Of course." The distinguished gentleman stood. "Well. You'd better go see her, Mr. Powell. Get us that first piece of the Triangle. We'll be needing it."

Powell bowed, and left the room.

"Lady Croft. Good evening."

Lara had been lost in thought, staring out one of the huge room's floor-to-ceiling windows. She turned now and saw Powell standing at the open doors to the Council chamber, Pimms a step behind him.

"Good evening," she replied, as Powell closed the doors, shutting out Pimms, whose face registered astonishment before it disappeared. "Illuminati."

Powell began walking the length of the black-and-white marble floor toward her, pulling a cigar out of his pocket. He stopped in front of a huge seal—the All-Seeing Eye—and cut the end of the cigar off.

"Do you mind if I smoke?"

"Yes." Lara folded her arms across her chest. "I do."

Powell grinned, struck a match, and lit his cigar. "Your father smoked cigars, I believe."

"One of the reasons I've come, Mr. Powell." She glared. "To hear you talk about my father."

"We'll get to Lord Croft, I promise you." He took another puff. "Marvelous. In the summer, this kills the stench of the canals. Well, masks it somewhat."

"I'm sure. About my father—"

"Soon." Powell puffed. "About the Triangle—"

"This. Illuminati headquarters."

Powell grinned. "You're with the Illuminati."

"I beg your pardon? The Illuminati?" He grinned. "There's no such thing. It's just a bedtime story."

"Really? What's all this?" Lara spread her arms wide, indicating the huge room. She pointed to the Illuminati seal on the wall. "And that?"

Powell didn't even look up. "Oh, that," he shrugged. "You know the Italians. A very florid people. Very inclined to the exaggerated gesture, the grand symbol, the—"

Lara had a tiny throwing knife in a sheath along the inside of her left arm. She pulled it out and threw in a single fluid motion. The knife pierced the eye of the Triangle.

Powell looked shocked. "That's a very important piece of artwork."

"Sorry, I'm bored—Illuminati."

He nodded and took the cigar out of his mouth. "Very well, then. You want to know about the People of the Light."

The two of them were still a good thirty feet apart. Powell started to come closer now, talking as he approached.

"Did you know, Lara, that there are twenty-two civil wars raging around the world at this moment? Terrible conflicts. Incalculable grief. Loss. Injustice."

The two of them were now toe to toe. He puffed on his cigar, and breathed smoke at her.

"Twenty-two wars. Without the People of the Light, there would be at least fifty, maybe sixty. More. The Illuminati work beneath the loom, as it were, to weave a golden thread through life's chaos. A life that tends for most people to be nasty, brutish, and—"

"Short."

"Yes. So short. Insultingly so."

"So you're the good guys?"

"Well." Powell smiled. "My colleagues like to think so."

"And you're a more practical man?"

"I'm a serious man, Lady Croft."

"Meaning . . ."

"Let's get down to business. Have you brought my Triangle?"

It was Lara's turn to smile.

"No," Powell shook his head. "Of course not. You've hidden it somewhere."

"Yes. Of course I've hidden the piece. Otherwise you'd try to kill me."

"I'm not going to kill you."

"I said you'd try." Lara smiled.

Powell smiled back. "You are a rare person, Lady Croft. Rare indeed. Do you mind if I call you Lara?"

"I do, actually. Mind."

Lara walked to the far end of the room, where seven chairs had been lined up in a row in front of a huge, floor-to-ceiling mural. The chairs were on a dais, slightly above the marble floor. A person sitting in them would have a commanding view of the rest of the room. The center chair was bigger than the others. Lara walked around behind, and put her arms on the back of it.

"You invited me here for a business proposal, Mr. Powell. I'm still waiting to hear one."

"Fair enough." He nodded. "It's a very straightforward proposition. You can keep the Triangle you have, and I will keep your father's clock, and we can be partners."

Lara gestured to the chair in front of her. "But who sits here?"

Powell ignored her question, continuing his thought. "We can be partners and go for the Big Prize. The Triangle of Light."

He started walking toward her.

"Yes," Lara said. "But who sits here?"

"It's an incredible dream. An awesome power. It could set right so many wrongs."

"I don't think you sit here, do you?"

Lara eased herself into the big chair.

"I think your place is somewhere else, perhaps." She patted the chair on her left. "Here, perhaps. Or here," she said, indicating the one on the right. Or maybe—" she gestured to a chair in the distance—"all the way down there, somewhere."

Powell shook his head, smiling.

"Oh, not down there." He walked up on the dais and sat down at the chair to her immediate right. "Here," he said. "My place is here, close to the action. On God's right hand, as it were. In fact," he puffed on his cigar, "I now sit exactly where your father used to."

His words were like a splash of ice water on her face. "You're lying."

"Actually, not." He smiled. "In fact, your father mentored me in the Order."

The room spun. Lara took a deep breath.

Soon you'll have discovered all my secrets.

"It was truly an honor," Powell was saying. "I loved him."

No. Her father? Powell?

"I don't believe you. My father was not Illuminati. He would have told me." Her head was shaking; her mind was racing. Would he have confided in her? She was a little girl.

"Your Daddy kept a great many secrets. Secrets not even your mother knew."

"Not from me."

"Oh, my dear." Powell shook his head pityingly. "Especially from you."

He leaned back in his chair; Lara leaned toward him, in hers. She studied his face, his eyes, the set of his mouth. He was enjoying himself, the bastard. Enjoying the surprise he'd sprung on her. Her father, a member of the Illuminati.

Was such a thing possible? The things he'd taught her, the life he lived, the way he made her laugh . . .

I ask only that you judge me with your heart, angel. And not too harshly.

"I know you so well, Lara. Perhaps better than yourself. And I know what you want."

Powell's words brought her back to the here and

now. "You? Know what I want?" She shook her head. "I doubt it."

"I do know, Lara. I think I do. Having had the advantage of knowing your father." He puffed. "And you are so like him, in so many ways The best I've ever seen."

Lara leaned back in her chair. "So why should I help you, Mr. Powell? My father never meant for you to have the Clock. He hid it from you."

"So it seems. He broke his oath. He lied to us. To me."

Powell looked down at his cigar. Lara thought she saw a flicker of actual emotion cross his face. "I think your father knew what result his actions would bring. He was scared, at the end."

"Of you, Mr. Powell? I hardly think so."

"No. You see, I think the more he came to understand the power of the Triangle, the more it worried him."

"And."

"Oh, it fascinated me." He leaned in closer to her. "The Triangle gives its possessor the power of God, Lara. Anything you wish for can be yours"—he snapped his fingers—"in an instant."

"I'm actually quite well-off now, thank you. And judging from your place in London, you're not doing too badly yourself."

"Don't joke, Lara. Think seriously. Think of what you can do." Powell lowered his voice, made it even more insistent, urging. "With the Triangle, you can change the world. You can rebuild; you can build; you can destroy. You can move back and forth in time; see the civilizations whose offal you spend so much of your time digging up in the full flower of their glory. Egypt. Rome. Athens." He was so close to her now they were practically nose to nose. "You'll not only have the power to right today's wrongs, but yesterday's. Imagine it. You can undo the past. Save the Parthenon from the Turks, the Temple at Jerusalem from the Babylonians, the Library at Alexandria from the Romans."

Powell smiled.

"You can even have another life with your father, Lara. A second chance. Imagine it: the two Crofts, re-united, exploring all the ages of the Earth. What dream could be grander?"

Lara shook her head. It sounded wonderful, but it was wrong, all wrong. She felt it deep inside her.

"I know what you're thinking, Lara. You should de-stroy the Triangle. You should destroy the Clock. But think it through. Life with your father. It will be within my power to give, and I will do it, I swear."

"But you don't sit in the big chair." Lara patted the arm of her seat.

Powell, ignoring her question completely, kept talking. "Lara. Help me, and you will get what I know you want."

"How do I know if I were to give you the piece you wouldn't try to kill me."

Powell suddenly had a blade of his own, and was holding it inches away from Lara's left eye.

"Would it make you feel better, on more familiar ground, if I killed you now?"

She fixed Powell with a steady glare. "As I said be-fore, you could try."

He grinned. "Lara, will you reconsider?"

"I might."

"Don't take too long." He turned and threw his knife. It landed in the seal on the wall, in the eye of the triangle, inches from hers. "This opportunity disappears in eighteen and a half hours."

Lara stood. "And won't be back for five thousand years."

"That's right." Powell took one last puff of his cigar, and stood as well. He walked down the dais, and stubbed the cigar out in an ashtray on one of the tables.

"I'll consider your offer, Mr. Powell. You'll have my decision in the morning." Lara picked up her backpack, and headed for the door. "One way or the other," she called over her shoulder.

"Lady Croft."

Ten feet from the exit, she turned. Powell stood underneath the huge mural, in front of the seven chairs, hands clasped behind his back.

"We leave here at 0700 hours. You should dress warmly; where we're going, it gets very cold indeed."

She nodded. "I'll keep that in mind."

"I'll see you bright and early. And don't forget the Triangle, please."

Lara pushed through the door, past an open-mouthed Pimms, and out into the warm night air.

21. Lara was walking in San Marco Square, pushing through a crowd of mostly couples, young and old, arm in arm, heads tilted upward, enjoying the spectacular light show. The Aurora. *Once in a lifetime stargazing spectacular*, screamed the headlines—roughly translated: Lara's knowledge of the Venetian idiom was spotty at best. More to come tomorrow, with the total solar eclipse. Everyone oohed and ahhed at the bursts of light from above.

If only you knew, Lara thought.

She walked through the crowd unnoticed, anonymous, except for the occasional, predictably lewd comment from the occasional, hormonally overloaded Venetian lad. There wasn't a snowball's chance in hell she could trust Powell. Giving him the Triangle would likely be her last act, in this lifetime anyway. Wouldn't it? He'd just pull out a gun and shoot her. Wouldn't he?

Probably. Except for what had happened back in Cambodia, where she'd saved his bacon. All right, he'd tried to kill her after that, but that was reflex; she had the Triangle, and he wanted it. Perhaps he really did want her as a partner. Perhaps. Only because it increased his odds of getting the second piece of the Triangle, though.

Lara left the square, walked down a small street, past a café. She was hungry. She stopped for antipasto and a glass of wine.

Always do the unexpected; it was the rule she lived by. So what was the unexpected move here?

Toss the Triangle into a canal and disappear? Or show up for Powell's joyride to her—almost certain—death?

She had taken an outside table; now she tilted her head upward, and looked at the Aurora. Spectacular. Awe-inspiring. A once-in-a-lifetime show. A once-in-a-lifetime chance.

And then she realized what the truly unexpected move would be.

Take the power of the Triangle for her own.

Destroy the Clock, Lara. Don't be tempted by its power, as I was.

She looked up, and scanned the café, almost expecting to see her father again, or hear his voice. But there was only a single waiter, an older man, folding napkins at a wait station.

Lara raised her hand, caught the waiter's eye.

"Signorina?"

She asked for the check, paid, and started walking again. A plan was forming in her mind. But before she finalized it . . .

She needed to gather together all the pieces in the game, and finalize the positions of all the players in her head.

She'd been heading east. Lara changed direction, and turned back toward the heart of the city, San Marco, the Grand Canal . . .

The Illuminati, and their associates.

Lara heard voices raised, laughing behind the door. She supposed she should check out the situation before entering, but she was hardly in the mood for that right now.

So she kicked the door down.

She couldn't believe it.

The bastard was playing poker.

There was a table set up in the middle of the room. Four men sat around it, heads turned toward her, mouths wide open in astonishment. Alex was one of them.

The three men she didn't know reacted quickly. They all had their guns out and trained on Lara even before the initial shock had fully registered on Alex's face.

Guns. She didn't have time.

"Not now guys, okay?"

The men all looked at each other, confusion on their faces. They had the drop on her—why was she giving orders?

"I need to speak with Alex," she said. "Alone."

"Okay, guys." Alex stepped forward. "Give the lady some air."

The men put away their guns, and began gathering up their money. One of them was openly gawking at

Lara. As they filed out, he reached out impulsively and kissed her hand.

"*Scusi. Bella.*"

Lara burst out laughing.

When he closed the door behind him, the grin on her face disappeared, and she sat down opposite Alex at the card table.

"Do you want to be a good guy, Mr. West? Or a bad guy?"

"Lara—"

"Because you've got to choose one pretty soon. You're working for bad, bad people, Alex. You know that, don't you?"

He lowered his head. "I know Powell's not the most likeable man, but—"

"Are you going to do it?" She bore in on him mercilessly. "Are you going to get the Triangle for Powell? Are you going to give the power to rule the world to that man?"

"Ah—"

"You're just doing it for the money, right? Not a good guy, not a bad guy, just a regular old guy, getting on the best he can, isn't that so? Well, here's the problem, Alex. Powell can't be trusted. And if you're anything like the man I thought you were, that should not be acceptable to you."

She stopped, folded her arms across her chest, and glared.

Alex looked hurt. "I'm just trying to get by. Earn a little poker money. Have a little fun."

"Of course."

Lara shook her head. That was not what she had hoped to hear from him. But now, at least, she knew where he stood. And how to play him.

She stood and picked a card off the table. The King of Hearts.

"I'm coming with you tomorrow, Alex. You, and Mr. Powell. So I'll be there, in your face, one step ahead of you, every step of the way. This is my business now."

She gripped the card between middle- and forefinger of her right hand, and threw it at him.

Alex ducked: the card spun around him, toward the window—

Unseen, Lara's left hand shot out and picked up a second card from the table.

—and then, like a boomerang, the first came back to her. She caught it in her left hand and slid it underneath the one she'd just picked up. Then she turned both over, showing him the second card.

The joker.

She slammed it down on the card table, then crossed to his bed, and retrieved, from underneath it, the first piece of the Triangle, which she'd hidden there earlier, when he was in the shower.

Alex, who'd turned to watch her, turned away again with a grimace.

Lara walked up behind him, and put a .45 to his temple.

"Just so you know," she said, bending low to whisper in his ear, "if you cross me on this one, we may not be able to stay friends."

She kissed him on top of the head, patted him on the shoulder with the piece, and left.

By six-thirty, Powell was dressed and in his office. At his desk, he collected his notes, and the clock. Outside, he heard the whir of a helicopter. He peered through the window, and saw a pair of twin-rotor Chinooks approach, and land in the courtyard.

Pimms burst through the office door, bleary-eyed and unshaven.

"I overslept!" He looked like he was about to cry. "Did she call?"

"For God's sake, man. Relax." Powell shook his head disapprovingly, and pressed a button next to his phone. A voice came back over the speaker.

"Yes, sir?"

Pimms was still wild-eyed. "Lady Croft, did she call?"

Powell set his pack on the table, and began loading it. "I think I'm all set, thank you for asking. Why don't you go see if our distinguished guest needs assistance?" He pointed at the door, Pimms left. There. Now he could think again.

Miss Holcomb's staff had copied a number of volumes from the library for the trip north: those dealing, in particular, with the original legends of the Tomb of a Thousand Shadows. He hadn't looked those over in months; it would be worth refreshing his memory before they actually arrived. Before the alignment.

Fifteen hours, twenty-six minutes, and counting.

His phone buzzed. "Speak."

"The helicopter is here, sir." It was Julius. "We're loading."

"Thank you, Julius. Everyone is prepared?"

"Yes, sir."

Powell smiled: he, Julius, and six carefully chosen men had spent an hour together yesterday afternoon on a borrowed fire-fighting barge, a totally secure location, making plans.

"Good. I'll be down in a moment." It took him ten; he was very careful packing the material from the archives. He also picked up a curio box he'd found in a London antiques store (hand-carved cherrywood, with inlaid paste jewels and the Illuminati crest) and put it into his bag. He had plans for that box.

As he left the office, he looked up at the clock. It was six-fifty.

The landing pad behind the building was a sea of activity: Julius and his men loading their gear; the Illuminati's mercenaries loading theirs; and there was Mr. West, standing a few dozen feet back from the helicopter, taking it all in with a rather grim expression on his face.

Powell walked over to him. West's expression, if anything, got only grimmer.

"Five minutes," said Powell. "And we're on our way. Fifteen hours, and we're in the tomb, making history. So cheer up, Mr. West."

"Huh." West grunted. "Sorry. Late night."

"Oh?"

"Yeah. Think I'll get on board, get some sleep."

Powell eyed him carefully. He had the feeling there

was more behind West's mood than a lack of sleep, but he wouldn't press.

He would simply keep a careful eye on his young charge.

"Go on, Alex." He smiled, and clapped a hand on West's shoulder. "Get aboard, then." West did.

And now here came Pimms, a step behind Gareth and their distinguished leader as they emerged from the building and headed toward the Chinook. Pimms was trying to help Gareth carry a suitcase; he kept reaching out his hand, and Gareth kept turning around and giving him dirty looks.

Pimms caught sight of Powell, bowed low to his charges, and walked over.

"I think we're in big trouble," Pimms said, sotto voce.

"Really? Hold this, will you?" Powell handed Pimms the curio box. Pimms took it, and inclined his head in the direction of Gareth and the distinguished gentleman, who were now boarding the Chinook.

"They think we have Lady Croft's piece of the Triangle."

"I know." Powell took a Cuban from his pocket, unwrapped it, and struck a match. He puffed it to life, walking toward the Chinook as he did so. Pimms fell in a step behind him. "They think it's in the box you are carrying right now."

Pimms looked down at the object in his hands. "And is it?"

"Why don't you worry about something else?" Powell took a slow, deliberate puff, and looked Pimms up and down. "Do you think you're dressed warmly enough? We're going very far north, you know."

Pimms stopped walking, and looked down at the box in his hands.

"The suspense is killing me," he said.

Powell sighed. "If you must."

Pimms sneaked a look. His face fell like a surprised soufflé.

"Remind me," Powell said, "to play poker with you."

"Oh my God." Pimms looked up. "It's empty. What are we going to do?"

"You're going to guard that box with your life. You've been entrusted with a huge responsibility."

"I don't understand. Is it still the case that we have no chance of success without that piece of the Triangle?"

Powell nodded, and rested a hand on Pimms's shoulder. "Zero. But you shouldn't dwell on it. Everything will work out."

"But—"

Powell touched a finger to Pimms's lips, shushing him.

"You see?" He spun Pimms around. Lara Croft, followed by a thin, bookish-looking man, was in astoundingly white arctic gear. The pair were crossing the courtyard, heading directly toward them.

"Lady Croft! I'm so glad you decided to join us." Powell turned and bowed in the direction of the helicopter. "Your chariot awaits."

Bryce frowned. "Good Lord, he's even smarmier in person."

"Wait till you really get to know him." Lara stopped

walking and turned to Bryce. "Wait here a moment, will you?"

"Not a problem," he said. "I'll just continue sweating. Unless I can get this zipper unstuck."

Lara grinned. Bryce had been struggling with his gear since they'd left the hotel. Actually, he'd been struggling with his gear since he walked into the hotel the night before. Just past one, she was sitting in the lobby, reading up on the tomb, and, hearing a loud thump and a curse, she looked up to see Bryce stumbling in. He was carrying half a dozen hardshell suitcases under, in, and hooked onto his arms, and giving instructions in French to a porter who was trying to handle a half dozen more such cases and a score of shopping bags and decipher Bryce's commands as well. Bryce's struggles had continued this morning as well; his problem right now was the zipper to his parka, which wouldn't unzip from its current uncomfortable position, jammed into his Adam's apple.

She left him struggling with it, and joined Powell and Pimms.

"Good morning, gentlemen."

"Good morning, Lady Croft. I knew you would change your mind."

"Did you? Amazing. Since I wasn't completely sure of it myself."

"I knew. Pimms." He snapped his fingers. Pimms held out a wooden box in front of her and opened it.

Without taking her eyes from Powell, Lara reached into her belt, pulled out the piece of the Triangle, and dropped it into the box. "My part of the bargain."

"So I see. Partner."

She fixed Powell with her gaze. "You'd better be ready for this. Partner."

"I am." Powell's gaze was steady. "Are you?"

"You'll see." She spun on her heel.

"Glad to have you aboard, Lara!" Powell called after her.

Bryce was muttering to himself and still fighting the zipper when she reached him. "Of course he's glad to have you aboard. You just gave him the only thing in the world he wanted."

"Have a little faith. Here, let me."

Lara gave a hard yank, and the zipper came loose.

"Oh, thank God." Bryce opened his jacket. "Thank you."

"You're welcome."

"And what am I doing here, anyway?"

Lara looked him over. A joke about setting a new trend in arctic fashion danced on her lips, but she stifled it. Bryce was here because she needed him: The dead zone she'd read about would likely break a great many things Bryce would be handy at fixing. Besides, it was good for her to have one friendly face around to look at.

"You're with me." She leaned in closer. "We're saving the Universe. Come on."

She started toward the Chinook. Bryce fell into step beside her, his woolly earflaps bobbing.

"Can we still do that? Even after you just gave the bad guy our half of the Triangle?"

"Trust me." She smiled. "I have a plan."

"An insane, reckless, damn-the-torpedoes, 'I see no

ships' kind of plan that you will not be sharing with me just at this moment?"

"Something like that."

"And we'll save the world and all?"

"Absolutely."

Bryce shrugged. "Okay, then."

"Moving out." Lara looked up and saw Powell's man—Julius—standing at the top of the cargo bay ramp. "You two coming?"

"Wouldn't miss it." She jumped up on the ramp, then reached out a hand to Bryce and hauled him up after her.

Julius pressed a button, the ramp lifted into the body of the copter, and the Chinook rose up into the sky.

22. The helicopter was a modified MH47E: Judging from the lines, it was a decade old, but Lara doubted it had been out of a hangar for much of that time, and it certainly hadn't flown any sort of hazardous missions. It was simply too spit-and-polish to have logged many hours in the air.

The twin-rotored Chinooks, in her experience, tended to get a lot of use as transport equipment. She'd seen a lot of specialized modifications among them, medical evac units, heavy equipment harnesses, some particularly inventive cargo bay reconfigurations.

But what the Illuminati had done with this chopper took the cake.

The front of the long, narrow interior was sectioned off, and climate control and custom furniture had been installed. It looked like the interior of a private jet. Powell, Pimms, and some other gentlemen who Lara could only assume were also Illuminati—along with Alex—sat there.

She and Bryce were riding coach, in military-style

jump seats, in the rear of the plane, which was still raw, unheated cargo space. The rest of the expedition team were with them.

An hour or so into the flight, Powell made his way back to them, carrying a tray of finger sandwiches.

"Terribly sorry for the seating arrangements. I hope it's not too uncomfortable."

"We're fine," Lara said. "Partner."

Powell grinned. "Something to eat?"

Lara shook her head. Bryce swooped his hand, and came away with half a dozen, which he quickly stuffed into his mouth, one after the other.

"I don't believe we've met," Powell said, handing the tray off to one of his men. I'm Manfred Powell."

"Mmmm." Bryce swallowed, chewed, and swallowed again. "Bryce."

Powell's hand reached down, Bryce's reached up, and they shook.

"Bryce—is that your first name, or last?"

Lara cut in. "I'd like to offer Bryce's services to the group, Mr. Powell. In the spirit of cooperation."

"That's very kind of you." He smiled, and looked down at Bryce. "What is it you do, exactly?"

"Electronics."

"Really?"

Bryce nodded. "Custom work, mostly. Security. Weaponry. A little of this, a little of that. Some repair work."

"Repair work?"

"Yes, that's right."

"Well. Perhaps you can help me."

"I can try."

Powell grinned. "I have this clock I've been having some trouble with . . ."

The cargo bay exploded with laughter.

Bryce glared.

"Mr. Powell," Lara said when the noise had died down. "I see we're headed north."

"That's right."

"Care to fill me in on our destination . . . partner?"

"Certainly. Novaya Zemlya. Are you familiar with it, Lara?"

"Can't say I am . . . Manfred."

"Novaya Zemlya." Bryce frowned. "Sounds Russian."

"Part of the federation, yes," Powell said.

"And where is it, in relation to, say—Moscow?"

"North," Powell replied. "Way, way north. I can get you a map, if you're interested, Mr. Bryce."

"No, that's all right." Bryce zipped his jacket back up, and visibly shivered. "I quite get the idea."

A few hours out, the Chinook refueled in midair, courtesy of a Russian army plane. Powell watched the operation from the cockpit; when he returned to the main cabin, West was talking with the distinguished gentleman himself.

"Quite a character, Lady Croft," the man was saying. "You know her well, I understand."

West nodded. "I suppose."

"She seems to have a flair for the dramatic, judging by what Mr. Powell has been telling me."

"Oh, yes." West grinned. "Lara has quite the flair."

"Still . . . I dislike so much enthusiasm. So much exuberance. I distrust it. I prefer a calm, considered approach." He turned to Powell. "We have the Triangle. Are we quite sure she's . . . necessary?"

"Well." Powell looked at the older man. *You coldblooded bastard, you. Take the Triangle, and toss her over the side?* He admired the impulse, but he remembered Cambodia. Lara had saved them from making a big mistake, a potentially fatal mistake. He'd give her a chance to do it again.

Then he'd kill her.

"One Tomb Raider is good." Powell clapped a hand on West's knee. "But two are better."

"Lara's the Tomb Raider," West said quietly. "Not me."

"Considering the stakes," Powell said. "It's worth having the both of them."

"The stakes are high." The Illuminati leader nodded, and turned to West again. "Can you two work together?"

"I suppose."

"You've never before pooled your resources?"

"No." West grinned suddenly. "Well, not like this."

"Alex. You devil, you." Powell grinned, reached over, and clapped West on the knee again.

West's smile disappeared as quickly as it had come.

Next to her, Bryce, who had been snoring, started, and opened his eyes.

"Whew."

"What?"

"A dream. A doozy. I was the Tomb Raider. My droid

was the butler. Kept breaking everything." He squirmed in his seat. "Ooh, my bum's gone to sleep again. All down the left cheek."

"Suck it up, soldier."

"Soldier? Me? I don't recall enlisting for infantry duty—not like those boys." He lowered his voice, and nodded in the direction of Powell's soldiers, who all sat ramrod straight in their seats, as they'd been the entire trip, Uzis on their laps, at the ready.

"Don't you feel like we're being guarded?" he whispered.

"We are," Lara whispered back.

Bryce frowned. "Are we on the team here, or have we been kidnapped?"

"Neither."

"Neither?"

Lara nodded. Across the bay, Julius caught her eye, and glared. She gave it right back.

She turned back to Bryce, who looked anxious.

"Listen." She smiled. "It's going to be fine."

"It is?"

"It is. Trust me."

"Oh yes." Bryce sighed. "The plan. I keep forgetting about the plan. Only natural, I suppose, since I don't know what the plan is." He folded his arms across his chest, leaned back in his seat, and closed his eyes again.

"Bryce." Lara leaned close to him, whispering again. "If it'll make you feel any better . . . ?"

One eye cracked open. "Yes?"

"I don't know what the plan is either. Yet."

"Oh, yes. That makes me feel wonderful."

He closed his eye, and turned away from her.

The Chinook refueled again. A tray of sandwiches was passed around. Powell took out the Clock. All three dials were glowing now: All the hands were spinning, counting down to the alignment.

"Here's an interesting thing." Powell looked up: Pimms was reading from a travel guide. "The biggest thermonuclear bomb ever was tested on Novaya Zemlya. They still have weapons-testing facilities there, too: that probably keeps the tourist population down, wouldn't you say?" He smiled. "Fortunately for us."

Gareth, who'd been staring out the window, turned to Pimms and started laughing: a few seconds later the distinguished gentleman, who up until that moment had been wearing a particularly sour expression, joined in. Powell found himself chuckling as well.

"What?" Pimms asked. "What's so funny?"

"Mr. Pimms," Gareth said, "there has never been a single weapons test on Novaya Zemlya. Not an atom bomb, not an H-bomb, not a stick of dynamite."

Pimms frowned. "But it says right here . . ." His voice trailed off. "Oh."

"Money buys privacy, young man." The distinguished gentleman cleared his throat. "Never forget that."

"Oh, I won't, sir. I won't."

"How much longer?"

Their distinguished leader was frowning, clearly impatient. Probably uncomfortable, too. His breath made steam in the air. The heaters were no longer powerful enough to keep the chill arctic air out.

"A few hours." Powell looked out the window. The Barents Sea was below them, dotted with icebergs. Novaya Zemlya—the southern island—should be coming into sight shortly. That was their jumping off point. "We'll have to take the last hour overland. The helicopters will not fly within two miles of the tomb's core."

Pimms, who'd been warming his hands over the vent next to his seat, started. "We can't fly?"

Powell nodded. "Electromagnetic effects. It's a dead zone."

"Mr. Powell. You didn't answer my question." The distinguished gentleman was still frowning. "How much longer, in total, until the alignment?"

"Sorry, sir." Powell forced a smile. "Three hours."

"Precisely?"

Powell sighed. "Three hours and three minutes. And twenty-five seconds, as of one second ago, when I began to say the word 'twenty.' "

The Illuminati leader stared at him, openmouthed. Powell supposed it was the first time in a good long while that anyone had dared upset the old man's applecart.

Possibly since Lord Croft himself, twenty-odd years earlier.

"Don't take that tone, Powell." Gareth, the toady, shook a finger at him. "Don't you ever take that tone."

Powell bowed his head. "Forgive me."

"Hey, let's all relax." West, who had said perhaps ten

words the entire trip, grinned. "How about we synchro-nize our watches? Anybody?"

The distinguished gentleman glared. "I hardly think that necessary. I simply want to be kept updated on the time remaining."

"Here's an update." Powell pointed out the window off to their right, where land was coming into view. "Novaya Zemlya. We'll be landing in twenty min-utes."

He stood, and turned to the rear cabin, intending to focus Lara's attention on their imminent arrival.

But she was already standing, and fastening straps on her gear.

As the cargo ramp lowered, a blast of frigid air rushed into the cabin, instantly dispelling whatever warmth it contained. Bryce stood at the top of the ramp, and shiv-ered.

"Oh my God." Powell's men pushed past him, un-loading. Bryce didn't move. Another blast of air came. "That's the wind from the helicopters, yes? Please tell me that's the wind from the helicopters."

Lara shook her head. "That's the wind, Bryce. That's what it's like up here. Better come on out, and get ac-climated."

He came, albeit slowly, and with a sour expression. Outside, at the bottom of the ramp, Powell's men had made a neat pile of everyone's equipment. Powell him-self was talking with a man in an oversize jacket and pants made out of animal skins. A native.

They'd landed right next to a native settlement,

Lara saw as she looked around. A fishing village, from the looks of it, teepees and cooking fires, and fish hanging out to dry on elaborately lashed-together branches. A short stretch of water—the strait he'd mentioned—lay directly ahead of her. Beyond that was a sheer cliff of what looked like ice. In all other directions around her, tundra stretched out, as far as the eye could see.

Alex broke off from the group of Illuminati and approached her. "Hello, Lara."

"Mr. West." If he'd forgotten their confrontation of the previous night, she hadn't. "Do you have something you wish to say to me?"

"Yes." He offered a smile. "Lighten up. We're in this together, aren't we?"

"Are we?"

He sighed. "Well, anyway. Come with me. We're in charge of picking out the teams."

"Teams?"

"You'll see."

He started off. She started after him

"Hey!" Bryce called. "What should I do?"

"Stay warm. I'll be right back."

Alex led her over a short rise, and into the middle of the native village. The smell of fish was overpowering. Everywhere Lara looked, someone was doing something related to fishing, cutting off heads, hanging nets, scraping guts into a bucket.

Alex slowed, and turned to her. "Listen, Lara—"

A gap-toothed old man, with a cigarette dangling out of his mouth, stepped right into their path.

"*Yukola?*" he asked, thrusting a desiccated fish at them. "*Yukola?*"

He looked at them expectantly; they looked at each other.

"I think he wants us to eat it," Alex said.

The old man broke into a big smile, and nodded. "Eat, yes. Eat."

Lara looked at the fish. "Risky."

Alex sniffed. "Very."

They looked at each other again.

"What the hell," Alex shrugged.

Lara nodded. "You only live once."

They each held out a hand. The old man pulled out a knife and delicately carved them each a piece, about two fingers thick and just as long.

"*Salut,*" Alex said, cramming his into his mouth all at once.

Lara shook her head. "Savage." She took a bite.

It was delicious.

It was, unless she was greatly mistaken, salmon.

"Oh, boy," Alex said, licking his fingers. "That's good stuff."

They both smiled at the old man, who reached into his jacket and pulled out an empty soda can.

"Coke?" He turned the can upside down, and shook it out. Empty. "Coke?" he asked hopefully.

Lara shook her head. "Sorry."

"Hold on a second." Alex was wearing a fanny pack: he pulled it around to the front and reached inside. He came out with a ginger ale. "Schwepps?"

The old man shrugged, and took the can.

"Striking a blow for the Empire," Alex said. Lara laughed. Then she frowned.

"For a second there, Mr. West," she said. "I quite forgot you were the scum of the earth."

His face fell.

They started walking again. On the other side of the village, they found a man sitting on a log, warming his hands on a fire, surrounded by dozens of the largest huskies Lara had ever seen. Sled dogs, for the last leg of their trip, Alex explained. Across the null zone, to the meteor crater and the tomb.

They began choosing dogs, each of them indicating their picks to the man on the log. At one point Alex chose a husky that was so fat it waddled, and Lara snorted. Alex glowered back at her, and chose another. The old nomad laughed.

In the middle of the process, a rumbling sound filled the air. Lara looked up to see a line of huge armored vehicles rolling across the tundra toward the village. A man jumped down from the first and hurried over to a waiting Powell.

Lara turned back to the dogs.

A little girl was sitting cross-legged on the ground, not two feet away, watching her.

"Where did you come from?"

The girl wore her long black hair pulled back in two pigtails, underneath a blue knit cap. She looked to be about eight years old.

"Are you going out across the ice-lake?" She spoke Russian; Lara replied in the same language.

"Yes."

"To the crater?"

"Yes, the meteor crater."

"There are devils out there. The Tomb of Ten Thousand Shadows."

"That's right." Powell and the Illuminati knew where the tomb was, that made sense, but the locals?

The girl reached up and tugged at Lara's arm.

"Time is broken there. You will lose your mind. Don't go."

Lara's head swam for a moment. She went to one knee, and steadied herself.

"Hang on a minute, I'm . . ."

Lara looked into the girl's eyes, and it was if she were falling into a whirlpool.

All she could hear was the sound of the rushing water, pulling her down, down, down. The sounds of the native village, of the dogs barking, Alex calling out his selections, the armored vehicles idling, all disappeared.

"You're risking everything," the girl said, and it was as if her voice was coming from underwater as well, muffled, and pitch-shifted down an octave, the sound of her words shifting as she spoke. "To see him. To be with him."

"To see who?" she asked. "Who am I going to see?"

"Your father." God, it was happening again. The air around the girl shimmered.

"One thought," the girl said, speaking flawless English, "fills immensity."

Lara caught her breath. "Where did you hear that?"

A shrill whistle sounded. Lara blinked, and shook her head.

"Lara! Come on!"

She turned to see the dogs being rounded up, and Alex looking at her strangely.

"Lara?" He frowned. "Are you all right?"

"A minute." She shook her head, trying to clear it, and turned back around.

On the ground, where the little girl had been sitting, was a single jasmine flower. The girl was nowhere in sight.

Lara picked up the flower, and inhaled.

Weird, she thought, climbing to her feet. *And only getting weirder.*

She hustled after Alex and the dogs.

23. **T**he strait between the two islands of Novaya Zemlya was frozen, but ice, as Lara knew all too well from personal experience, was treacherous stuff, especially at this time of year, so she kept a sharp eye out. Next to her, in a second amphib, she saw Alex doing the same. Pimms and Powell were with him. Bryce was with her. Julius drove the third vehicle, one of the other Illuminati the fourth.

The amphibs were a Red Army version of the old U.S. Navy DUCKS from World War II. They looked like Coast Guard launches with two axles' worth of tractor-trailer wheels: go on land, go on sea, go on just about anything. Lara was in the glassed-in cockpit; Bryce, who had been below, came up on deck and sat beside her.

He reached into his pack and pulled out his laptop. He powered up.

"What are you doing?"

"Thought I'd check my e-mail, while we've got a minute."

"Bryce . . ." Lara shook her head. "What would you ever do if the power went out?"

He grinned. "We'll find out soon, won't we?"

A horn honked.

Lara and Bryce both looked up. Alex's amphib was cruising past them; he turned and waved.

"Little boys. Always in a hurry." Lara grinned, and punched up her amphib. It lurched forward.

"Whoa!" Bryce, unprepared, flew back. He landed on the deck with a solid *thump*.

"Christ, Lara," he said, rubbing his rear. "My bum's going to be sore for a week."

Ten minutes later, they left the ice and were back on dry land. The northern island was all snow, rock, and glacier. Spectacular scenery, but Lara couldn't really enjoy the view; she was too busy thinking.

Where did Powell, and his Illuminati friends, and Alex—yes, let's throw him in there with them, that's where he belongs—expect to find the Triangle?

One possibility occurred to her: Perhaps this piece of the Triangle had a guardian like the first, a nasty creature whose responsibility it was to see that the Triangle remained hidden. Maybe, Lara thought, she was along as bait for that creature: a sacrifice, as it were.

Not a pleasant thought.

They crested the lip of what she thought at first was a massive basin, the remnants of an inland sea, and then realized it was the outer edge of the meteor crater. The inside was a barren, featureless field of snow.

They drove on.

"Got a GPS uplink: infrared view of the terrain, in

case you're interested," Bryce said, swiveling the laptop screen around so she could see it. It was the first time either of them had spoken in minutes. Lara realized she'd been dangerously close to drifting off, hypnotized by the endless, unchanging white-on-white scenery before her.

"Sure." She turned, and caught a peek of a hazy reddish-blue image that vaguely matched what she'd just been watching through the windshield. Then the image distorted, and disappeared for a second.

"Oh come on. Not yet." Bryce jiggled the laptop; the image came back, but fizzled out again.

Lara shook her head. "Welcome to the dead zone."

Bryce sighed. "Okay." He looked up from the laptop. "About a hundred yards, I reckon."

Lara shook her head. "I'm betting fifty."

"Eighty, perhaps."

The amphib's engine died; they continued coasting forward. Lara looked around and saw the other amphibs slowing to a stop as well.

"All right." Bryce closed his laptop. "Fifty it is."

But Lara wasn't listening. Even before they'd come to a complete stop, she'd grabbed her backpack, and jumped out onto the snow. It was much, much colder here, she realized; ten degrees colder, she would bet, and with nothing to halt its progress, the wind when it came was the very definition of bone-chilling.

She loved it.

"Come on, Bryce!"

He stood at the guardrail, making a face.

"Now?"

"Now. Come on, you lazy git. Chop-chop."

He turned and gingerly made his way down the stepladder to the snow below.

"It's very cold, you know."

Lara started walking.

"It's invigorating, you mean. Come on Bryce, this is life!"

He snorted. "This is a large ice cube."

There was a smudge of black on the horizon: Lara pulled out her pocket telescope, and peered through it. The smudge became a dent in the landscape, a huge black hole, probably a couple of miles away.

The amphibs unloaded; Alex and Julius harnessed the sled dogs. They had half a dozen teams, half a dozen sleds. Lara took the first, Alex the second, and Powell the third. Two of the Illuminati, including the older gentleman, took a fourth, the soldiers and Pimms spread out over the last two.

"Come on Bryce. Hop on." Lara nodded to the back of the sled.

Bryce rubbed his bottom. "I'm not going with you. You drive too fast."

"I prefer a more sedate pace as well." That was Pimms, who looked at least as uncomfortable and out of place as Bryce did.

"Well, naturally," Bryce said. "On such a rickety contraption, it's the only way to go."

Pimms, for the first time Lara had seen, smiled. "Pimms. Roderick Pimms."

"Bryce." They shook hands.

"Perhaps we could ride together," Pimms suggested.

Bryce agreed, and to Lara's surprise, actually took the reins.

"Bryce," she heard Pimms say as she clambered onto her own sled. "Is that your first name, or your last?"

And then they were off.

They were well above the Arctic Circle now, the sun a huge yellow disk hovering over the horizon. This time of year it didn't set at all; civil twilight was the phrase, she believed.

Ten minutes into their trip, she looked again, and its rim was being chewed away by the edge of the moon.

The eclipse—the final phase of the alignment—was beginning.

24. Fifty minutes of mushing brought them to the black smudge that was the crater's epicenter, where the original home of the People of the Light, had—supposedly—once stood. All that remained now was a mass of blackened, melted, fused rock, a ring of devastation hundreds of meters wide that was somehow managing to hold the arctic ice at bay.

Lara brought her sled to a stop, and climbed out. Powell's men were unloading their sleds of what looked like unnecessary gear. Lara followed suit, stacking the cases neatly next to Bryce and Pimms, who were both ignoring the frenzied activity around them and looking up into the darkening sky. Bryce wore black welder's goggles, to shield his eyes from the growing eclipse: Pimms was peering through a dark viewing glass.

"Hmmm." Pimms frowned. "There are no birds here. At all."

"Because there's no life here."

The landscape around them lit up with an orange

glow: Lara turned to look at the sky just in time to see the wisps of Aurora light fading.

"Twenty minutes, people!" Powell stood at the hole that marked the entrance to the tomb, the clock folded open in his hands. "Let's make haste."

"Bryce," Lara grunted, pulling down a particularly heavy equipment case that he had packed. There were two more next to it on the sled. "Could you give me a hand?"

He and Pimms were still talking.

"According to the ancient Egyptians, after death, you have six souls. Your second soul represents energy, power, and light. Its name is Sekem."

Pimms visibly shuddered.

"I wouldn't know," he said. "I find things like that a litle spooky."

Bryce lifted his goggles and stared at Pimms. "And you joined the Illuminati?"

Lara strapped down the remaining cases and climbed back on the sled. At the entrance to the tomb, she saw Powell's men—who had ridden separately, split among the half-dozen sleds during the ride across the crater—huddled together, talking amongst themselves.

She didn't like the looks of that.

"Bryce," she called. "A couple things."

He was still talking.

"The sixth soul is Khaibit, the Shadow. Khaibit is your memory, and all your pasts."

Pimms nodded, intent. "Go on."

"All your deeds; good and bad. All that you ever were, all that you—"

Lara reached down, made a snowball, and threw it. It hit Bryce square in the face.

"*Owfff.*" He sputtered, spit snow, wiped his goggles off, and glared at Lara. "Was that really necessary?"

She grinned. "Come here."

He came. Pimms, as if suddenly realizing where he was, ran off to assist Powell.

"You're staying up here." Lara told him. "In case."

"In case what?"

"In case things go wrong."

Bryce finished wiping his face. "And how will I know if things go wrong?"

"Well. If Powell comes back up alone, for example."

"And what do I do then?"

"Send in the cavalry."

"And who would that be?"

Lara got back on the sled and grabbed the reins. "That would be you."

"Yikes."

Lara lowered her glasses. "Did you just say 'yikes'?"

Bryce sighed. "I may have."

She nodded behind him, at the stack of crates. "There's extra ammunition in there. And another set of these," she said, patting her guns.

"I know. I packed them."

"Lady Croft!" Powell's sled was poised at the entrance to the tomb; the others were in line behind it, waiting.

"Well." She smiled at Bryce. "Keep warm."

He nodded, looking miserable. "Good luck."

She cracked the reins, and the dogs shot off, heading toward the mouth of the tomb.

* * *

The tunnels banked, spiraling down, down, down. In the old books, the High Priest had ordered the remains of the once-great city buried, after seeing the devastation and death the Triangle had caused. And so it vanished beneath the Earth, presumably lost forever, except, of course, you couldn't really lose anything forever, at least not a ruin of such surpassing importance as this one—witness the Valley of the Kings, or Chichen-Itzá, or even Angkor Wat, for that matter.

Powell wondered if there was more of the city intact, underneath the earth. There was a vast network of tunnels already; the Order had carved them out over the centuries in search of the tomb. Some of the tunnels led nowhere, dead ends abandoned once the temple ruins had been found. They might be worth reopening, afterward. The legends of the Triangle also hinted at other, powerful artifacts that the People of the Light had used. He would want searches mounted for those as well, afterward.

"Mr. Powell!"

West was in the lead sled, a barely visible shadow in the light cast from the torches they were carrying.

"Mr. West!" he called back. "Exhilarating, isn't it?" It reminded Powell of the luge, which he'd done for the first time last winter in Switzerland. Not quite as steep, and not quite as stimulating but then, this trip wasn't about pleasure, was it? The pleasure—and there would be quite a bit of it, Powell promised himself—would come later.

This trip was about power.

"How long do these tunnels go on?" West didn't

sound the slightest bit exhilarated by the ride. He sounded impatient.

"Don't worry, Mr. West," Powell called ahead. "We're almost there."

And they were, in fact, one sign of which was that the temperature was markedly increasing. Powell slipped off his hat, and turned to address Julius in the sled behind him.

"You gentlemen may want to remove your gloves now," he said.

Behind Julius were the rest of the Illuminati: the soldiers, Gareth, and the distinguished gentleman. Powell shot a hand up, and waved. Their leader nodded back, looking even more uncomfortable than he had on the plane.

Lara's sled was behind him. Powell could only catch an occasional glimpse of her, before she disappeared around the curves.

She stood ramrod straight in her sled, urging her dogs forward.

Powell thought that, if he were her, he wouldn't be in quite so much of a hurry.

The tunnels were carved out of solid rock—how, Lara couldn't quite imagine. The walls were smoother than anything but the most modern equipment could have managed, and the grade steeper than she would have expected as well. And from the papers Powell had shown her, the tunnels had existed for hundreds, if not thousands, of years. It was almost enough to lend credence to some of the wilder tales about the Illuminati and the things they were supposedly responsible for. Almost. Particularly if the Order had been composed of men like her father.

She thought of the little girl at the native village.

You're risking everything to see him. Your father.

And as she followed the tunnels ever downward, she realized she was, in fact, risking a great deal—her life, for one thing—for Lord Croft. Not to literally see him, of course, that was impossible, but to give the last few acts of his life meaning. To stop the Illuminati—Powell, in particular—from gaining the power of the Triangle. Of course she hadn't been able to plan exactly how she was going to do that, just yet. It seemed that she was going to have to improvise, which she had no problem with, although it was a good thing she had left Bryce up top, because he would probably be fainting at her feet right at this moment if he knew that she was still winging it. And speaking of Bryce . . .

She should have told him to call Shugrave. Or she should have called Shugrave herself. There was the real cavalry, and no matter what he was involved with, Shugrave would drop it and come if she called urgently enough. He was a real friend, not like Alex West, up there in his sled, leading the way for his Illuminati masters.

The sled in front of Lara's slowed. She pulled back on her reins, and saw, up ahead, the tunnel widening, the slope lessening, and the sleds coming to a halt. She drifted forward a few more meters. The tunnel ended.

They had emerged into a huge cavern, easily twice the size of the tomb in Cambodia. No, bigger: on one end, it stretched off into infinity. The walls here were not the smooth rock of the tunnels, but blackened, twisted, distorted rock, melted into the shapes of—

"Good Lord." Alex had climbed off his sled, and brought a torch up close to one of the walls. "What the hell are they?"

Lara joined him. "They," she said, tracing a finger along the rock, "were the original enemies of the People of the Light. Annihilated. By the power of the Triangle."

A power that had vaporized these ancient soldiers instantaneously, leaving only their blackened remains on the wall, their mouths wide, their eyes open in endless, unseeing horror.

"Death was everywhere . . ." Lara said, echoing the line her father had read to her so long ago.

Alex swallowed hard. "Whoa."

"That's right, Alex." Lara stared into his eyes. "That's what we're here to fetch for your masters."

He looked back, rattled.

"The Tomb of Ten Thousand Shadows—an apt name, wouldn't you say?"

Powell, who had silently padded up behind them, now thrust his head between them and squinted at the wall. Then he straightened up, and smiled. "Come along children. We've seen the sights. Now let's get to work."

He clapped a hand on each of their shoulders.

Lara glared, and picked his hand off hers. "I'll get my things."

She turned back to her sled.

"Thirty-one minutes," Powell called after her. "And counting."

25. The cave was even bigger than Lara had thought, though it narrowed at points to a passage small enough that they were forced to leave the sleds behind, and walk. They left the dogs behind, too, but before they'd gone twenty meters the huskies began howling piteously, setting up such a racket that Powell sent two men back to unharness them. The dogs bounded forward, the lead dog from Lara's sled—a particularly solid-looking husky she'd nicknamed Boris—rushing to her side, and butting her with his muzzle.

"Poor fellow." Lara reached down and rubbed his head. "Were you frightened?"

"Sure you were, weren't you boy? And why not? Yes, you as well, I know, I know." Alex, next to her, was patting two dogs simultaneously. "This big, empty scary place."

"Oh, I don't know," Lara said. "Kind of reminds me of your loft."

Lara saw Alex's lips forming a reply, but before he could speak, the soldiers walking in front of them lit a series of chemflares, and both she and Mr. West stopped dead in their tracks.

No one spoke for a good five seconds.

"Make a note of it," Powell said, looking down at the clock. "Eighteen-fifty-seven Greenwich Mean Time, we have arrived at the center of the tomb."

"Wow." Alex was walking around the machine, staring up at it, shaking his head. "Look at the size of it."

"Magnificent," said the distinguished gentleman.

Powell cleared his throat. "Eleven minutes until alignment. Mr. West, Lady Croft . . ."

Alex stepped forward: Powell handed him the Clock.

"Be careful with this, Mr. West."

He nodded, sticking it in his belt. "Right. I'm going to shuck some of these clothes, it's gotten awfully warm in here. Lara?"

"Yes, a moment." She continued to stare up at the metal orrery that loomed over them.

It was immense, easily fifty times the size of her father's, maybe a hundred times as large. It sat in the center of a frozen pool, raised up a good twenty feet off the ground. Each planet rested on an immense metal arm, projecting up and out from a central point. The planets were huge, and the Sun larger still. It seemed quite capable of holding two dozen people within it.

"Mr. Powell?" The distinguished gentleman spoke. "Is not the orrery supposed to be in step with the heavenly alignment?"

Which was a fancy way, Lara supposed, of saying "Shouldn't this be working?"

"There must be some obstruction." Powell turned to Julius. "Find it, please."

Lara began removing the outer layer of her clothes as well, the cape, the parka, the snow boots, watching as Julius and two men stepped forward and began clearing away some sort of moss that hung from the machine's lower arms.

She was about to tell Julius that they should concentrate their attentions on the actual mechanism that drove the orrery, which was probably somewhere under the model of the Sun, when she noticed that one of the men had left the laser sights on the team's rifles activated. As they worked, red beams swept across several of the planets.

One struck a point somewhere between Mars and Jupiter, and fractured, and twisted into a knot, and veered off toward the ceiling, and the pool, and the far wall of the tomb.

Lara stopped and watched.

The laser beam moved on: it struck the Sun, dead-center, and disappeared.

It swept between Neptune and Pluto, and fractured again, this time into a dozen different directions.

"Alex." Lara touched his arm.

"I'll bet the piece is hidden in the Sun." Alex had produced a tin of chalk powder and was rubbing it into his hands.

"Earth. Sun's too obvious. But look," she said, pointing.

He raised his eyes just as Boris, who'd been playing with another husky on the far side of the orrery, chose that moment to come bounding back to Lara. He passed right beneath Mars and Jupiter to do so, directly under the point where the laser beam had fractured.

And disappeared in mid-leap.

"Holy shit," Alex said.

Boris reappeared, but all wrong, like he'd been put together inside out.

Lara's stomach turned.

Boris disappeared again. And then reappeared, landing on the ground, everything back to normal, but with a very, very confused look in his eyes.

"Timestorm," Lara whispered. "Time is broken here."

He trotted right past Lara, whimpering, and sat down in a ball against the far wall.

Alex looked up at the orrery, and then back at her.

"What the hell was that?"

"We have just witnessed an interruption in the normal flow of time."

"An interruption in the normal flow of time. You say that like it's an everyday occurrence, and we'll be back on schedule momentarily."

"It is an everyday occurrence. Here."

"But I mean . . ." He shook his head. "Holy shit."

Lara pulled out a coil of rope, unslung one end of it, and tested the coil's weight in her other hand.

"Try to avoid those areas. Or you can wait here. Watch my stuff."

Alex shook his head, refocused. "Not bloody likely." He took out a coil of rope himself. "My fifty pounds says the piece is inside the Sun."

Lara remembered how the laser beam had struck there, and chose her words carefully. "Incorrigible."

"In-what-a-bubble?"

Powell walked up to them. "Five minutes. Places, please."

Lara threw her rope; it caught high above, on the arm suppporting Saturn. Alex threw his line up, next to hers.

"Do we have a bet, or what?"

"Race you to the top," Lara said, starting to climb.

Gareth walked over to Powell, his gaze on Lady Croft and West as they scaled the orrery. "You're sure it's inside one of the planets?"

Powell nodded. "That is my reading of the material, yes. I'd be happy to entertain other suggestions."

"Hmmm. No, no other suggestions. You are the expert here, Mr. Powell. I concur with your deductions." Gareth attempted a comradely smile. "You deserve great credit, Mr. Powell, great credit indeed, for securing both pieces of the Triangle. I commend you, sir."

Powell smiled, and nodded his head in acknowledgment. Some sort of response was warranted, he supposed. His preference would be to return to the mouth of the tomb, collect his sword, and chop out Gareth's tongue. But there was hardly time for that, and besides, what was the point?

"Commendations to you, as well, Mr. Gareth." He lowered his voice. "I know it was you who pressured our leader to let me see this project through to the end—despite my earlier difficulties locating the first piece—and I want you to know I greatly appreciate it."

Gareth looked momentarily flustered. Then, predictably, he puffed up like a bullfrog.

"Well. I must say." He leaned closer. "I too feel appreciative, to have my efforts acknowledged, Mr. Powell. Working behind-the-scenes as I do, all too often one feels as if the breadth of one's work is never quite appreciated. Now don't take this as a complaint, because—

"Mr. Gareth! Mr. Powell!"

Gareth suddenly stood up, ramrod straight, as if a steel pole had been inserted into his posterior. Across the chamber, the distinguished gentleman was glaring at the two of them.

He had the first piece of the Triangle out and in his hand.

"Time remaining until the alignment, please?"

Alex had the Clock, so Powell consulted his wristwatch.

"Eight minutes, sir!" he called back. "Approximately."

"Then focus, please."

Powell nodded. The man was right.

He snapped his fingers, and pointed upward.

His men focused their guns on Alex and Lara, shimmying up their rope lines.

Alex looked down at him, confusion on his face.

"Powell? What—"

"Trust me." Powell took a Cuban out of his pocket, and lit it. "It's not that I don't trust you."

But he didn't.

Alex glared, and started climbing again.

Powell motioned Julius over.

"Sir."

"There's a chemistry between those two," he said, indicating Alex and Lara. "I don't trust what they'll do up there."

"Then let me send some of my men to accompany them," Julius suggested.

Powell smiled, and clapped him on the shoulder. "Just what I was thinking."

Julius barked out the necessary orders. Three of his men threw up ropes of their own, and started to climb.

Powell felt a bumping at his knee.

He looked down and saw Croft's sled-dog, the one that had gone through—what was it she had called the phenomenon—the timestorm. It still had a dazed look on its face.

He bent down and ruffled its fur.

"Hey doggie. Did you go to hell and back?"

The dog whimpered, and nuzzled him again.

Powell nodded. "So tell me—what was it like?"

26. Reaching out her right hand, Lara pulled herself up and onto the single solid piece of metal that represented Saturn's rings. She was on the far side of the planet, farthest away from the Sun.

And there came Alex, pulling himself up and over onto the rings, on the planet's near side.

They got to their feet and faced each other.

"Well." Alex bent over, put his hands on his knees. "That was pretty easy."

"Then why are you huffing?"

"I am not huffing."

"Of course not." Lara took stock. The ground below seemed very far away, Powell and the distinguished-looking gentleman and all the soldiers looking like action figure-sized versions of themselves, their movements stiff, and mechanical. The planets, on the other hand, seemed even more massive and solid. Talk about the miracle of the Pyramids, how on earth did they manage to build this thing?

"Not much longer now," Alex said. He glanced below, at the three soldiers who were still climbing up. He seemed to have something on his mind, something he wanted to say before the soldiers joined them at the top. "Lara—"

She held up a hand. Every second was critical now, if she wanted to stop Powell from getting the Triangle. If she wanted to save herself and Bryce, and—she glared over at him—possibly Alex, who was even more naive than she thought if he expected to walk away from his dealings with Powell carrying anything but a bullet in his skull. And Powell wasn't the only danger she had to be prepared for. Time was broken here, and from reading her father's notes, and seeing what had just happened to Boris, that could be a very dangerous thing indeed.

Perhaps that was the trap this tomb held. Avoid the areas of temporal discontinuity, and you won the prize, that being the second piece of the Triangle, hidden in time and space, as the other half had been. Avoid them, or . . .

Hmmm. She looked down along the orrery, at the gleaming surface of the Sun.

"Five minutes and change." Alex was holding the clock. Lara could see the dials were all glowing.

"It's going to be inside the Sun, I'm telling you. The second piece."

"We'll see about that."

"We will. Very shortly." He looked across the length of the orrery. "It's a cakewalk from here, Lara. A giant jungle gym. Where's the challenge?"

At that moment, a rumbling, grinding noise filled the chamber. Gears rumbled. The planets lurched.

After five thousand years, the orrery had started to move again.

The sudden motion threw her. Lara lost her balance, righted herself, and leaped from the rings onto Mars, which was just barely small enough for her to get her arms around.

Powell's men weren't so lucky.

All of them slid from their ropes, and into the mechanism below, screaming as they fell.

Blood stained the snow.

Alex lost his footing as well, and fell to his knees, scrambling to find a hand-hold on the slippery surface of the rings. He couldn't, and went flying through the air, slamming into Jupiter with a loud thump that made Lara wince.

He lost his flashlight, which fell and was crushed in the mechanism as well.

"Whoa." Alex got to his knees, and balanced himself, still holding the clock.

Gunfire filled the tomb.

"Focus!" Powell pointed a semiautomatic in their direction. "There are two hundred and fifty-six seconds till alignment. Find me that Triangle!"

"I'm on it, Mr. Powell!" Alex shouted back. Then he winked at Lara.

And before she could say a word, he jumped.

Halfway across the orrery, it seemed to her, clear over to the model of the Earth.

Lara took a running leap, and landed on Mercury.

The orrery sent the two planets hurling toward each other.

"Hey!" Lara called out. "What are you doing?"

Alex tapped the sphere beneath him, and shook his head. "You said it was in the Earth. I won!"

"Oh, for—" Lara rolled her eyes. "We don't have time for this."

They didn't have time for much, in fact, and Lara had concluded that he was right, the piece had to be inside the Sun, hidden in space and time, but the problem was how to get at it? The laser beam from the rifle sight had shot into the giant globe and disappeared, while the falling stones had just bounced off it.

The two planets passed each other, and then drifted apart. The glowing dials of the clock caught Lara's eye.

And she remembered her father's diary entry.

The clock is the key that can open Time itself.

"Alex!" she called after him. "I need the clock to find the second piece! Give me the clock! You were right!"

He looked confused. "But—did you just say you were wrong?"

"I said, you were right!"

He disappeared on the other side of the Sun. When he reemerged, he wore the most serious expression Lara had ever seen from Alex West in his lifetime.

"You know what, Lara? Forget about the clock. I just wanted to win. And I did. But now I'm with you. Now we save the world, right?"

"Alex." Her voice trembled with frustration. Of all the bloody times for a spiritual awakening. "Not now!"

Alex twisted around on his perch to maintain eye contact.

"But we can't let Powell get the second piece. The eclipse'll be over in a few minutes, and then we're off the hook for another five thousand years. Yes? Or no? Lara—"

"Alex, trust me. Throw me the Clock!"

"I don't understand! I'm being a good guy! Aren't I?"

"Alex! Give me the bloody Clock!"

"West!"

They both looked down at the same instant. Powell had his gun trained directly on Alex. "Give her the Clock!"

"Okay." Alex shrugged.

He threw it.

Lara leaped as it arced downward, caught it in midair, and twisting her body, jumped toward the Sun. She caught a glimpse of something that looked like, yes, it could be, the keyhole, the place to insert the Clock, and she stretched out toward the Sun's golden surface—

And vanished.

Blackness swallowed her.

27. Lara landed on a floor of polished stone.

The sun was shining high above her.

A vast army was spread out at her feet.

The clock in her hand was running forward.

Lara blinked. She was in the Illuminati City, in the temple, the pictures from her storybook come to life. There was a man in silk robes with his back to her, on his knees, praying up to the sun, the edge of which was being eaten away by the beginnings of a solar eclipse, a total eclipse, alignment. She raised her hand to blot out the corona, and—

The world cracked.

She was standing on desert sand, looking up at the sun and the Sphinx. This Sphinx's nose was intact, its huge stone feet not buried in the sand, eroded by time, but resting on a platform of huge sandstone blocks. She looked around, where were the pyramids, there were no pyramids, there was only the sun, and the sand beneath her feet opened up and swallowed her and she was falling and—

Lara stood before her own home, Croft Manor, and a man was coming out the front entrance, and looking up at her. Her grandfather. Look at those clothes, look at how young he was and she blinked again and—

She was in a jungle, the air around her alive with insects and the sounds of animals nearby. Now, she had her bearings, well, not exactly her bearings, but at least she knew what was happening, she was falling through one of those areas of temporal discontinuity, bouncing back and forth through time the way Boris and the laser had. Then there was a huge rushing sound, and she looked up, and the sky was falling, no, not the sky, a giant meteor was heading right for her and—

She was back in the temple, looking down at the city, but it was shattered beyond all recognition, cracked, and twisted, and blackened. Before her, a man sat on a throne, an impossibly ancient, wizened man, shrunken to the size of a child, hands folded across his lap, head bowed to study the thing he held. She took a step toward him, and realized two things.

He was dead.

And the thing in his hands was glowing.

"Where is she? Where is the Clock? Where is the second piece?"

The distinguished gentleman was screaming. Powell had never seen the man so worked up. Not without reason; there were twenty seconds, according to his watch, till alignment. Twenty seconds till they had to start the whole thing all over again, five thousand years and counting. True, whoever was running the Order would have the first piece this time, which would make things a whole lot easier for them, but frankly, Powell didn't care about that. He'd be long dead and gone.

So he was wondering, as well, what had become of Lara Croft.

Up above, West had jumped onto the Sun, and was crawling along it like some sort of spider, searching every inch for some kind of seam, a way in to rescue Lara. He seemed, if anything, even more frantic than Lowery.

"Look." Gareth spoke, pointed up at the Sun. "Something's happening."

The man was right. The huge yellow sphere was starting to glow. One side of it actually, not the whole thing, just a single, circular patch.

The patch blossomed outward, and a split second later, Lara burst from a hole in the side of the Sun. She tumbled in midair and landed on the Earth, high above.

In one hand she had the Clock.

In the other was the second half of the Triangle.

"Lara!" Alex jumped down on the ground beside her. "What the hell happened?"

She shook her head. "You wouldn't believe me if I told you."

The distinguished gentleman stepped forward.

"You can tell us all, Lady Croft. Later. Now, if you please . . ."

He held out his hand. Lara had only a moment to consider. She had her rope, coiled around her belt. She had a knife, hidden in the small of her back. She had her guns. She had the Clock, and she had the second piece of the Triangle, the other half of the sightless eye.

She considered, and then dropped the piece into the older gentleman's outstretched hand.

"Here you go . . . partner."

He looked surprised, as if he hadn't expected her to give it up quite that easily. Then he smiled.

"Thank you."

Now the older man stepped back, followed closely by the two bodyguards. Water, Lara noticed, had begun to fill the tomb.

The Illuminati Leader stood beneath the orrery, and raised the two pieces of the Triangle above his head, one in each hand.

"For five thousand years, the members of our sacred Order have awaited this very moment. For five thousand years, we Illuminati have stayed hidden, keeping the unsuspecting masses of the world safe from their own folly. But the time for concealment is now over. Now we will unite these two parts, the past and the present."

Lara saw Powell turn his head. She followed his gaze across the tomb, to where Julius and a half dozen of his men stood.

"Let us twist all of time into this one moment," the Leader continued, "to fulfill our sacred promise to our ancestors—"

A shadow flashed across her face, and she spun around. But no one was there.

Her imagination? Or . . .

Colored lights sparkled. The tomb suddenly seemed to be alive with strange whispering noises. And now shadows flashed everywhere, dozens of unseen creatures darting this way and that, gathering in the tomb for this one, long-awaited moment.

Alex's eyes were wide.

"What the hell?"

Across the tomb, the distinguished gentleman's voice rose to a crescendo. "What is now proved, was once only imagined . . ."

Lara gasped.

Directly opposite her, behind the Illuminati Leader, she had seen something—strange cowled figures, their robes emblazoned with the All-Seeing Eye, their hands twisting together in barely suppressed excitement. Colored lights flashed.

Timestorm. The Illuminati ancestors, she realized.

"As a new heaven is begun," the distinguished gentleman continued, "eternal hell revives. To every man is given the key to the gates of heaven. The same key opens the gates of hell."

Lara heard a sudden, incongruous sound.

The click of metal on metal. A gun magazine, sliding home.

Powell stepped forward. "Enough of this twaddle."

The tomb filled with gunfire, a good ten seconds worth. Then silence.

Powell stepped forward, over the corpses of the

Illuminati and their soldiers, and retrieved the first piece of the Triangle.

"Got what you wanted?" Lara asked icily.

"Oh yes." He looked down at his watch, and smiled.

"Alignment," he said, and joined the two halves of the Triangle.

28. The two pieces fused together into one, and promptly stopped glowing.

Powell looked down at the reformed Triangle in his hands, and frowned.

He lifted the Triangle and held it above his head.

Water pooled around his feet as he looked around the tomb, searching for some kind of clue, something, anything to let him know what to do next, there was nothing about this in the archives, how in hell could the blasted thing not work?

"Not what you hoped for, Mr. Powell?"

He looked up at West, who was smiling.

But it was the enigmatic expression on Lady Croft's face that interested him most.

"Lara."

Holding the Triangle at his side, he sloshed across the tomb toward her.

"Oh, Lara. I have a gut instinct about this."

She folded her arms across her chest. "Do tell."

Powell smiled. With his free hand, he reached into his belt, and pulled out his throwing knife.

West's smile disappeared.

"What's that?"

"This?" Powell flipped the knife up in the air, caught the hilt as it came down, tossed it again, and caught it. "It's a knife." He circled the two of them, tossing it as he went. "Now. Lara. My instincts tell me you know what is happening with the Triangle here—" he held it up for a second, lowered it again—"why this supposedly all-powerful artifact is behaving like an ordinary hunk of metal. Hmmm?"

He stopped in front of her, holding the knife inches away from her eye.

"Haven't we done this dance before?" she asked.

"You're not answering my question." Powell lowered the knife. "After all, you are the daughter of a genius. Surely you have some ideas."

She shrugged. "Nothing comes to mind at the moment."

"Lara, Lara, Lara." He shook his head. "I think you're lying. Let me test my theory."

Powell took the knife, spun, and threw it directly into West's chest.

Pierced the heart, he thought. First time.

Alex collapsed and fell backward into the water, at the base of the orrery. The device shuddered slightly, the arm holding up Saturn collapsed.

The planet hurtled to the ground, its rings pinning him in place.

"Alex!" Lara screamed, and ran to his side. She threw herself against Saturn. It didn't move.

West looked down at his chest. Blood dribbled out of the side of his mouth.

"Lara." He gurgled. "I'm good."

"You're good?" The idiot. Good? He was dying.

"You lost the bet." Alex leaned his head upward: the water was closing around his chin. "You said Earth, and it was the Sun."

"I was wrong."

"You owe me fif—"

The water surged again, and closed over his head

She turned to Powell.

He mimed a tear, rolling down his cheek.

Lara took a gulp of air, and dove down beneath the water.

Alex was thrashing about madly, trying to free himself.

She pinched her nose, and pointed to her mouth.

He didn't get it.

She pointed to his mouth, and a light dawned in his eyes, she could see it, and then he pinched his own nose shut, and she, still holding her breath, still holding all that good sweet air inside her, bent over Alex and put her mouth over his, and he opened it, and she exhaled, filling his lungs with oxygen.

When she was empty, she looked up, and saw Alex smile. She smiled back, and surfaced.

"Very touching," Powell said.

Lara shook water from her eyes, took a few deep breaths.

"What do you want?" she asked.

"I'm pretty sure you have figured out the answer to the," he waved the inert triangle at her, "problem. You have that insightful look about you."

Lara dove, and filled Alex's lungs once more.

"You can't keep breathing for him forever, you know. He's bleeding to death," Powell said as she surfaced.

Lara took a step toward him.

"Careful." Julius had his gun leveled at her.

Lara stopped, and collected herself.

"Show me how to complete the Triangle, and have a chance to change his fate. If you deliver me the Power of God, I will spare him. *Cogito Ergo Est.*"

Lara collected as much air as she could, and dove again. When she reached Alex, though, his eyes were closed. She prodded him awake, and breathed in what air she could to his lungs.

She rose up out of the water, gasping for breath.

"If I'm wrong," Powell was saying, "which I doubt, you can go home toting a body bag. But if you solve this puzzle for me, I could change that. In fact," and here he caught her gaze, pinned it with his own, "your father . . . I could change that too."

Lara stared at him. Above, the orrery quivered. The nine planets still holding in a line, the final phase of their five thousand year journey complete.

"But you must decide soon." Powell looked at his watch. "There's only about a minute left of the alignment. And then Mr. West's chance at life is gone. In fact, when the minute is up, if I am still holding a worthless piece of metal here," he waved the Triangle again, "your chances at life get fairly low as well."

Lara dove under again, without responding.

The water around Alex was clouded with blood. She moved through it, and found his face.

She kissed him good-bye.

Coming out of the water again, she strode right up to Powell, till the two of them were nose-to-nose.

"You better be ready for this."

He smiled. "Five thousand years worth of ready, I am."

Then she walked past him, and right up to one of Julius's men.

"Unhook your laser sight," she demanded.

"Do it," Powell said immediately.

She had the Clock in one hand: she took the laser sight in the other, and began sweeping the red beam across the tomb.

The Clock is the key to time itself, her father had written.

And, she was betting, to the power of the Triangle. But the key had to lie within the Clock, and so the question was how to get under its impenetrable surface.

The beam swept across the tomb in a straight line, and then—

Twisted on itself, knotting, in the same spot where Boris had leapt before. Lara held up her father's clock, judging its weight, and then reached back, cocked her arm, and threw it in one swift motion.

The Clock flew through the air, straight along the line of the laser beam, right into the timestorm, where it exploded into a thousand tiny parts.

All of which remained frozen in midair.

Lara dropped the laser sight.

She started running, one two three steps across the tomb, gathering up a full head of steam. And just in the shadow of the orrery, where she gauged the area of temporal discontinuity began, she leaped into the air. Her arm extended, reaching with her hand, and grabbing the tiny, glowing crystal that shone at the center of the fragmented mechanism. As her hand passed through the timestorm, it turned translucent, like a living, 3-D X-ray. She lost all feeling in it, but her momentum carried her forward, to safety. She rolled, and landed on her feet, holding the crystal safe in her hand.

"Bravo," said Powell as she walked toward him. "Bravo. And now . . ."

Lara brought the crystal toward him. It glowed brighter as the distance closed: ten feet, five, and then they were facing each other an armsbreadth apart.

Powell held out the Triangle.

Lara looked down at it, at the center of the eye, where there was a barely visible depression. The pupil of the All-Seeing Eye.

Her father's words came back to her.

To see the world in a grain of sand . . .

She inserted the crystal into the eye.

All at once it began to glow, a fiery white heat that spread instantaneously to the iris, then the entire eye, and finally to the Triangle itself. The light was brighter than the Sun, brighter than the white-hot flame at the very tip of a welder's torch.

Lara raised a hand to shield her vision.

"The All-Seeing Eye," whispered Powell, his eyes shining. "The Power of God."

"Here's a power for you," Lara said.

She cocked her fist and drove it straight at his face, right through the Triangle.

The room exploded in a burst of incandescent light.

29. Time was broken.

Venice, the High Council Chamber of the Illuminati.

On the dais were seven chairs. Her father sat in one, to the right of the distinguished gentleman. They leaned their heads together and spoke.

She stood next to Powell—a much younger Powell— whose eyes blazed with jealousy.

"That chair," he hissed between clenched teeth, "is mine."

The Library in Croft Manor.

The sun was shining brightly. A figure stood in front of a window, features washed out by the light.

The door opened, and a little girl ran through, straight for the man at the window, who bent, laughing, and picked her up in his arms.

The little girl was her.

The man was her father.

* * *

The Tomb of Ten Thousand Shadows.

Her father, pacing carefully underneath the giant orrery, pausing every few seconds to consult a sheet of paper he held in his hand. He took one step forward, then another, and stopped. He looked down at his wristwatch.

"Three. Two. One. Now."

He reached up into the air. His hand seemed translucent for a second.

He smiled, and pulled down the Clock of Ages.

Again, the Library in Croft Manor.

And now it was her—the adult Lara—embracing her father.

"Lara. My Lara." The sun blazed behind him: she rested her head on his shoulder.

"Oh God. Daddy. What's happening?"

"Angel." He stroked her back, whispered in her ear. "It's no use. Yield. Give in to the Power of the Light. Give up. Surrender."

The voice wasn't her father's.

She pulled away from the embrace, and stared up at Manfred Powell. He grinned at her.

"Let go of the Triangle, Lara."

Powell raised a revolver, pointed it square at her forehead, and pulled the trigger.

The Tomb of Ten Thousand Shadows.

Her father, hands raised in the air, defiantly staring down Powell.

Who raised his gun and fired.

* * *

The Library in Croft Manor.

She and Powell stood face-to-face.

The Library was on fire.

A little girl was screaming.

Lara turned and saw her younger self, stranded on the other side of the Library, behind a wall of flame, tears running down her cheeks.

"Don't be scared," the adult Lara called.

"Oh, I think you should be scared." Powell came around behind her, addressing both her and her younger self. "You're going to die."

Lara turned and faced him.

"You died in a fire like this, when you were seven years old." Powell shook his head. "You never lived at all. No tombs, no Pulitzer Prizes, no fancy cars. Just the cold, cold dirt you were buried in."

Her younger self screamed again, and Lara remembered an incident, when she was seven years old, a fire she accidentally started in a wastepaper basket in the Library, but her father—

"He never came, Lara. And you burned to death." Powell's gaze bore into her. "This is the power of the Triangle, Lara. The Power of God."

And Lara suddenly realized what was behind all she was experiencing. Powell and she were fighting for control of that power.

"You died, Lara. You never lived. Never."

She smiled, and shook her head. "In your dreams."

Lara concentrated.

The image of Powell burst into flames then, and he was gone. Then so was the fire.

The Library was quiet.

Lara turned around, looked into the eyes of her younger self, and smiled.

Then she closed her eyes and concentrated.

Interlude

ℏ
ᚹ
⚶
⊕
♈
♀
♊
⚶

He'd sent the artfully disguised clock off yesterday with instructions, and so that part of things, the preparing for the worst, was all set.

But Lord Croft had renewed hopes today, listening to Mrs. King and Gareth talk. They seemed to understand, in a way that some of the younger, rasher members of the Order did not, the dangers of possessing such limitless power. The ethical conundrums one inevitably confronted. The slippery slopes that one all too easily started down. Croft felt empowered to voice some of his own opinions. They had all listened, it seemed to him, very attentively.

Through the tent flap, he saw a flash of color, the Aurora. He was up late again—too late. Tomorrow was an early start again, and now he was debating whether or not to tell the Council about the temporal anomalies he'd discovered in the tomb. Perhaps . . . he would have to consider it in the morning. Now he was simply too tired to think clearly.

"Oh." He yawned. "I am getting too old for this."

Colors flashed again, at the tent flap. Croft looked up.

A young woman stood there, a woman with long, flowing, dark hair, and piercing, blue eyes. His wife's hair. His eyes.

Croft's heart leaped into his throat.

"Good Lord."

He stood. The young woman stared at him, and then her eyes moved, around the tent, to his cot, his books, his instruments laid neatly on the writing desk, and then finally settled back on him.

"Daddy."

Her eyes were full.

"Lara. But how . . ."

And then he knew.

She had found the clock, had put the pieces of the Triangle together. She was using its power. So he had failed, after all.

He was dead.

She took a step forward, and looked around. "It's hard to tell if this is real or not."

He sighed. "Real enough. It is . . . a crossing. Of past—my past—and your present." He looked her up and down. "My God, you've grown up beautifully. Your mother, all over again."

"A little bit of you, too, I hope."

"A little bit of me, yes." His expression grew serious. "You used the clock. You found the Triangle."

"I—" She smiled then, and shook her head. "It's a long story."

Through the tent flap, the Aurora flashed again.

"Why didn't you tell me about the Illuminati?"

Croft sighed. "You were only a child. Not even your mother knew."

"But you could have written it in your journals. You never mentioned it. Not once."

"By God." And despite everything, Croft started to laugh. "You're still talking back! Didn't I teach you better?"

She smiled too, and then that smile dissolved into tears.

She came into his arms, and he held her, rocking her gently.

"Lara. Precious." He squeezed her with all his strength, feeling tears well up in his own eyes. "I would have told you everything, I swear. But I only wanted you to know that which would inspire you. And keep you safe. I loved you. I love you." He sighed. "When you were a baby—after your mother died—I suddenly saw the Order through new eyes. Your eyes, Lara. A child's eyes. And I didn't like it—at all. The urge for power had eaten away at our souls. I was ashamed."

Croft realized, quite suddenly, he didn't want to talk about the past. That this was the only time he and Lara, the grown-up Lara, had. Or would ever have.

Unless . . .

"No. This is wrong." He stepped back from the embrace.

"Daddy?" She looked confused.

"You and I," he shook his head, "we're not supposed to be here, like this. It can't happen, mustn't happen."

"But why? Why can't I use the power—just this once? So I can see you again? We never—"

"With power like this, there is no just once, Lara. You have to destroy the Triangle."

"But—"

"Listen to me, dammit!" He glared, and then he smiled, because the look on her face now, that stubborn "why-can't-I" was the exact same one he'd seen on her as a little girl. "Do it now, before you're sucked in even further. Before I can't stop myself from—"

And then, he was crying too. Dead, by God, dead, and a failure.

"Daddy? What is it? What's wrong?"

He collected himself, and took her hands in his.

"Lara. The power of the Triangle is the power of a god. Take that power, and every other person in the world becomes a bit player on your stage. Their lives become figments of a dream that you're having." He reached out, and brushed her cheek. "Listen to me. Destroy the Triangle."

She nodded, her eyes misting.

"Suddenly I feel so alone."

Croft shook his head fiercely. "Now you listen to me. You're never alone. I'm with you—always. Just as I've always been. And don't pretend you haven't heard my voice!"

They looked at each other, and suddenly Lara laughed.

"So now . . . Lara fight on! Be brave! Have fun!"

He extended his arm toward her. She stretched out and touched his fingertips with her own.

And then she was gone. And Manfred Powell stood in the opening to the tent, in her place.

"Lord Croft." He bowed at the waist. "Our leader sent me to fetch you."

"Now? At this hour."

Powell nodded. "Yes. I'm afraid so. Something about the orrery. He's waiting in the tomb."

Croft shook his head. "No. It's simply too late. We'll deal with it—whatever it is—in the morning.

He turned away from Powell, his mind already racing. Too late, and there was too much to do. By God, if he was going to die—and he hadn't quite worked that through yet, the consequences of a time paradox, Lara coming back to warn him and him not dying after all. But he would certainly explore it—if he was going to die, there were things he had to do, for one thing his notes, the Order mustn't get their hands on—

"Lord Croft."

He turned.

Powell had taken out a gun.

"I'm afraid it will have to be now." He waved the pistol toward the tent flap. "Right now."

30. Lara concentrated.

The Tomb of Ten Thousand Shadows.

The orrery was underwater. Two figures struggled just beneath the surface, working at something caught beneath one of its arms.

No. That was wrong.

She tried again.

The Tomb of Ten Thousand Shadows.

Her father, lying on the floor, blood pooling around his head.

Powell, laughing, turning his back, and heading toward the surface.

No. Wrong. Try again.

The tableau faded—and as it did, she thought she saw her father move, pushing himself backward with his legs, trying to get underneath the orrery . . .

* * *

The Tomb of Ten Thousand Shadows.

The instant before Powell killed Alex, the three of them still as figures in a wax museum.

The knife, frozen in midair, inches from Alex's heart.

Ah. Here she was.

Lara concentrated again, and stepped forward.

Powell and Alex remained frozen.

She drew her guns, and walked in front of Powell.

"Hello, Manfred." His eyes stared at her, frozen, yet somehow unseeing. "I've got a little something for you."

She fired. Round after round after round, emptying one clip and then another, straight into Powell. It was overkill but this was the bastard who killed her father and—

The bullets weren't having any effect.

They passed straight through Powell, his clothes, his person, without leaving a trace.

She holstered her guns.

"Okay." In the silent, dead air of the tomb, her voice echoed back to her. "That's not going to work."

Lara thought a moment, then walked over to the knife.

"Have to work with what we've got."

She grabbed the blade with both hands, and yanked.

"Ow!" She stepped back, surprised. The flesh on her palms was seared. The knife hadn't moved at all.

She closed her fingers around the blade, and—

It burned her flesh.

Newton's laws, a memory from physics class, came back to her; objects at rest tending to remain so. The knife was frozen in time, about as at rest as you could make it.

Forget the calculations, forget the searing, burning smell she was suddenly aware of, Lara's resolve was rock.

She closed her fist around the blade, and threw her whole weight behind an incredible effort to rotate the knife, twisting it like it was a rusted faucet. The harder she pushed, the hotter the knife got.

Lara pushed very hard. She felt something wet trickling down along the inside of her wrist, and her arm.

The knife moved, about a millimeter, but it moved.

Lara gritted her teeth, and tried again.

She pushed, strained, dug into the ground with the balls of her feet, felt her muscles quivering from the stress. The pain was too ridiculous to even consider, so she ignored it.

Blood flowed down her arm, and she had the strangest sensation. She felt as if the knife wasn't moving, that the world itself was rotating, ghostly, weirdly, somehow catching up to itself.

She lost track of all time . . . and at last, when she looked up, the tip of the blade was pointing not at Alex, but at Powell.

Then Lara stood, wiped her hands on her shorts, and stepped back into place, next to Alex.

She closed her eyes again and concentrated.

31. Powell threw the knife directly into West's chest—just as a sharp pain pierced his shoulder.

Powell looked down, and saw the knife sticking out of him.

Him, not West.

How?

He staggered backward, and dropped the Triangle.

It fell to the floor, and shattered into dust.

He collapsed next to it.

"Well now." Lara smiled at him. She had West by the shoulder and was helping him steady himself. "You ought to be more careful with your things, shouldn't you?"

"No." Powell shook his head, refusing to believe what had just happen. "It can't be." He stared at the place where the Triangle had been, and then looked up at Lara Croft.

He had never, ever, hated anyone as much in his life.

"*Kill her!!!*" he shouted at the top of his lungs.

Gunfire exploded.

Lara dove, grabbing a still surprised-looking Alex by the arm and taking him with her. As bullets raked the ground, the water started to rise all over again. She rolled to her feet, as did Alex, and they started running.

The whole tomb shook. Lara looked up and saw the orrery wobbling. A huge stalactite fell to the ground in front of them, kicking up a cloud of frost and ice. They dove behind it, just as bullets plowed into it.

"Lara, Lara, Lara." Alex, crouching next to her behind the stalactite, looked up at the orrery and shook his head. "Looks like you've broken something again. Can't we take you anywhere without . . ." His voice trailed off. "What? Why are you looking at me like that?"

Because you're alive, you bastard, was what she wanted to say.

Instead, she punched him on the arm.

"Hey! What was that for?"

He looked confused, which was nothing compared to what she felt right then, so she simply said, "You stole my prayer wheels," unholstered her .45s, and handed him one.

The tomb rumbled again.

She looked up and saw cracks were beginning to appear everywhere: on the walls, going up to the ceiling above. Ice chips were falling. Now a whole series of stalactites joined them on the journey to the ground.

"Lara . . ."

Alex was holding out his gun to her. "If you're not too busy contemplating the wonders of creation . . . may I have another clip—please!!!"

She ripped a half dozen off and tossed them at him, then turned and began firing again herself.

But Powell's men were too well-armed. Two of them hung in the shadows of the tomb, laying down a hail of protective fire as the rest advanced. She had to do something, or they would be on them in about twenty seconds—

The tomb rumbled again, and a huge shower of ice and dust fell from the ceiling. The orrery was collapsing now, and that collapse was not only destroying the chamber, it was doing something to the temporal anomalies as well. Fixed in place at the moment of its construction, the mechanism's destruction appeared to be setting them free.

Flashes of light and color swirled about in the air, like miniature Auroras. As the falling stone and ice fell through the anomalies, they transmogrified. The stones crumbling to dust, the ice changing to water. One tiny sliver of stalactite dropped through a swirling, eddying, whirlwind of time. It popped out on the other side as a massive dagger of stone, a baby rock suddenly all grown-up.

The dagger pierced one of the planetary support arms. Mars came loose, crashing down, smashing through the surface of the frozen pool, sending up a shower of frigid water.

"I'm new at this hero thing, Lara," Alex said, "but it seems to me we ought to be thinking about making our exit right about now."

Apparently Powell's men shared his thinking.

Julius suddenly lowered his gun.

"Exfiltrate! Plan C!"

He and his men turned and began to race for their sleds.

Powell, still lying on the ground, wounded, couldn't believe it.

"Julius? What are you doing! What the hell is 'Plan C'?"

Julius turned to him.

"Our mission is compromised, sir. We have failed."

Oh. Powell got it now. "You're abandoning me."

"Yes sir."

Powell couldn't believe it. Ten years, he'd worked with the man, and now, when the going got tough, he was walking out?

"I'm disgusted."

"It's nothing personal sir."

"Glad to hear that."

"You have failed," Julius said simply. "I must now take care of my men."

The tomb shuddered again.

"Time's up. Good-bye, Mr. Powell."

Powell raised his eyes. "Go then. Go."

Julius left.

"And thank you!" Powell called after him. "Thank you for nothing!"

As Julius and his men left, Lara was surprised to see Bryce entering the tomb with—what was this?—Pimms trotting along right beside him.

"Well done," she said to Bryce. "Good cavalry."

He shrugged. "It was nothing."

Pimms hung back a second, eyeing Lara nervously. Then, he took a step forward, and affected Bryce's non-chalant air. "It was nothing at all," he repeated. "Easy as pie. A walk around the park. A trip to the moon on gossamer—"

"Mr. Pimms."

He smiled nervously. "Lady Croft."

Lara fixed her gun on him, and grinned. "Are you still one of the bad guys?"

"Absolutely not." His voice went up an octave.

"Promise?"

"Promise. Oh yes, I promise."

"Cross your heart, and—"

"Hope absolutely to die. Absolutely." He nodded enthusiastically. "Not that I hope to die, really, you understand, but that what I'm telling you is—"

Lara lowered the gun, and winked at him. "Good."

Pimms sighed with relief. Alex clapped him on the shoulder.

"Pimms, buddy! Good call!"

"Good work all around," Lara said. She looked toward the tomb's exit. "Now let's make haste, before this place—"

"Lara!"

At the sound of Powell's voice, Lara turned. He lay helpless on the ground, staring up at her. Hatred consumed his features.

"Good luck, Mr. Powell," she said simply. "You're going to need it." Alex, Bryce, and Pimms moved past her, heading for the tomb's exit.

Powell, surprisingly, grinned. "I thought you'd like to know. Your father begged for his life."

Lara stopped dead in her tracks.

"Like a baby."

"I don't think so," Lara said.

"Well." The man shrugged. "Now you'll never know, will you?"

"Go to hell."

He pulled something out of his pocket, and began twirling it in the air. It looked familiar.

Powell held it up so she could get a better look.

It was her father's pocket watch.

"You bastard." The watch was her father's most prized possession. On the off chance that he hadn't taken it with him on his last trip, she had torn the Manor apart, almost stone by stone, looking for it. The fact that Powell had it now—

The man grinned.

"He seemed particularly concerned that I shouldn't take this from his cold, dead body." As he spoke, Powell lifted the watch to his lips and kissed the image on the inside of the lid.

The picture of her mother.

That tore it.

"Lara! Leave him! No, no, no!"

She heard Alex yelling at her to stop, she heard rocks raining down around her, she felt the water rising up her legs, but none of it mattered.

What mattered was the watch, and ripping it from Powell's grasp.

A good beating, she decided, was also in order.

32. "Don't pull the 'Who Dares Wins' stuff on me now, Lara!" Alex was running alongside her now, still yelling. "Please! We gotta get out of here. This whole place is going to collapse."

She nodded. He was right, of course, but all she needed was ten more seconds. One to snatch the watch, and nine to administer a satisfactory beating to Powell.

She reached the man's side, and glared down at him. Powell stared right back up at her, smirking, still twirling the watch.

"Lara!" Alex pleaded. "We're gonna be freakin' pancakes in about two minutes!"

Which was plenty of time.

She reached down to snatch the pocket watch away from Powell—

And he lunged forward, and slashed her with his knife.

Pain shot through her body, and Lara almost fell.

"Hey!" Alex kicked Powell in the head.

The man shrugged that blow off, and rose to his feet, waving a second knife in the air.

The bastard, he'd been faking his injury the whole time.

Lara regained her balance, and pulled out her own knife. Then she stepped between Alex and Powell.

Alex tried to step back in front of her, to take on Powell himself.

"No," she said, shaking her head. Powell—and the watch—were hers. He apparently felt the same way. He began circling her, holding his own knife expertly.

"You've got to be kidding," Alex said.

"And you've got to be going."

"Lara. This is insane! Let me shoot him." She was aware of Alex pulling out a gun, but she waved it away, keeping her eyes focused on Powell.

"Leave right now. Get the others out of here safely. I'll follow."

"But—"

"Right now," Lara said. "Go."

Alex, thank God, knew her well enough to know she meant business.

"I'll leave you a sled. Hurry."

"What about me?" Powell asked. "After all, Mr. West, if I don't get out of here, you don't get paid."

Alex was silent a moment.

"Kick his limey ass, Lara," he said.

And then he was gone.

"You inspire such loyalty, Mr. Powell," Lara said. "Alex. Pimms. Julius. The list goes on."

"Point taken, Lara." Powell lunged forward with the

knife. She stepped back smoothly. "I shall address it in the future."

"In your next life, you mean."

He shrugged. "I wouldn't worry about my fate so much, Lady Croft." He put down his knife suddenly: What the hell? "I'd worry about yours."

From the small of his back Powell produced a gun, and held it on her.

Of course, the second she saw him reach, she'd drawn her own .45.

His smile fell.

"Stalemate, I believe," Lara said. "We could both pull the trigger, but the .45," she waved it at him, "has a much larger caliber bullet. I like my odds of survival better than yours."

He dropped his gun to the ground.

"Lady Croft. As we only have a few spare minutes before we both die, I suggest we use our time creatively.

"Unarmed combat," he said. "The two of us. Mano a mano, or in your case, womano. Winner take all—the watch, the sled, West, Powell, Pimms, and whoever—"

Lara holstered her weapon. "You're on."

Powell smiled, and began circling her again. "What I fear I neglected to tell you, my dear," he said, "is that I am an expert in seven forms of unarmed combat. Last year, in China, I took on two of the world's foremost blackbelts at the same time, and beat them easily. Broke one man's spine, poor fellow. Now he's eating through a straw, and crapping into a bag." He smiled. "I look forward to seeing you in a similar position."

"Oh my God," Lara said. "You've tricked me. I'm trembling in my boots. See?"

He looked.

She drop-kicked him in the face.

She punched him in the stomach.

She kicked out a knee, and then, for good measure, punched his wound several times.

He fought back as best he could. He did have a nice spin kick that caught her on the chin, and sent her reeling. Mostly what he did, though, was fight dirty. She had him in a headlock, and he tried to bite her.

She pushed him away, and punched him square in the mouth. A tooth fell out.

His eyes rolled back in his head.

Powell fell to the ground, and didn't move.

She bent down, and pulled her father's pocket watch from his body.

"This belongs to me," she said.

Powell cracked an eye open. "Take it. It runs a little fast, anyway."

To her right, she saw a flash of color.

A temporal anomaly—it whirled and brushed the wall of the cavern. The entire cave shook as a chunk of rock as big as a good-sized car suddenly just vanished.

Powell looked over and his eyes widened.

Lara smiled, grabbed him by the leg and—dragging him like a sack of potatoes—hurled him into the timestorm.

He screamed.

Lara opened the pocket watch and smiled.

"Oops. Time to go."

"Lara! Lara, for God's sake! Why won't you kill me!" he yelled. "I'm as good as dead."

She stopped a moment, and stared at the flashing swirls of color. The effects of the anomalies varied so widely: some of them seemed to act as corridors through time and space—witness what had happened to Boris—while others simply were chaotic. Time-storms, as the little girl had dubbed them.

The one that had Powell was one of the latter.

It was actually sucking him into it. She would love to stick around to see what happened.

Unfortunately, it really was time to go.

"Dead's not good enough," she said, bending down to pick up her backpack. Wouldn't do to forget this. "Not for the man who killed my father."

"Kill me!" he cried after her.

"Good luck, Mr. Powell," she said, under her breath. "As I said, you're going to need it."

The sled was ready to go, as Alex had promised.

And at the top, the three men were waiting for her.

Interlude

MAY 15, 1981
NOVAYA ZEMLYA

♄
�£
✲
⊕
♈
♀
♊
⚶

The bullet struck Croft right in the forehead. He was falling backward before he felt anything and then suddenly all feeling was gone and he was lying on the ground looking up at the orrery, the right side of his face covered with blood, warm and sticky. Suddenly, he was covered with pain, every millimeter of his body shrieking in agony, and no last-minute life flashing before his eyes, there was just Powell and the knowledge that he had failed. But Lara at least had gotten the Triangle now, if she would destroy it—

His eyes closed. Everything went black.

Lara, he thought, picturing his daughter as he had seen her mere moments before, so alive, so beautiful.

Croft opened his eyes again, and there was color, right above him. A miniature Aurora, wildly spinning in the air.

Timestorm. What would happen if . . .

He raised his arm, and reached up, toward the light.

Epilogue

Lara stood in front of her father's memorial.

"No more clock, Daddy. No more Triangle, and no more tomb, and no more Mr. Powell, either. They're gone, all of them."

Gone as in disappeared off the face of the Earth. When she had reached the lip of the crater, they'd turned around, and saw something shoot up out of the ground, where the tomb had been. Whatever it was—a meteor, the granddaddy of all temporal anomalies, or something else entirely—it left a trail of fire behind as it flew into the sky. She had a feeling that when the Illuminati sent their next expedition to Novaya Zemlya—and there was no doubt in her mind that an expedition was going, was in fact probably already on its way—they would find no trace of the tomb whatsoever. The hole in the ground itself, she suspected, would no longer be there.

A butterfly fluttered past, landing on top of the

stone tent. Its wings beat slowly up and down in the afternoon sun, resting, recharging, before it fluttered off again.

Lara felt recharged too, though she had only returned to the Manor this morning. Amazing how a long, hot shower and clean clothes could make you feel like a whole new person.

She knelt down next to her father's headstone.

LORD CROFT
DIED IN THE FIELD 15TH MAY 1981
LOST BUT NEVER FORGOTTEN

"Never forgotten," she whispered. "And not entirely lost, either." She kissed her hand, and then touched her fingers to the stone. "I love you, Daddy. I'll be back soon."

She stood and walked into the house.

Hillary and Bryce were waiting at the top of the stairs. Both of them wore huge grins.

"What?" She set her hands on her hips. "What are you staring at?"

Hillary held out his hand to Bryce. "Money, please."

Bryce reached in his pants, pulled out a wad of bills, and passed them over. "I don't mind, you know. This is worth the price of admission." He raised a camera then, and pointed it at her. Click. "Alert the *Tattler*. Lara Croft in a dress."

"So I'm wearing the dress. So what?" She frowned at Hillary. "If you'd see to the laundry more often, I'd have more than one option when dressing."

Though she had to admit, she was looking forward to

Alex's face at dinner that evening when he saw her wearing it.

Bryce and Hillary were still smiling at her.

"Don't you two have anything better to do?"

Hillary looked hurt. "I've been very busy cleaning, I'll have you know."

He had been busy. The Manor looked good as new.

She glared at Bryce. "And you? What's your excuse for laying about?"

"Oh no, no laying about. Not me. I've been busy too."

"Really?" Lara folded her arms. "Doing what?"

She heard a clanking sound behind her, and turned.

Bryce's droid walked out from the equipment room, all shined up good as new. Even better, in fact.

The droid's fists were no longer drills. Now they were cannons.

Lara tossed Hillary her straw hat.

"Hold this for me," she said, and kicked off her shoes.